A HEALER'S PROMISE

Books by Misty M. Beller

HEARTS OF MONTANA

Hope's Highest Mountain
Love's Mountain Quest
Faith's Mountain Home

BRIDES OF LAURENT

A Warrior's Heart
A Healer's Promise

BRIDES of LAURENT

HEALER'S PROMISE

MISTY M. BELLER

BETHANYHOUSE
a division of Baker Publishing Group
Minneapolis, Minnesota

Published by Bethany House Publishers
11400 Hampshire Avenue South
Minneapolis, Minnesota 55438
www.bethanyhouse.com

Bethany House Publishers is a division of
Baker Publishing Group, Grand Rapids, Michigan

Printed in the United States of America

Library of Congress Cataloging-in-Publication Data
Names: Beller, Misty M., author.
Title: A healer's promise / Misty M. Beller.
Description: Minneapolis, Minnesota : Bethany House Publishers, a division of
   Baker Publishing Group, [2022] | Series: Brides of Laurent ; [2]
Identifiers: LCCN 2021053582 | ISBN 9780764238055 (paperback) |
   ISBN 9780764240126 (casebound) | ISBN 9781493437290 (ebook)
Subjects: LCGFT: Novels.
Classification: LCC PS3602.E45755 H43 2022 | DDC 813/.6--dc23/eng/20211029
LC record available at https://lccn.loc.gov/2021053582

Scripture quotations are from the King James Version of the Bible.

Cover design by LOOK Design Studio
Cover photography by Aimee Christenson

Author is represented by Books & Such Literary Agency.

Baker Publishing Group publications use paper produced from sustainable forestry
practices and post-consumer waste whenever possible.

22   23   24   25   26   27   28   7   6   5   4   3   2   1

*To my dear friend and amazing author Lacy Williams.
This book wouldn't have been finished without
your unending encouragement and accountability.
You are such a blessing to me,
and I'm thankful God brought us together!*

A merry heart doeth good like a medicine:
but a broken spirit drieth the bones.

Proverbs 17:22

1

The sound of animal hooves shattered the quiet morn, and a flock of chickadees shot from the trees near Audrey Moreau. Recoiling, she slipped behind a brushy cedar. That noise reverberated much too loudly to be an elk or caribou, even a whole herd of them. Her breath puffed in icy clouds as she peeked through the snow-covered green needles, her heart thumping in her ears.

Down the creek a distance from her hiding place, a man sat atop a horse, letting the animal drink from the rushing stream. Her chest seized for a half second until recognition settled in.

Evan MacManus. Her friend Brielle's betrothed had returned already. Brielle had been watching for him for days, but Audrey hadn't really expected his arrival for another few weeks at least. His trip must have gone smoothly. And his desire to see Brielle had likely driven him to travel faster than he might have otherwise.

Audrey stepped from behind the tree and raised her hand

to call out to him, but as her mouth parted, another figure caught her notice—this one much closer and tucked in the shadow of the woods. He, too, sat atop a horse.

Beneath the brow of his hat, his gaze locked on her.

Audrey's breathing stilled as her entire body tensed. Who was this stranger? Their village was hidden deep in the mountains, unknown to anyone except the local Dinee natives. And Evan. And perhaps Evan's superiors, whom he'd gone back to report to about the mineral he'd found in their caves.

This man must have been sent to accompany Evan. Maybe he was the first of the miners and scientists who would come to harvest the pitchblende to help America win the war against Britain.

She raised a tentative hand in greeting, though her heart thundered with awareness that she'd walked out here alone, with nothing for protection save a small knife to harvest barks for her medicines. That single blade would be little help against a man like this one. She'd been raised to believe all strangers intended to cause harm, like the ten Englishmen who'd invaded their village a decade before, killing and wounding a host of innocents before they, too, were killed.

But if this man was Evan's friend, he must be safe. Right?

He didn't return her smile, nor raise his own hand in greeting. He did nod, but something about the way he was tucked just inside the edge of the trees made it appear he was trying to keep himself separate. Maybe even hiding from Evan.

She glanced downriver to where Evan watered his horse, but he'd gone.

Icy dread crept through her, but she did her best not to

panic. She had to find out who this stranger was. If he didn't go with Evan, why would he be here? How had a stranger come to this remote area?

She forced her posture to relax and curved her mouth into as close to a welcoming smile as she could manage. "Hello." She used English, as it seemed most likely he was from the American states.

The man studied her for a heartbeat. Then his gaze flicked toward where Evan's horse had stood, then refocused on her, all within the space of a single breath.

He nodded once more. "Hello." His voice held a different cadence than Evan's. He didn't seem to intend to say more. Did he think she ran into strangers on horseback every day in these woods?

She lifted her chin. "I am Audrey Moreau. You are?"

His response came quicker this time. "Levi. Levi Masters." That unique cadence was even stronger, more stilted than Evan's speech. But then, Evan had grown up in Scotland, so maybe that accounted for the difference.

She offered another welcoming smile. "And from where do you hail, Levi Masters? Are you traveling with Evan?"

His expression didn't shift, and he didn't flick his gaze again to the place Evan had been, but something in his eyes seemed to distance himself before he responded. "I've been traveling with Evan from America. It appears he's about to leave me behind, though. I'm pleased to make your acquaintance, Miss Moreau. Perhaps we'll meet again soon."

As he nudged his horse forward into the clearing along the stream and turned the direction Evan had gone, a frisson of worry slid through her. He probably *was* traveling with Evan. What reason would he have for lying about that? But it was that slight shift in his eyes that raised the head of caution inside her.

Brielle reminded her so often to be careful not to overlook a person's ill intentions just because she sought to see the good inside them. There were enough odd details in Levi's actions to give Audrey pause.

Maybe this stranger simply wasn't comfortable around people. She well understood that condition, as her father also struggled with the pressures other people's expectations placed on him and how he thought others expected him to act in public. Perhaps this man simply felt ill at ease meeting a new person.

Yet, the safety of her people might be at stake. Levi Masters rode directly toward Laurent's gate, the direction Evan had gone. She should catch up with him, surpass him even, and sound the alarm before he entered the village. Her people had created a signal for this very occasion—when an outsider who may be dangerous approached the gate.

She started forward, quickening her step to catch up with the lanky stride of his horse. When he glanced back at her, she slowed. If his intentions were nefarious, would he change his plan if he thought she was following him?

She was no good at stealth, that was for certain.

She kept her gait as normal as possible, even though she dropped farther behind the man. If she ducked into the woods where she wouldn't be seen and tried to run around ahead of him, he would suspect her motives. At least this way, she could call out to the village before he entered.

Lord, let them be listening for me. With the joy surrounding Evan's arrival, the guard stationed by the wall might not have his ear attuned to a signal.

Heavy clouds gathered on the horizon, threatening more snow. Along with the frigid wind against his back, Levi Masters could sense the woman trailing behind him, though he didn't let himself glance at her again. Perhaps he'd made the wrong move in saying he'd been traveling with MacManus. When she'd asked the question, it seemed like the perfect cover to allay her suspicions about his presence in the woods.

Technically, he *had* been traveling with the man, though MacManus hadn't known it.

Had the beauty by the stream suspected his duplicity? Part of him almost wished she'd seen through him. Then he could finally be honest and forthright.

His gaze sought out the tracks in the snow ahead to ensure he was still following MacManus's trail. The habit had become second nature these long weeks that he'd followed the man from Washington. He'd perfected his ability to stay far enough behind that MacManus didn't hear him, but close enough not to lose the trail. When they reached the snow-covered ground of these northern mountains, his job had become easier. Though, at times, more treacherous as the horses maneuvered over the icy stone.

A shrill whistle from behind him pierced the air, filling the open space around him so its source was almost hard to detect.

But he knew.

The woman trailing him must have signaled someone ahead of his presence. Did she intend to warn Evan Mac-Manus? Or the people of her village?

He scanned the landscape before him, but all he could see

was the cliffside of a mountain, with shrubby brush clustered in sections around its base. Were the caves the people lived in somewhere in that mountain? He'd overheard enough of MacManus's report to his superiors to know of the caves and the mineral he'd found within them.

A mineral the US government thought would give them power to win any war.

Those words had resonated so strongly within Levi that he knew he had to follow MacManus and learn more of this situation. Other information he'd overheard in the past from this particular American spy had proven quite valuable. Though this American war might be behind them, who knew when another battle would arise? This intelligence might finally give Britain the upper hand they needed. British Parliament needed to know what the Americans were plotting now.

A shift at the base of the mountain ahead drew his focus. Beside a cluster of skinny-needled trees, he thought he spotted a slight movement.

His imagination? Maybe, but he tightened his grip on the rifle resting across his lap. MacManus had traveled that exact direction, which couldn't be a coincidence. This must be the entrance to the cave village.

He would have preferred to sneak around the edge of the woods to see what he was up against before making his presence known, but Miss Audrey Moreau had taken that advantage away from him with her alert.

Tingles ran across his shoulders and down his back. How many sets of eyes watched him?

Lord, what should I do? Station your angels around me for protection and give me wisdom about how to speak to these people.

When he'd neared ten strides from the place where he'd seen the movement, what he'd thought was the mountainside separated at the top to reveal a V of sunlight. The sight made no sense but must be part of their entrance.

Sitting deeper in his saddle, he eased back on Chaucer's reins to slow the gelding. Any moment, he would likely be stopped at gunpoint. Or worse.

A man stepped out from the stone and planted himself, legs spread, arrow drawn tight in his bow and aimed at Levi. He barked a sharp command. "Halt."

Levi halted Chaucer as he studied the fellow. He wore furs, as anyone who lived in this frozen land would, though his light brown hair proclaimed him to be of European descent. Not one of the natives. And his accent . . . he spoke the word with a lilt, maybe French or Italian.

"Who are you?" The fellow still held his bow lifted and drawn, ready to let the arrow fly at any moment. They must not have muskets here if they still used bow and arrow.

At least Levi had that advantage. "I've come from the south looking for a village of caves. Is Evan MacManus here among you?" Maybe giving the man's name would allow him entrance, or at least keep that arrow from flying yet.

Once he got inside, though, he had no idea what he would say to MacManus. The American hated him. He'd worry about that when the time came. Working in the intelligence division had given him plenty of practice at coming up with creative stories to keep his neck from the noose. Yet most of those stories were lies.

The man's chin shifted, as though he was listening to someone behind him speak. Then he refocused on Levi and lowered his bow, though he still kept the arrow tight against the bowstring. "You may enter the courtyard." The fellow stepped to the side and motioned with the arrow for Levi to ride forward.

Did he dare? Approaching whatever opening was hidden in that stone would be riding into a nest of vipers. But did he really have a choice? If he spun Chaucer and made a run for safety, this man would likely plant that arrow in his back. And Levi, if he survived, would have lost his best chance to see the village and find out more about the mineral—the secret tool that would win any future war for America as MacManus had claimed.

He had to take this chance. He was a Masters, after all, practically bred to sacrifice his life for Britain. His grand-father and uncle had died for the motherland, and most days his father wished he'd paid that ultimate sacrifice instead of being left without the use of his legs.

Levi nudged his mount forward. He would do what he must to serve his people, though he might be riding to his death. If that happened, perhaps his father would finally be proud of his efforts for their country.

2

"Dismount!" The guard with the bow and arrow motioned for Levi to halt as his mount reached him. The man had finally pulled the arrow away from the bowstring and slipped it back into his quiver. Now, he clutched a knife in one hand.

Levi nodded to show he planned to obey, then eased down from the chestnut gelding. He kept his musket gripped casually in his right hand. If these people were so separated from civilization, maybe they wouldn't even know what the weapon was.

But the man reached out for the gun. Perhaps they weren't so naïve.

Levi flicked his gaze toward the gap in the rocks that he could see better now. The opening ran all the way to the ground at an angle that made it impossible to see until you were standing directly in front. Sunlight and muddy ground appeared through the sliver of opening—the courtyard the man had spoken of.

He handed the rifle over, and the fellow snatched it away. Levi kept his voice friendly. "My intentions are peaceful. I mean no harm."

The man ignored his words, motioning for Levi to proceed through the opening. He called out in French to someone on the other side. "The stranger enters." That must have been a French accent Levi had detected before.

Levi led Chaucer forward. Surely the man realized the gun wasn't Levi's only weapon. Any person traveling through this wilderness would need to carry at least one knife. Three were concealed on Levi's person, but only the hunting knife would be easily found. The guard must feel confident in however many armed men stood on the other side of that wall.

As Levi turned to maneuver through the sideways opening, the first of the armed men appeared in the courtyard ahead. Then two more. Yet something seemed unusual about those two. . . .

His mind took a second to interpret what he saw. The one in front appeared to be a woman, though she was dressed like a man with her bow drawn and an arrow aimed at him. Behind her stood Evan MacManus, musket pointed at Levi's head.

He halted in the middle of the opening, his hands sliding away from his body in an automatic reaction to show he had no weapon at the ready. "I mean no harm." His gaze lifted to MacManus, eyes locking with the enemy spy.

One look at the man's expression made it clear he'd not forgotten that bit of intelligence Levi had overheard. The information that had given the major the upper hand. Well, the dislike was mutual. He'd never forget the day MacManus had led a wagon full of explosives into a fort full of not only soldiers, but women and children. Only a man with no conscience would do that.

The war may have ended, but some things were impossible to forget.

Levi shifted his focus back to the other armed guards. MacManus may hold sway among these people, but the villagers still possessed greater numbers. If he could convince them he wasn't a threat, maybe they would give him a chance to talk peaceably.

The woman stepped sideways to stand by herself, drawing Levi's attention to her. She spoke with bold command. "Who are you? What is your purpose here?"

Levi dipped his chin in deference to her. "My name is Levi Masters. I've been traveling northward, and I saw horse tracks leading this way. My curiosity bid me follow them." None of that was a lie exactly, but it didn't match what he'd told Audrey Moreau. How could two completely different statements stem from the same reality?

Because neither were the full truth. This lying had to stop.

Maybe he could steer the conversation to topics that wouldn't require hard answers on his part. "Can you tell me where I am exactly?"

The woman's chin lifted, and she motioned to the ground in front of her. "Come farther in." Her voice held an indisputable command. No invitation to tea, this.

As the old saying went, in for a pence, in for a pound. He took three strides in, nearly to the place she pointed. Chaucer, ever the obedient steed, trailed along behind him.

"Andre will care for your horse." A lad of around a dozen years stepped forward and took Chaucer's reins.

Levi allowed him to pull the leathers from his hands but raised a palm to stall the boy. "Let me take off my packs first." Apparently they were allowing him to stay—or maybe holding him here? It might be a while before he was allowed to retrieve his things if he didn't take them now.

"They'll be safe. And your horse well cared for." At her words, the young man turned and led Chaucer away. The gelding's obedience no longer felt like a blessing to be thankful for. A bit of loyalty might have been preferred.

"Where have you come from?" The woman's sharp tone pulled his attention back to her.

Should he say Washington? If MacManus didn't already suspect he'd been followed, that would seal his opinion. "From the States. America." He did his best to sound like a Yankee, but it came out sounding more like he was speaking with food in his mouth. He'd never been good at taking on the American drawl.

An older man stepped beside the woman. "You're from England, aren't you?"

A knot formed in Levi's belly. If he told the truth now, what would they do to him? As far north as these people were, maybe they held British sentiment. Though if they spoke French, they might be bitter about Britain taking over the French colonies of Canada. And if they gladly harbored an American spy . . .

Still. He'd already come to terms with the fact he might not make it out of this place alive. If he died today, he'd rather do it with a clean conscience.

He met the man's gaze. "I've not had what I'd called a real home with roots for a while. I mostly travel with my work. But I grew up in Yorkshire, near Kettlewell."

There. They could run knives through him for his ties to Britain if they wanted to.

The older man responded, "We're not accustomed to visitors. In the past, our experience with people from your homeland has been deadly. For that reason, sir, you will understand why we have questions for you before we can allow you to roam freely among our villagers." The fellow nodded toward the woman, which appeared to be a sign for everyone.

Two men stepped forward on either side of Levi, and one at his back.

"To the assembly hall with you." The fellow on his left motioned for Levi to step forward.

If they were simply cautious about strangers, maybe it wouldn't take long for him to set their minds at ease. Whatever had happened to them in the past was unfortunate, but he certainly didn't plan to hurt these people. His only goal was to find out what MacManus had learned and exactly how the US thought it would give them so much power.

The armed men led him across the courtyard, toward the sheer cliffside of the mountain ahead. Doors had been cut at the base of the stone, and they led him to one on the left. One of the guards pulled the wood open, then they stepped into a long stone hallway. Torches flickered off the walls, mounted at intervals to light the corridor. Noises ricocheted from the stone on all sides—the sounds of their steps, the rustle of clothing, even their breathing. Levi worked to make his breaths as quiet as possible. The last thing he wanted was to appear nervous before the villagers.

At the end of the corridor, they turned left, then stopped at a set of tall double doors. His escort opened one, then ushered him into a dark space, though the echoes of their movements proclaimed it to be much larger than the hallway.

"Stop here."

Levi obeyed as darkness enshrouded them. After a moment, one of the men carried a torch into the room, moving along one wall to light torch after torch. These people must not have kerosene lanterns. Did they even have candles? Their system of wooden torches reminded him of the old castles that dated back to England's earliest days.

As the perimeter of the room began to take shape in the glow, the two guards flanking him led the way toward a table near the middle of the room.

He sank onto the wooden bench, the weariness of riding for weeks on end soaking through him. Now was hardly the time to succumb to exhaustion, but how long had it been since he'd sat in a real chair, with velvet upholstery and goose down stuffing? Or laid on a feather bedtick? Their country home had always been modest, but his mother had ensured their comfort as much as she could. He'd never appreciated those small things like he should have.

Not until he left England. Though a few American inns prided themselves on luxuries, most of the country seemed to have no idea what inferior accommodations they suffered under.

Sleeping on pine boughs spread over stony ground, or sometimes even on snow-covered rock, had been a pleasant reprieve from the flea-infested boardinghouse he'd stayed in the week prior to setting off after MacManus.

What sort of homes did these people live in? Would he be offered a place to stay or sent away before nightfall, locked outside their stone walls?

The door widened, and a man stepped in, the older fellow who'd spoken in the courtyard. He must be a leader here, possibly the governor himself.

Behind him entered the woman who dressed nearly as a man and had taken the lead at first. And following her was Evan MacManus.

Levi's chest tightened at the sight of him. Whether these people cast him out of this village of caves or not, he had to learn what MacManus knew.

A few others filed in behind them, all men. Most didn't seem to carry weapons, so perhaps they were elders of the village, come to hear what he would say and make a decision about him. This would be Levi's chance to ask his questions if he could lead the conversation well enough.

The group formed a half circle around him, some of the men taking seats on benches. Those who appeared to act as guards or soldiers remained standing, including the woman, with MacManus by her side. He stood close to her, far nearer than two acquaintances would stand. There must be something between them, an attachment of some sort.

How long had the American stayed here with these people? Had he lived among them? He couldn't have stayed here more than a few months, for Levi had seen him entering and leaving the Army headquarters several times through the course of the war.

"Now . . ." The older man sat directly across from him, his hands on his knees as he studied Levi. "I'm Chief Durand, and these are members of the council. You said your name is Masters?"

Levi nodded.

"And you come from Yorkshire, which is in England?"

Again, he dipped his chin to confirm.

"What is your business in Laurent?"

Levi's chest clenched. He knew what he *should* say. The answer that might save his life and help him learn what he'd come here to discover. But when he tried to summon the words, bile rose instead. A twist on the truth had never been this hard before.

He couldn't stall any longer, so he answered from his heart. "I overheard Mr. MacManus speaking of a village of caves that possessed a unique mineral." He let his gaze shift to the American long enough to catch his narrowed glare.

Levi refocused on Chief Durand. "I found the idea intriguing enough to learn more." He didn't have to say outright that he followed MacManus. They would realize it. The conclusions they would draw likely wouldn't be far from the truth.

The chief looked to MacManus, and his gaze must have given him permission to speak, for he took a step forward. "You're a British spy."

Levi tried not to show the cringe that tightened his insides. The comment wasn't posed as a question, but he had to answer. If he spoke the truth, he would be labeled a concern if these people sided with the Americans.

Yet MacManus knew the war had ended. Surely he would abide by the Treaty of Ghent. Of course, this area was so remote, nothing required these people to follow an agreement signed between two countries thousands of miles away. If Levi simply disappeared, no one would know why—or even where. He'd not known exactly where he would end up, so he'd only written that he'd be heading northwest in his note to his superiors.

As a surge of possible answers rose within him, that growing voice inside pressed the truth forward. "I report to the British War Office. I'm not a spy—at least I've never been called such. I simply research information they request." This was the first time he'd ever taken the initiative to track down a promising detail on his own, though he'd often been told he had the liberty to do so.

MacManus seemed to be working hard to maintain a calm façade, though his gaze shot sparks across the space between them. "A spy. A man I know from experience to be untrustworthy and devious."

The words hung in the air, coiling like a noose around his neck. MacManus knew Levi had been the one to overhear the plans for the Battle of Stoney Creek. Levi couldn't regret sharing those details with the officers in charge. He'd saved lives that day.

Yet MacManus wouldn't feel the same about the event, not when he'd been working for the opposite side. And with a spokesman like this to represent his character, Levi's fate in this place would be almost certain.

3

Levi had to find a way to shift the focus away from himself and move the conversation far from anything involving MacManus. He kept his expression light, then scanned the chamber around them. "This is quite a remarkable room you've built in the mountain."

The ceiling rose in a dome. Surely something as grand as that must have been crafted by the Lord's hand, not chopped out with hammer and chisel.

He dropped his gaze to Chief Durand. "How long have you occupied this area?"

The lines across the man's brow deepened. "We appreciate your kind words, but our council needs time to discuss your presence here before we will consider answering your questions. First, though, we have a few more things to ask."

Levi raised his brows. "I'm expected to answer inquiries when you refuse to respond to my own?"

The man tipped his chin. "You approached our gate of your own accord. We didn't summon you."

Touché.

Levi acknowledged the truth with a respectful dip of his head. "What do you wish to know?" He would answer honestly, place the outcome of this inquisition in the Lord's hands. *I have set the* LORD *always before me: because he is at my right hand, I shall not be moved.* He'd claimed that as his banner verse when he first left England to pursue this work. Now he would finally live it.

The chief's gaze narrowed, taking on the look of a shrewd judge. "How is it you overheard Evan speak of our village? What were you doing at the time?"

Levi swallowed, pressing down the knot in his gut. "I sometimes keep watch outside the Army headquarters building. I saw him enter, and his appearance proclaimed him fresh from the frontier. It intrigued me enough that I followed him. The room where I hid stood two doors down from the chamber in which he met with one of the officers. I . . . might have removed one of the ventilation pieces to better hear." Heat flared up his neck at the obvious spying he was admitting to.

Lord, you promised to protect me, right?

But protect him from the results of his intentional deception? How did that work in God's eyes, exactly? If only he'd never accepted the intelligence commission. He could kick his brother for recommending him for the assignment. Levi had been so eager back then, relieved that he'd finally found a way to serve his country, something that might give him more acclaim than his brothers' multiple merits of valor. A way that he could finally make his father proud.

He'd had no idea the miry pit he was sliding into.

But no more. From this moment forward, every word and every action would be matched up against God's guidance through Scripture.

"And your purpose in following Evan so far was . . . ?" The chief left the sentence for him to finish.

This time, the truth wasn't as hard to push out. "I felt my country needed to know about this new discovery and what America planned to do with it. Evan spoke of a mineral, but I don't know how that would help America win a future war. That's what I came to find out." With each statement of truth, a weight lifted from his chest. Though the scowls around him grew darker, especially the one MacManus aimed at him, the lightness inside meant he could finally breathe freely.

A motion by the door caught the edge of his focus. He didn't let his gaze flick that way immediately but swept his attention around the group until he glimpsed a single figure standing by the door.

Miss Audrey Moreau.

She must not be one of the elders or soldiers, or she would have been invited into the room. Of course she wasn't. She didn't look aged, nor did she dress as a man and wield a knife. She looked like a nymph standing in the shadows. But the darkness shrouded the beauty he'd seen so clearly outside. A brown-haired angel with wide green eyes. Had he frightened her hiding in the woods like that? With everything in him, he hoped not.

"What did you plan to do when you discovered the information you sought?"

Levi forced his focus back to the chief, struggling to clear the muddle from his thoughts.

"I . . . had planned to take the details back to my superiors. With the war over, my commission is also ending. I had hoped this would be my last bit of intelligence." He'd also hoped it might earn him an award of merit.

Consternation flicked across some of the faces around him, and he hastened to say more. "I'm assuming whatever news there would be to share would not endanger your village. Britain would not wish to bring harm."

He sent a glance toward MacManus. "Perhaps my country has not always been fair to its colonies"—he returned his gaze to Chief Durand—"but Parliament wishes to bring aid and protection to its remaining colonies in the New World. I suspect your village is outside the border of the Canadian colonies, but our government would wish to extend the same kindnesses to you, I'm certain."

Levi didn't dare a glance at MacManus again, but the heat emanating from him made the room downright stuffy.

Durand rose, and with him the rest of the group. He looked to the woman. "Have him held until we reach a decision. Once he's secure, I would like you and Evan to join us for the meeting."

One of the guards who led him there stepped forward to grip Levi's upper arm and haul him up. He almost scowled at the fellow's roughness, but with so many around, he had to do his best to stay quiet and follow orders.

Audrey slipped out the moment Papa Durand gave his final instructions. She shouldn't have listened to the questioning, but curiosity about the stranger had stirred too strongly within her. Not that any of the elders would object to her presence, especially since her father hadn't felt up to attending this unexpected council meeting. Every family was allowed a representative on the council, after all, though she rarely attended in her father's stead.

But now the curiosity had turned into unrest, with a

churning inside of her building with intensity. Everything the man had said would likely turn the council against him. Though not for the reasons Laurent would have worried about six months ago.

No, since Evan's coming, her people had finally opened themselves to the possibility that strangers didn't always mean danger to their people. Now they were more willing to hear out a newcomer before planting an arrow in his gut.

But having promised pitchblende to the United States, they'd essentially thrown in their lot with that country. This Levi Masters worked for England—the United States's primary enemy. And the fact that the group that massacred six innocent Laurent citizens a decade ago were also from England would not encourage the council to extend grace to this man.

Yet didn't everyone need grace? None of them were good in the sight of the Lord on their own power. Only the great God who freely offered mercy through the death of Jesus allowed any of them to live.

So who were they to condemn any man based on his country, or even his past? Levi Masters should be condemned or acquitted based on his character and current actions. His honest response to questions that he must've known would condemn him had spoken much for his character. Maybe she could get Brielle to allow her to speak with Levi. Perhaps bring him food and allow her the chance to learn more about him. Then, if necessary, she would exercise her family's right to have a representative on the council.

She would speak for this man if she had to. With the grace she'd been given so many times, both by her heavenly Father and her earthly papa, she couldn't sit by while another person was judged according to something they had no control over.

She padded to the apartment she shared with her father, then slipped inside. Papa sat in his wicker chair by the fire, carving a wooden bowl.

He straightened when she stepped in, and his face wreathed in a welcoming smile as she made her way to the shelves of dishes mounted beside the fireplace. "Bonjour, my girl. You look like you're set on a task."

She reached for a mug and bowl, then set them on a tray and carried it to the fire. She kept a pot of stew always warming for times like this, or if someone in the village took ill. "Evan's come back. And another man followed him here."

Papa's gaze sharpened as she shared the details. He stroked fingers over his close-cropped beard when she finished with, "He's being taken to the storage room for holding until his fate is decided. I imagine he's hungry."

"I suppose the council will be meeting to discuss him?"

She nodded but kept her focus on the stew she scooped into the bowl. Should she encourage Papa to go share his opinion? If he went, she had to make her thoughts known to him. But would he plead on the stranger's behalf if she asked him to?

An image of Levi Masters's earnest face slipped through her mind. When he'd been speaking of his plans to the council, something in his tone, his expression, rang true in her core. He'd lost that veil of deception that had covered his features when she'd met him by the creek. This was the real Levi Masters—she would stake her reputation on it. And she was almost as certain the council would vote against him. Either against his freedom, or possibly even against his life.

She couldn't let that happen.

Yet Papa needed to represent their family on the council if he was able. So many times, his melancholy kept him from taking on that role, whether from an excess of drink or simply fear of what the others thought of him. The rest of the village knew his quirks and took it all in stride, but Papa couldn't always overcome his fears. If he could do so today, she should encourage him.

She placed the dishes and a serviette on the tray, then turned to face her father. "You should go to the assembly room and join the conversation. I hope you'll vote in favor of this new man. He spoke honestly to the council, and I feel confident he's not holding back important details. Even more so, I don't think he means us any harm. We can't punish an innocent man who intends no harm to our people. Yet I fear Evan's influence and the commitment the council made to America will affect the others' judgment. Will you stand up for this Levi Masters?"

Her father studied her, and his jaw seemed to tremble the slightest bit—something she'd noticed a few other times recently. Was he so deep in thought he'd lost his ability to control his bodily reactions? Or did this mean something more ailed him? Maybe there would be enough valerian in the herb garden to help him with these trembles.

"I wish I could meet this man who seems to have captured your regard."

Audrey met his solemn gaze, even as she tried to ignore the heat rising up her neck. "I'm taking this food to him now. Would you like to walk with me?"

Papa shook his head. He rarely made unexpected appearances around the village, staying home most days. With a sigh, he laid his woodwork on the table beside his chair and pushed up to his feet. "I had better see what's happening with the council. I'm surprised Durand hasn't sent someone to summon me."

Her gaze followed her father as he shuffled to the wall beside his bed where his clothing hung on hooks. With slow movements, he pulled on his best frock and ran a comb through his salt-and-pepper locks.

When he turned to her, straightening the tails of his coat, she sent him a warm smile. "You look well, Papa."

The way her words brought a lightness to his face made her throat burn. If only she could make him feel half as loved and appreciated as he'd done for her through the years.

If only she could take away the darkness inside him that made his life such a challenge.

4

When Papa left their chamber, Audrey turned her attention to the pot bubbling beside the fire. Perhaps she should ask Brielle before taking food to their visitor, since he was technically a prisoner.

Surely feeding Philip and Monsieur Masters would be acceptable. Her role had always been to prepare meals for newcomers to Laurent, as they were usually trading parties of Dinee natives. Why should this man be the exception?

With the tray in hand, she rose and made her way out of the apartment and down the chilly hall. Sounds drifted from behind doors she passed along the way—the Mignots' two young boys must be squabbling again, and their mother's voice rose above their bickering with a hearty reprimand. As she passed the Thayers' door, an elderly man's chuckle drifted through the wood. Louise's father-in-law had come to stay with them, giving his home to his newlywed grand-daughter and her husband.

The newly cut apartment for the Chapuis family sat on the left side of the corridor. It was the only home built that far into the mountain so far, though Brielle said Evan would soon be constructing their own home across from the Durands' quarters.

As they continued to excavate deeper into the mountain, more families would be able to spread out. Space had become a precious commodity for some of the growing families. They would all be grateful at the end of winter, when they could spend more time outdoors.

It grew quieter as she neared the storage room at the far end of the hall. She strained to hear voices inside, mostly to make sure she wasn't interrupting something important.

No voices, but a light scuffling noise sounded that might be footsteps.

She tapped on the door. "It's Audrey. I've brought food."

The footsteps neared from the other side. The bar clanged as it slid open, and the door parted to reveal Philip. Audrey glanced around the room, but no one else seemed to be inside except Monsieur Masters, sitting on a fur mat in the center of the room. Philip was one of the most trusted guards, as proven by the fact he'd been left alone to guard the new prisoner.

Audrey stepped in and did her best to lighten the mood with a smile. "I suspect our visitor is in need of something warm and nourishing." She glanced at Philip. "I can come back with a tray for you, too, if you'd like."

Philip shook his head, then glanced at the man watching them from the fur. "I'm not sure this is the right time for him to eat. I'd rather wait until Brielle comes back from the council meeting."

Unease curled in her middle. "I'm sure it can't hurt to let him eat a bit of soup and drink warm tea while we wait. I won't even ask you to untie him. I can help him eat."

Philip's gaze turned uncertain. Before he could voice another protest, she shifted to the man on the floor. With his ankles tied, he sat with his knees bent before him and his hands behind his back. Such a position couldn't be comfortable. Wariness cloaked his expression as he watched her, as though he suspected she might have an ulterior motive.

She offered a warm smile to thaw his suspicion as she lowered the tray to the fur beside him, then dropped to her knees where she could spoon soup into his mouth and lift the cup for him to drink.

"I always keep a stewpot warming, so this is full of all manner of goodness for the body and soul. I added a bit of echinacea to the tea to ward off winter's chill. I know you've been outdoors for a while and may have picked up a sniffle or two."

The guarded look in his eyes eased as she spoke, turning to something like gratitude, or at least the beginnings of it.

She lifted the cup to his lips, letting her gaze roam his face as he drank. She'd done this act for others in the village hundreds of times, nursing those too sick to help themselves. She always tried to use these moments of closeness to see the real person, to look beneath one's weary, lined face to the beautiful soul beneath.

But with this man, she didn't have to look far to see outer beauty. The chiseled jaw, the strong cheekbones, the sharp intensity of his eyes—all of it made her heartbeat speed up. Without his fur hat, his tousled brown locks lay in loose waves, the perfect thickness to run her fingers through.

She jerked her gaze down to his face again as something flipped in her middle. She shouldn't be thinking of such. This might be her only opportunity to gauge his character, to find out anything more that would help her plead his case.

When she focused on his eyes, she saw he already watched her, his Adam's apple bobbing with each gulp of the tea. She lowered the cup to allow him a chance to breathe and to provide some much-needed space between them.

What could she ask him to learn more? Perhaps she should start with allowing him a chance to correct his earlier lie to her.

Reaching for the bowl and spooning a hearty scoop of potato and meat, she kept her voice casual. "So, traveling with Evan, were you?"

His expression took on a proper level of chagrin. More than chagrin, even. Closer to shame. He dipped his chin, his eyes falling too. "I'd never realized how much lying was expected in my profession. Not until I got away from Washington, away from the need for so many falsehoods. The Lord's been working with me on that very thing all the way up from America. That lie I told you was my first in months, and it brought back all the guilt I've been feeling for years now. Between when I saw you by the creek and when I reached the gates of your village, I finally decided *no more*." He met her gaze, his eyes rich with earnestness. "I'm sorry for lying to you. I've asked God's forgiveness, and now I ask yours."

Her chest squeezed as she studied the rich brown of his eyes. "Of course."

She could trust this man. His eyes held no guile. No sign of anything feigned. And now she should be equally forthcoming. She spooned a bite of stew into his mouth. "I'm afraid our people aren't very open toward the English. We had a bad experience with some of your countrymen, and I'm not certain our citizens will be willing to trust you."

Monsieur Masters's brows lowered in concern. "I suspected

your people were sympathetic to America with the way they welcomed MacManus. They do know the war is over, right? Both countries signed the peace treaty not two months ago."

Hope surged in Audrey's chest. The two countries no longer fought? Surely this news would help his cause with the council. She had to make certain they knew. Evan likely had told them, but she had to be sure.

Though every part of her longed to leave the man and run to the assembly room, she held her self still long enough to spoon one more hearty bite into his mouth. "I think Evan would have told them, but perhaps I should go check."

Hope flared in his gaze, the same as what swelled inside her. "Go, then. Don't waste time on me."

She hesitated, glancing from the mostly full bowl in her hands to the half-drained cup on the tray. Leaving the man with food, yet without the ability to feed himself, went against everything within her.

"Go, if you think it'll make a difference. Please. Food can wait."

His final words sent her into motion. She placed the bowl back on the tray and rose, glancing at Philip as she strode to the door. "I need to take care of something. Cut his hands loose, Philip. Please. At least until he finishes eating."

She didn't wait to see if he obeyed, just slipped through the door and sprinted down the long corridor.

When she neared the tall double doors, she slowed, forcing in deep, steady breaths as she collected herself. Would the council reprimand her for barging in? Surely not if she possessed a piece of pertinent information. She had to make sure she didn't come across as an impulsive schoolgirl, eager to spread gossip.

Lord, grant me favor with them. She smoothed her hands over her skirt and inhaled a steadying breath, then reached for one of the doors and pulled it wide enough to slip inside.

Perhaps it was the sound of her step on the stone floor, or the rustle of her skirt, or simply the flash of movement as she stepped into the room, but the eyes of every council member turned to face her. They sat in the same area where they'd questioned Monsieur Masters. All families were represented as far as she could tell, including her father. Brielle also sat in the circle, as she sometimes did in her role of Le Commandant, leader of the guards and hunters. Evan sat beside her.

She did her best to keep her poise and not let her trembling hands show as she stepped forward. Chief Durand stood and approached her. His eyes always held a kindness, especially when he looked at her. With as close as she and Brielle had always been, he'd practically adopted her as another daughter.

Now that kindness in his gaze blended with worry as he met her partway across the room. "What is it, Audrey? Has something happened?"

She swallowed the knot in her throat as she slid a glance toward the others, then readjusted her focus to him. Maybe she shouldn't have come. Surely Evan had told them the news already. No matter how she worded it, her presence would seem unnecessary.

But she'd come this far. She met Chief Durand's gaze. "I took food to our new guest, and he said the war between Britain and America is over. They've signed a peace treaty."

The concern of his eyes slipped away, replaced with seriousness. Almost a sternness as he regarded her. "Yes, Evan brought this news to us."

She nodded. "I wanted to be sure you knew. With the two

countries no longer at war, we shouldn't hold animosity toward him for his nationality."

The lines deepened across his brow. "That's what we've been discussing." He laid a fatherly hand on her shoulder. "Thank you for coming to make certain we knew. We've much to talk through."

That was her command to leave. Did she dare press harder?

She had to. If she didn't speak for Monsieur Masters, would anyone? She stood straighter. "I would like to stay and hear the discussion." The words came out almost like a demand, so she softened them. "Please."

Chief Durand's expression turned troubled again as he studied her. "Your father is here." In other words, their family's single representative already attended. The only time more than one person from a family was allowed would be a case such as Brielle's, where she attended in her position as Le Commandant.

"I'll hold my tongue unless there's information I believe no one else is aware of."

His brows rose. What might she know that these others didn't? Maybe nothing. But she had to stay. Something inside pressed her with the need. She couldn't explain exactly why, but she had to speak up for Levi Masters if the conversation turned the wrong direction.

At last, he sighed. "You may sit with your father as an observer." He turned and strode back to his seat, impatience marking his gait.

Relief slid through her as she followed behind him, then slipped onto the bench beside her father.

Chief Durand scanned the faces in the group. "Now, I believe Monsieur Rochette was speaking."

The man leaned forward, hands on his elbows. "That man came here with evil intent. He said so himself. He can't be trusted. He knows our location now. Who knows what he'll do with that knowledge? We can't just let him leave. He'll be back with an army—or worse."

Audrey squirmed in her seat. The very fact that Monsieur Masters told them the truth pointed to the fact he could be trusted.

"In your opinion, what should be done with him?" Papa Durand kept his voice measured.

"He must be silenced. He can't be allowed to leave here. And he certainly can't be allowed freedom among our women and children."

Audrey clenched the bench beneath her. They were back to this? Pure distrust of all outsiders, especially Englishmen?

"So, you think he should be put to death?"

Audrey cringed at the strong statement. Surely not. The man had done nothing deserving.

Rochette straightened, drawing back. At least hearing the blatant words gave him pause. "Well . . . yes, if that's the only way we can silence him. We can't put our people at risk of the same slaughter as ten years ago."

Audrey's heart ached. Rochette had lost a daughter in that massacre, so it made sense he would encourage caution. But death to an innocent man? Simply because of his fear?

Chief Durand scanned the rest of the group. "Who else wishes to speak?"

She glanced sideways at her father. Would he raise his voice now? Or had he already done so? She had no idea what had been said before she came. Had *anyone* spoken in favor of the Englishman?

Papa caught her gaze and rested his hand over hers. He clearly meant the gesture to soothe her, but it only tightened the clench in her middle. Was he saying he'd already spoken for Levi? Or trying to keep her from raising her voice?

A shuffling sounded to her left, and she glanced over as Evan straightened. His face held a look of steel. "I know the man. At least, I know of him. He works with the British army, and he stole information from me—troop plans I was carrying for the Battle of Stoney Creek. He took them to the British commander, and it nearly decimated an entire regiment of our men. I don't trust him. He followed me all the way up here, staying hidden the entire time. That's not a small thing—neither the journey nor the great effort he took to conceal himself. I'm not sure why he would do all that then appear to come clean and tell us exactly who he is. Something's not right. I can't figure any motive that's not malicious, or at least sneaky."

Audrey's chest compressed even more as Evan spoke. His words made sense. If you looked solely at Masters's actions, they appeared suspect.

Yet the taking of information to use for the British army's benefit . . . wasn't that typical during a war? Each side was trying to gain news about the others' movements so they could better their own strategy.

And she couldn't deny her overwhelming feeling about the man. He'd not hidden anything from them as he answered their questions. He meant them no harm.

But could a feeling be trusted? This seemed even stronger than a feeling. An instinct? A sign from God?

The latter felt more accurate than anything, as strong as this sensation pressed.

Chief Durand studied the faces around the room once more, giving everyone a final chance to speak. She had to take this opportunity.

She lifted her hand enough to gain his attention.

A new crease formed on his brow, but he nodded toward her. "Miss Moreau."

It would be easier to speak boldly if she stood up, but no one else had risen when they talked, so she lifted her chin and stiffened her spine. "I understand the manner in which he came here raises concern. But he answered every one of your questions with the utmost truthfulness—even when those answers showed him in a poor light. As I listened to him speak, I had such a strong feeling here—" She pressed a hand to her chest. "Too strong for anything I could have summoned on my own. An impression I believe wholeheartedly came from our Lord. This man is not a danger to us. If we shed innocent blood, that evil will be marked to our account. He must be set free."

She could sense the stirring among the others in the group. Not only was she a newcomer to the council—an imposter, really—but she advocated the opposite of what the others wanted. She didn't dare meet anyone's gaze except Chief Durand's.

He regarded her for a long moment, his thoughts surely spinning. But in which direction?

At last, he shifted his focus to the rest of the group. "I believe a great deal of prayer is in order here. We cannot take lightly a man's life, nor can we disregard the safety of our people. I ask that we take time for prayer and fasting. Beginning at sunrise tomorrow, let every adult in the village fast until the sun rises the following day. Pray with your families.

Beseech the Lord for His will. Ask Him to set aside our own desires and fears and make His guidance plain. We'll meet here again in three days at the noon mark. That will give sufficient time for us all to hear the Lord's leading and discuss the matter with our families." He sat back and looked around the group once more, allowing the opportunity for any final comments.

The others were nodding. Chief Durand had delayed decisions for prayer before, although she could only remember one other village-wide fast. That had been during the harshest winter she could remember, when their people had been near to starving.

As she rose with her father and followed the stream of people exiting the room, she sent a glance to Brielle. Her friend was speaking with Evan, though from the softness in her expression, their conversation had nothing to do with the prisoner locked in the storage room.

A new tightening clenched within her. Now that Evan had returned, Brielle would marry soon. How would that change the friendship Audrey had treasured since girlhood? Not that Brielle would change, but her focus would be on her new husband. On their new home. Their new life.

Audrey pressed the longing away. Whatever Brielle needed, Audrey would be there for her.

Another thought slipped in. Brielle surely wanted to spend time with Evan now that he'd returned. How would that affect their prisoner? Brielle likely wouldn't have time to stand guard. She wouldn't be spending time in the man's presence to decipher his motives and intentions. Instead, she'd depend on information from others.

Audrey would have to talk with the prisoner in her stead.

She wanted to learn more about the man anyway, so extra time with him would be no hardship.

If only she could find a way to get him out of the village so he could be on his way and the council wouldn't be forced to make a difficult decision. The moment the idea surfaced, she pressed it away. That couldn't be the answer.

Could it?

5

"I imagine Brielle is occupied." Audrey kept her hands furiously kneading dough while she waited for Chief Durand's answer. He'd come to their apartment for a visit with her father after the council meeting. Chief Durand was one of the only men her father knew well enough to relax in his presence.

"She and her beau have gone for a stroll outside village walls. I'm sure they've much news to catch up on."

Audrey didn't glance up to see the twinkle in his eye, but she could hear it in his voice. She had a feeling Brielle and Evan would be catching up on more than just news. How wonderful for Brielle. She deserved this happiness, and Audrey wouldn't wish it away for anything.

But with Brielle so distracted, who was caring for Monsieur Masters? Not that Brielle would focus on more than securing him and learning his intentions. Audrey handled the meals. And that's exactly what she was preparing now, food for her father and Monsieur Masters. Yet not having Brielle as involved with the prisoner felt odd, like there was too much chance something could go wrong.

As she spooned meat into the *Breton galette*, the men's voices slipped into the background. Papa Durand seemed more focused on the stranger's background and how that might influence his future behavior than on the fact that he'd been honest in all the details he shared.

At times, she itched to speak up and remind the chief of that truthfulness. But he'd been there just as she had. And this was his own conversation with her father. She respected both men too much to interrupt as she might have when she was ten.

When she pulled the first round of meat pastries from her new cookstove oven—a wonderful apparatus from the outside world Evan had taught them about—she used a break in conversation to catch Chief Durand's attention. "Will you stay and eat with us?" It had taken her a while to perfect the baking in the new cookstove Papa Durand constructed for her, but now baked goods came out even lighter than from her handmade stone oven.

He gave her a fond smile. "Charlotte will have a meal ready for me soon. Thank you for your hospitality, though." He raised the mug he'd been sipping tea from and handed it to her. "I should head back to our quarters now."

As he rose and made his farewells, Papa followed him to the door and the two men clasped hands. Papa Durand held the grip a moment longer than usual. "It was good to see you at the council meeting, Martin."

The warmth in his voice brought a sting to Audrey's eyes. If only Papa had ten friends like Chief Durand, men who fought through the distance he placed between himself and others. Men who saw the good in him and encouraged it, instead of only the way he secluded himself and sometimes hid in strong drink.

After Papa closed the door, he stood with his shoulders a little straighter, though the shuffle of his step had slowed. "I'm not quite ready to eat, I think. I'll rest a while first. You go ahead, though."

She worked for a smile to offer him. "I'll take food to the guard room first. We can eat together later."

With a weary nod, Papa turned to his bed. Once again, she was on her own.

Levi itched to do something. Anything. All this waiting drove him mad.

Ropes still bound his wrists and ankles. The guard hadn't released him to eat, as Miss Moreau had suggested. Instead, the man had stood beside Levi and poured the stew from the bowl into his mouth. The fellow hadn't been rough in his handling, but he possessed none of the bedside manner Miss Moreau had used.

The stew had settled well in his hungry belly, so he knew it wasn't food that caused the unrest now stirring inside him.

Though the guard stood by the wall, casually leaning against the stone with his arms crossed and one foot cocked, his stare on Levi remained constant. The large hunting knife strapped at his waist and the tomahawk on the other side made him appear fully armed, especially since he likely had additional blades secured in places no one could see.

Sitting quietly on the fur, Levi kept his gaze casual as he took in the room around him. There seemed to be only one entrance—the door that led to the long hallway he'd been escorted down. Would they keep him guarded at all times?

Did they plan to hold him long? No one had come to tell him whether the council had made a decision. Maybe they were still deliberating, although several hours must have passed by now. Surely they couldn't find this much to discuss about him.

A soft tread sounded in the hallway, and the guard straightened, coming to full alert.

Levi focused on the door but kept the corner of his eye aware of what the guard did. The bar clanged as it slid open, then the door cracked to reveal the same lovely face that had come before.

Her smile struck him anew, its sweetness heightening her pleasing features so much that she looked like an angel. An angel bearing another tray of food.

She graced him with the smile first, then turned to the guard. "I've brought food for you both." She spoke in French, but her words were easy enough to follow. Levi had never been across the channel to France, but his father made sure all three of his sons were fluent in that language, and at least passable in Spanish.

The guard studied Miss Moreau. "Is the council still meeting?"

She shook her head. "They discussed the situation and have chosen tomorrow as a day of fasting and prayer. They'll meet again in three days to reach a decision."

The guard frowned. Did he disagree with the plan? Or maybe he simply wished he weren't locked in this room all day with a stranger.

Miss Moreau gave the man another of her angelic smiles. "I'm sure Brielle will come soon to speak with you. In the meantime, I brought Breton galette and warm tea."

She turned toward Levi and lowered the tray onto the fur beside him. The aromas of pastry and some kind of meat rushed up to him, and his body reacted viscerally. His stomach rumbled, and Miss Moreau glanced up at him with a knowing smile.

His grin felt too much like a schoolboy's as he did his best to cover. "I must be hungrier than I knew."

"Let's feed you then." She turned back to the guard. "Cut him loose please, Philip, so he can eat." Her tone commanded, and surprisingly, the guard seemed to be considering her words. This woman must be highly respected for even the armed guards to show her such deference.

She motioned toward Levi's arms and shifted to allow the guard—Philip—better access. "Please. A man should be allowed to feed himself." Again, her tone brooked no opposition.

After a moment, the man stepped near and moved behind Levi. "Only while he eats."

He gripped one of Levi's wrists, then after a moment of pressure, the strap loosened around that arm. The man unwound the cord from the wrist, then stepped back. The rope remained looped around his left arm, which would make it easier to retie him. But for now, Levi could move.

His upper arms ached as he pulled his hands around in front of him.

Miss Moreau beamed as she extended a plate loaded with two meat pastries. Again, the whiff of warm savory aromas flooded his senses.

He reached for the plate, then lifted one of the galettes to his mouth. Though he'd been prepared for a pleasant taste, the infusion of flavors that spread across his tongue sluiced through his body, drawing his eyes closed as he savored each nuance. He'd not eaten anything this delicious since . . . he couldn't remember when. Maybe nothing had ever been this good. Perhaps his hunger enhanced the taste, but this woman was proving she possessed a remarkable talent with food.

After the bite slid into his contented stomach, he opened his eyes to find her watching him, a secret smile curving the corners of her mouth. He lifted the remainder of the pastry. "You made this?"

She nodded, her cheeks pinking as her eyes dipped. As adorable as the look was, part of him wanted to reach forward and nudge her chin back up. She should be proud of such skill.

Instead, he settled for giving her a few paltry words. "It's excellent. Better than excellent." Then he focused his attention on his next bite.

As Levi filled his mouth with meat pie, Miss Moreau stood with a second plate and turned to the guard. The man took it but placed the dish on the floor by the wall with a simple, "Thank you. I'll eat later."

"I'm sure Brielle will come as soon as she's able to give you more details and a guard schedule." Miss Moreau dropped her voice and switched back to French as she spoke to the man. Surely they didn't think they hid their words from him by speaking that language. Many Englishmen spoke fluent French. But would they know that all the way out here?

Philip nodded, though something in his expression seemed frustrated. Brielle must be the woman who dressed as a man. A leader among them, it seemed.

As Levi finished off the first pastry and started into the

next, Miss Moreau moved back to kneel by the tray. She appeared to be organizing things, but something in her manner told him she mostly watched him.

At last, she gave up the pretense and raised that angelic smile to him. "So, Monsieur Masters. You said you have family back in England?"

He nodded, swallowing the bite so he could speak. "Mum and Dad have a home near Kettlewell. My younger sister is still there. My two older brothers work abroad."

She raised her brows. "Spies like you?" Her lips drew together in a pert expression that made him want to tweak her nose.

"Not spies. The eldest is a captain in His Majesty's Navy, and the other has a desk job in the war office. It's because of him that I obtained my commission." Levi's stomach twisted with that last bit. This commission hadn't been the blessing he'd expected.

She studied him, as though she could see some of what he felt. "Do you regret the work you've done?"

Her words crept in, weaving through his mind in a way that overturned what he'd always told himself. *Did* he regret the mission he'd devoted himself to these past three years? As his mind sifted through the things he'd accomplished, the intelligence he'd been able to pass along—one piece that had possibly saved a battalion of troops in the Battle of Stoney Creek—he tried to sort through his feelings about the job. "I . . . Some of the information I've learned has saved lives. I don't regret that. War is an awful business. I understand when it's necessary to maintain safety and quality of life for the citizens, but I despise battles fought to gain land and satisfy greed."

Bitterness crept into his tone, and he paused to gather himself again. He focused on the clear green of her eyes, reminding him of bright, cool moss on a stone. "I don't regret helping save lives, but I do regret every lie I've told along the way. I'm glad my commission is over. Glad the war has ended too."

"What will you do now? Return to England?" Her expression held curiosity, no sign of hidden intent. Even if she was probing to report back to her people, he'd committed to honesty. And the fact that she spoke as though he would be released soon boded well.

"I think so. At least, that's what I'd planned. I suppose I'll go back to Yorkshire and see how I can help Mum. The town is small, so it's hard to find work there. Dad is lame in both legs and can't earn enough to support them, so Mum and my sister are clothmakers."

Audrey's brows drew together as sorrow swam in her gaze. "I'm sorry to hear about your father's struggles. From illness or injury?"

The familiar cloak of weariness pressed over him. "Shot in one of the French revolutionary wars. The bullet hit in his lower back, and he lost feeling in both legs."

"How dreadful." With the pain in her expression, Miss Moreau truly seemed to mean the words. "There's a man in our village, Louis, who suffers from a similar challenge. It's made life so much harder for him and his entire family."

The way she spoke and the emotion in her voice wound through him, as though she really might understand what it had been like growing up with his father bound to a chair. The physical challenges had been hard, but Dad's moods had been the worst. "It's been hard on Dad and Mum both.

My sister helps a lot, both with Dad and with their business. That area is known for its wool, you know, and they've built up a reputation for beautiful fabrics."

Her face perked. "Really? I've always thought how fascinating it must be to create fabric from loose hair. Most of our clothing comes from animal hides." She brushed the leather of her skirt. "This village you come from . . . Kettlewell, did you call it? What is it like? Bigger than Laurent?" Her voice held a wistfulness. Did she want to see more of the world?

He chewed a bite of pastry as he thought through what little he'd glimpsed so far of this place. "I've only seen a few of your people, so I'm not certain how large your village is, but Kettlewell is a small farming community of about twenty families. We lived a couple miles outside of it, yet close enough for easy trade."

Movement from the guard, who stood nearby, brought Levi's attention up to the man. He pointed at the last half of the meat pie in Levi's hand. "Finish. I need to tie you again."

Levi nodded and returned his focus to eating. When he'd swallowed the last delicious bite, Miss Moreau nudged a mug closer to him.

His mouth watered as much as it had for the food. Finding a decent cup of tea had been a challenge since coming to America. The drink she'd served earlier had been different from English tea but possessed a strong welcoming taste. She could make a tidy sum by selling it as a specialty drink in the genteel markets of London.

With his first swallow, the flavors bit just enough, then went down with velvety smoothness. He breathed out a contented sigh, then eyed her. "What do you put in this? I've never tasted a tea quite like it."

She graced him with another angel smile. "Echinacea mostly, and a few other leaves to smooth the taste. It keeps us healthy through the winter."

The guard moved behind Levi to retie his hands, so he downed the rest of the drink in three gulps. As he handed the mug back to Miss Moreau, he gave her a grateful smile. "A fine meal, ma'am. Thank you."

She gathered up her tray and stood as Philip re-bound the cord around his wrists. With the leather cutting into his flesh, he watched Miss Moreau send a final sad smile, then step out the door.

He couldn't help thinking of her as a friend. His only friend in this place of suspicion.

6

Audrey couldn't remember the last time she'd had such unrest in her spirit as she returned the tray and used dishes back to her apartment. Her heart told her Levi Masters was not only innocent, but also a good man. Their conversation over dinner had confirmed that suspicion.

But what would the Lord have her do with the knowledge? She'd made her opinion known to Chief Durand and the council. Should she have been more vocal during the meeting? Perhaps, but it hadn't seemed the right thing at the time. Her father served as their family's representative.

Maybe Brielle could do something. She would likely still be with Evan, which meant Audrey should leave the two sweethearts to their reunion. Yet, this business with their visitor was urgent. Most of the villagers and council members would have their opinions set by tomorrow, even though Papa Durand allowed three days for discussion. Brielle could help influence those decisions, but Audrey had to speak with her soon to set things in motion.

Evan's prior experience with Monsieur Masters would hold weight with Brielle. But she and Audrey had been friends their entire lives. The closest of friends—sisters in so many ways. Surely that would carry weight as well.

After placing the dishes to soak in the wash water, she wiped her hands on a cloth and made her way back into the rear corridor. The Durands' apartment sat one door down, and she knocked gently on the door, then waited. Usually, she would enter after that first knock, as though this were her own home. But with Evan having returned . . . she didn't want to walk in on something better left in privacy.

"Enter." The voice inside belonged to Charlotte, her sweet tone barely carrying through the door.

Audrey opened the door and stepped in, sweeping her gaze around the room. Charlotte worked by her food shelves, while the rest sat around the table—Papa Durand, Andre, and even Brielle and Evan. The tension in her shoulders eased, and she smiled at the group. As natural a smile as she could manage. She'd located Brielle; now she just had to get her alone to talk.

Papa Durand and Evan both rose as she entered, then Andre hastily followed suit, stuffing a bite of food in his mouth as his chair nearly toppled behind him. She motioned them all down again. "Don't bother yourselves on my account. I've come to see if I could borrow Brielle a moment." She glanced at her friend and gave a hopeful look.

Brielle nearly glowed, the happiness of the return of her betrothed showing clearly in her expression. "Of course." She pushed to standing, and her gaze slid to Evan as her voice lowered. "I'll be back soon."

The besotted look Evan returned to her tightened something in Audrey's belly. It should be happiness for her friend, but Evan's words against Monsieur Masters still rang in her memory. *I don't trust him. Something's not right.*

Brielle followed her into the hallway, but Audrey kept going until they reached her own apartment—the only place they would have privacy to speak plainly. Papa still snored on his bed, but she and Brielle could keep their voices low.

"What is it?" Brielle's tone held a mixture of curiosity and frustration.

Audrey turned to face her. "I'm sorry to pull you away from your beau on the night of his homecoming, but this is important."

Brielle's expression turned worried, and she sent a glance to Papa's sleeping form. "What's wrong?" More than once, Brielle had stepped in to help when Audrey was at her wits' end with her father. Sometimes she simply listened to Audrey's worries, but other times she'd come up with ways to make things better, to ease Papa's angst or keep him from using up all her winter supplies.

This time, though, she needed help of a different sort. "It's the newcomer."

Brielle's attention jerked up to her face. "The British spy? What has he done?"

Audrey reached out to lay a soothing hand on her friend's arm, anything to ease the tension coiling through Brielle. "He hasn't done anything. Nothing bad, that is. It's just . . . I don't think he means us any harm, Brielle. I know Evan had a bad experience with him, but I've spoken with the man—several times, actually—and he—"

"You've spoken with him several times? Why?" Brielle's tone was half-curious and half-wary.

Audrey started to make light of her time with the man but paused just before the words slipped out. This was Brielle. They'd spoken of their deepest secrets. Their innermost fears and dreams. She would understand if anyone would. Audrey inhaled a steadying breath. "Something doesn't feel right about his situation, Brielle. The way we're treating him, as though he's come to infiltrate our town and kill us all . . . that's not his plan, Brielle. I really think he's a good man."

Now the curiosity had stolen completely over her expression. "How can you know that? What has he said?"

"He's struggled with the lying involved in his work for the army. He's relieved the war is over and he can return to his parents and sister in Kettlewell. His father is confined to a chair, his legs unable to hold him—the same way Jeannette's husband is—so his mother and sister make cloth to sell. He seems just like one of us."

Little by little, all hint of emotion slid away from Brielle's face. This was her Le Commandant expression, the one where she honed her focus to protecting and providing for Laurent. She would show no mercy to their prisoner in this mood.

Audrey reached for Brielle's arm again, but it took everything in her not to shake some sense into her friend. "Please, Brielle. Speak with him yourself. See what you think, but do it with an open mind."

Brielle shook her head. "I'll speak with him eventually, but my father and the council have determined what shall happen. A fast tomorrow, then the vote in three days. I'll share my opinion by voting with the others." Then the solidity of her face eased, and her eyes softened. "That's one of the things I've always loved about you. The way you want so much to see the best in people, even when it's not there. Just . . . please be careful, Audrey. Don't let yourself get too worried about his situation." The encouraging smile Brielle gave her turned joyful. "I'd better get back now."

But as she left, she pulled all hint of that joy from the room, leaving only thick foreboding that wrapped around Audrey like a smothering fur. Brielle would do nothing to help. Where else could she turn?

Audrey stifled a yawn as she curled in her chair by the fire. She'd been up since the wee hours of the morning as usual, but with today being a day for fasting, she'd not begun her typical baking. She'd missed the scent of pastries filling their apartment in those sacred early hours.

Not today, though. She'd spent the morning seeking God's will in the situation with Levi Masters. Pleading for His guidance. Searching Scripture.

Yet nothing had presented itself as direction from the Lord. The Scripture had nourished her spirit, of course. The Psalms always did that, especially the ones written by David. She could relate so well to his cries for righteousness, for God's hand on his life. *Purge me with hyssop, and I shall be clean: wash me, and I shall be whiter than snow.*

Her own soul cried the same, yet it gave no answer in the situation with Monsieur Masters—Levi, as she'd begun to think of him in her prayers.

Papa still snored from his bed, but enough time had passed that the prisoner and his guard should be awake. She could take them fresh water. Maybe the path the Lord intended for her would make itself known along the way.

With two large mugs in hand, she slipped out the back

door into the corridor. This hallway had been built in the rear of the apartments so no one would need to go outside during the winter snowstorms to visit their neighbors.

She kept her tread soft to keep the sound from echoing off the stone walls. No one else should be out this early, but the stirrings of families beginning their day drifted through many of the doors she passed.

When she reached the storage room at the end of the hall, she tapped her knuckles, then slid the bar open.

Leonard must have been assigned night duty, for he lifted groggy eyes to her when she stepped inside. He was one of the newer guards, a year younger than herself. Brielle didn't usually give him night shifts. Only a few of the men could manage them well, Philip among them. Perhaps Brielle hadn't fully focused on her duties yet since Evan's return. Audrey had seen her only in passing the night before, just long enough to ensure she planned to check on Philip and the prisoner.

Audrey shifted her gaze to Levi, and something inside her clenched at the sight of him. He sat much as he had the evening before, hands tied behind him, knees bent with his ankles also bound. But he didn't look quite as . . . put together. Maybe the feeling came from the stubble on his jaw or the rumple of his dark hair. Her fingers itched to comb through it, though to do so would be dreadfully improper.

To cast that thought away, she turned to Leonard and held out a cup. "I brought you both water."

He pushed up to his feet and took the mug, then she shifted to help Levi drink. Behind her, Leonard's voice gave her pause. "Audrey, I need to run down to my quarters for a minute. Can you stay here with the prisoner? It's been quiet all night. Just keep him tied and the door locked. I'll leave you a knife in case you need it."

Leonard looked tense, perhaps as though he needed a chamber pot. Heat flushed her neck at the thought, and she nodded. "Of course. Take as long as you need."

After handing her his hunting blade, he strode across to the door, and awareness sank through Audrey. She would be alone with Levi Masters. She had the ability to set him free if she chose.

If she dared.

Is this your leading, God? Maybe the idea and opportunity were the direction she'd been praying for. Everyone in Laurent seemed set against the man. If she set him free now, she might even be saving his life.

The moment the bar clanged across the door and Leonard's footsteps faded, she spun to the prisoner and moved into action. "We have to go quickly." She dropped to her knees by his feet and sawed through the cord binding his ankles. Leonard kept his knife sharp, which made the task easier.

When she had his legs free, she dared a glance at his face as she rose and strode around behind him. His expression proved hard to read. The line between his brows could be from his focus, yet she found none of the joy there she'd expected. Did he not wish to be set free? Surely he understood what she was doing.

The seconds to cut through the binding at his wrists seemed to take hours. At last, she'd released him. "Get up and follow me."

She grabbed the inside lever to lift the bar from the door. She cringed at the soft clang it made, then eased the partition open. A glance down the hallway showed no one out. The early hour worked to their advantage. As long as Leonard didn't come back while they were in the corridor . . .

She motioned Levi to follow, then crept down the corridor as he fell into step behind her. Using long strides, she covered as much ground with each quiet step as she could. She'd learned the art of walking softly from Brielle, but would the large man behind her be able to do the same?

Yes. Maybe they taught that skill during spy training, for she barely heard him behind her.

They would have to pass four doors on the left and one on the right before they reached her own. She dared not chance going all the way down to the short connecting hallway that led outside. They could cut through her apartment. Surely Papa would still be sleeping, and she could gather food and warm gear for Levi to take with him.

Then she would have to make sure none of the hunters were outside before she sent him into the courtyard. This early on a winter morning, when the muddy tones of morning light barely colored the air, no one would likely be out . . . she prayed.

But she would address that challenge if it came. For now, they had to make it down the corridor.

The first door they passed belong to the Rochette family. The children were all older, so only a quiet murmur sounded through the door. She glanced back at Levi to make sure he was keeping up. He gave her a nod, only a step behind.

She pushed out a breath and kept moving. The chatter of children's voices sounded through the second door. A man spoke from behind the third—Monsieur Thayer always thundered when he talked.

At the fourth door, the latch bobbed as she passed. Her heart lurched into her throat, and she reached back for Levi's hand. She grabbed his wrist and tugged him forward so anyone who saw them from behind would see a pair walking together.

She didn't dare look back. Maybe someone had only been preparing to open the door and hadn't actually stepped out. She didn't breathe, her entire body squeezed tight except for her legs nearly running beneath her.

At last, they reached her door. She tugged the latch string and pushed inside, pulling Levi with her. The moment they cleared the opening, she spun and pressed the door shut.

Her entire body trembled, and she could only draw tiny breaths. Papa's snores still rumbled from the corner—a small relief.

But Leonard would be striding back down to the storage room any minute. She had to get Levi Masters out of village walls before the guard sounded an alarm.

She spun and ran to the shelf where she kept food, grabbing a satchel and throwing in rolls and pastries, nuts and dried berries, and smoked meat. That would have to be enough.

She motioned him toward the door leading outside as she ran that way herself. Setting the food bundle on the floor, she grabbed Papa's coat. Her own would never fit on him, and she'd already been working on a new garment for her father. This would have to do.

She thrust the coat into Levi's hands. "Put this on. Quickly."

As he obeyed, she donned her own coat. She finished before him, so she grabbed up the food bag, then reached for the door latch.

"Miss Moreau." This was the first time Levi had spoken

since she released him, and his voice rumbled deep enough
to stop her short.

She glanced back at him, raising her brows even as her
heart thundered in her chest.

His expression looked worried. "Will you be in trouble
for helping me?"

A weight pressed in her chest, slowing her ragged pulse.
She'd not let herself think about that. She'd only seen an
opportunity and grasped it.

"What will they do to you?" His voice grew tighter, and
his words were like a hand around her own throat.

She shook her head, working to clear the panic. "I'll be
fine. We have to get you across the courtyard." She would
work out her own problems after he'd gone.

Surely once she explained her reasons for aiding him . . .
The villagers knew her well—knew her heart to help those
in need. Wouldn't they trust her instincts?

Too much worry answered that question. She couldn't let
fear slow her down now. She'd gone too far to turn back,
and she still believed strongly that Levi should be allowed
to go free.

"My horse?"

She frowned as she thought through where they might
have taken the animal. Laurent didn't own any livestock.
"Evan's horse was limping badly, so they kept him in the
courtyard. He's not fit to travel. I suspect your horse was tied
somewhere outside the village walls where he could graze.
Either to the southeast, or maybe to the west." She pointed
each direction she named. "I don't think you have time to
look for him now. Once Leonard finds you missing, all the
men will begin searching. You have to be gone by then."

They couldn't waste another minute. Cracking the door, she peered outside. Apartments lined two sides of the square courtyard, and the stone wall formed the other two sides. A gatehouse had been built in one corner where dwellings met the wall. Would it be occupied right now? Even though the council put a great deal of importance on safety, she knew better than anyone that the guard manning the gatehouse didn't always actively scan its tiny windows for threats. Especially this early on a morning so cold.

No motion appeared in the courtyard. She scanned the fronts of the apartments once more to make sure no one stood quietly in front of their quarters.

Then she pulled the door wider and stepped outside. After Levi followed, she closed the door, then strode toward the front gate. Everything in her wanted to sprint forward and be done with this final leg of the journey, but if they kept to a walk, anyone glancing outside might think she was strolling with her father. Of course, anyone who knew Papa would find it very odd that he would be up and moving so early.

She glanced sideways at Levi. "Pull your hood up. People might think you're my father."

The way the words sounded struck her the moment they left her mouth. Anyone who got a look at this man's face would never think he looked like her father. His shoulders were broader too. But they only had to convince people from a distance.

They'd nearly reached the gate when shouts sounded from behind.

She grabbed Levi's arm and broke into a run. By the time they stepped through the opening, he'd switched to pulling her.

Outside the wall, she scanned the open area. There was no sign of his horse grazing nearby. "Go. Run through those woods. There's not enough snow to leave tracks and you can stay under the trees for quite a distance. Then you'll see a row of mountains in front of you. Go past the first one, then on the east side of the second peak, there's a cave. There's a cliff just below it that makes it look impossible to reach, and a juniper tree blocks the entrance so you can't see the opening until you're standing at the branches. You'll find a steep path to the left of the cliff that will get you up to the tree. I don't think anyone here knows about the cave behind it. I only found it when I was gathering juniper bark. God go with you."

He spun to face her, his eyes almost fierce. "I don't like leaving you in danger. What will they do to you?" Worry formed deep lines across his handsome face.

Her chest ached, partly from breathing the icy air, but mostly from the fear that now gripped her insides. Again, she shook her head to clear it away. "I'll be fine." Although this new pounding in her chest didn't feel fine. It felt like she would face severe punishment.

"Come with me." The earnestness in his voice drew her gaze to his. "I'll keep you safe."

The thought appealed to her more than it should, so much so that it scared her. She pulled back and shook her head once more, breaking their gaze. "Go. Quickly." The pounding of footsteps behind them gave urgency to her words.

Without another sound, Levi turned and sprinted into the trees.

As the crackle of his feet stamping twigs faded, she prepared to face the oncoming hoard.

7

Leonard burst through the gate first, sliding to a stop when he saw her. As he panted, Brielle plunged through behind him, Evan nearly stumbling on her heels.

"Where is he? Did you see him?" Brielle pushed past Leonard and scanned the area around them.

Then she turned to Audrey. "Where did he go?" Both her tone and her glare said she knew Audrey had something to do with the escape. But recapturing the man remained her primary goal at present.

Audrey released a steadying breath. "He means us no harm, Brielle. Let him be."

Anger flashed across her friend's face, and she shifted her attention to the ground around them. Looking for tracks, no doubt.

Audrey fought the urge to step in front of the path Levi had taken so Brielle wouldn't see his prints in the snow. Once in the woods, his trail would be harder to find.

But true to her usual ability, Brielle found the tracks within seconds. Striding forward, she broke into a run as she headed toward the woods. Evan and Leonard followed in her wake, and the glare Leonard sent Audrey as he passed made her want to wrap her arms around herself.

The three disappeared into the trees, and she could do nothing but watch. Was Levi far enough ahead to get away? Would he find the cave? With so much snow on the ground to reveal his tracks, hiding up there on the rocky mountain might be his only hope of staying protected.

More footfalls sounded from inside the village wall. Philip and Wesley sprinted through the opening but slowed when they saw her.

She motioned the way Brielle had gone. "Into the trees." Attempting to stop these two would be futile, especially when Brielle had already located Levi's trail. If Audrey appeared to go along with things now, perhaps her penalty would be lessened.

Her insides clenched. What would they do to her for helping the prisoner escape? Physical punishment, like a whipping? The knot in her middle tugged tighter. Would they send her away? She'd been following her conscience in saving an innocent man. Maybe she should have waited and pleaded his case with the council once more. Would God have turned the hearts of the people during the day of fasting and prayer?

I'm sorry if I ran ahead of you, Lord.

But perhaps God's plan all along had been to use her to free Levi Masters. Why else would she have felt such a strong certainty that he was innocent?

She didn't know the right course anymore.

The pressure inside made her want to vomit. And part of the turmoil still came from worry for Levi. If Brielle found him and brought him back, this would all be for naught. She would have risked her position in the village and, worse yet, Levi's very life for nothing.

Lord, let him find safety.

Perhaps she should go back into the village, but she couldn't bring herself to yet. She wasn't ready to face the disappointment and anger of those she loved. Had Papa awakened and been told what had happened? She could imagine Chief Durand pounding on the door until her father rose, then the two of them discussing the matter, serious concern on the chief's face and pain wreathing her father's.

The knot in her middle pulled even tighter, if that were possible. She wrapped her arms around herself and began to pace.

Levi sprinted through the trees, ducking under branches and doing his best to avoid patches of snow or mud where his tracks would be obvious. They would be able to follow him if they slowed down to focus on finding his trail, but Lord willing, he would be tucked in that cave by then. If he found the place.

Lord, let me find it. Don't let this be my demise.

He never would have run if the opportunity hadn't practically forced itself on him. Perhaps he should have said no. Waited for God to work on his behalf among the council. But when Miss Moreau had sliced through his bindings and motioned for him to follow her, it had seemed like a miracle only God could orchestrate. Like in the book of Acts when God sent an angel to lead the Apostle Peter out of prison. Miss Moreau had looked like an angel from that very first time he saw her. Maybe God truly had sent her to free him.

If so, Lord, help me to keep from being recaptured.

Brighter light shone through the trees ahead, which meant he was nearing the edge of the woods. He slowed as an open stretch of snow spread before him. He couldn't travel across that without leaving obvious prints. Beyond the flat stretch rose the first of the mountains Miss Moreau had described. He could just see a second peak beyond it. That would be the one with the cave on the eastern side.

His gaze swept back to the tree line, first to his right, then to his left. Maybe if he followed the edge of the woods for a while, he could get closer to the mountains. Perhaps even find a place where the snow had melted, and he would have a better chance of getting across to the rocky peak. From there, he should be able to find a path over the stones and avoid snow-covered areas.

Aiming left, he moved back into a jog, picking his way carefully and ducking low to avoid the branches.

Was that the sound of footsteps tromping through the woods behind him? With his heart pounding so loud in his ears and his own feet heavy beneath him, he couldn't be certain. He didn't dare slow enough to look back.

The line of evergreens seemed to be curving away from the mountain. He might have to simply charge across the snowy expanse and count on the rock-covered cliff beyond to hide his tracks.

There appeared to be some kind of dip in the open land ahead, and as he neared, the indentation turned out to be a barely trickling creek running from the mountain to the trees. This might be exactly what he'd been looking for.

The small stream of water wove through puffy sections of snow on either side. If he ran through the liquid, he would leave no mark that he'd been there. But the thick leather of his boots wouldn't hold up against so much moisture. His feet would be sodden by the time he reached the mountain. He could go a while longer with wet boots, but not too far or frostbite would take over.

Once he got up on the rocks, he could strip off his tunic and undershirt and wrap his feet in them. This thick fur coat would keep his upper body warm.

Armed with that plan, he sprinted the last stretch to where the creek met the woods, then charged into the water. In some sections, the tiny stream barely spread wider than his foot, but he was careful not to bump against the snow on the sides of the bank.

His feet burned as water soaked through the leather, then seeped into his wool stockings. It didn't take long before his feet grew numb.

He allowed himself to look back at the trees once. No one appeared there. He tried to hunker low as he ran, but he would be seen if anybody looked. Finally, he neared the rocky base of the cliff. He might make the escape yet.

As he reached the first few knee-high stones that signaled the base of the mountain, his numb feet had grown so heavy he was beginning to stumble. *Give me strength, Lord.*

Using his hands, he climbed up on the rocks. The mountain didn't rise very steeply, but with his feet so frozen, he would be more surefooted if he kept going on hands and feet. Tiny streams of water ran down the slope from several directions to form the creek he'd been walking in. He followed one up the slope, so his wet boot tracks weren't so obvious on dry rock.

As he maneuvered, he finally had to leave that line of damp rock to veer around the east side of the mountain. He needed to reach that second peak. Only then could he find safety.

A shout sounded in the distance. A man's voice echoed across the open space.

Levi spared only a quick glance over his shoulder, enough to see at least two figures standing at the edge of the woods. One began sprinting toward him, and the other leapt forward to follow.

He refocused his efforts on maneuvering around the mountain. He'd already traveled a quarter of the way around and at least a third of the distance up. He shouldn't go any farther up, as he'd just have to go down again on the other slope. But if he could put the mountain between him and his pursuers . . .

The faster he moved, the clumsier he got. Not only were his feet numb, but his gloveless hands burned from so much contact with the icy stone. Rocks skittered from under his feet, and he stumbled to his knees more than once. But he still made progress.

His pursuers wouldn't have wet feet to slow them down, though. They could travel twice as fast as he could over this mountain.

His only hope was to hide. He no longer had time to find the cave.

He straightened and scanned the area around him. Boulders littered the slope, several of them large enough to conceal him. But his pursuers would see him the moment they passed wherever he perched. Could he shift around a rock so he always kept the stone between him and his pursuers?

Perhaps. That seemed like a questionable possibility, but it might be his only option.

The echo of stones clattering behind him brought his attention around. The two men had reached the base of the mountain, and a third had joined them now. One appeared to be the woman who dressed like a man, but he didn't take time to recognize the others. He didn't have a second to waste.

Spinning back around, he glanced from boulder to boulder to pick the best choice. A rock that would shield him completely and allow him to shift around it when his pursuers passed.

There. The stone about fifteen strides forward and a little down the slope should do.

Just as he started forward, a force slammed into his side. He stumbled to the left and barely kept from tumbling.

A piercing pain penetrated his awareness, like a knife between his ribs. He twisted to see an arrow protruding from his right side. His breath came hard. His thick fur coat had stopped the missile from going in deep. He could pull out the head and keep moving.

Fumbling with the buttons of his coat, he finally worked enough to pull the right flap away from his body. As he moved the coat, the arrowhead shifted inside him, biting deeper into his flesh.

He reached for the place where the shaft met his side. The stone head penetrated his skin but hadn't fully submerged in his flesh. *Thank you, Lord.*

Locking his jaw, he wrapped his hand around the base of the shaft and gave a hard outward tug.

The arrow pulled out of his flesh, leaving behind a fresh burning. He pressed his shirt to the area to staunch any blood flow. He could bandage himself later. The arrow still protruded through the hole in his coat, but he didn't have time to work it out now.

Sounds of footsteps on rocks drifted toward him, but his pursuers had disappeared temporarily behind boulders on the slope. He had to move now.

Ducking low, he scrambled forward and down to the boulder he'd chosen to hide behind. He reached the stone and tucked behind it, then forced himself to still. His breath came in deep gasps, the icy air burning his lungs and making his vision wavy. His side still stung, and his feet felt like limestone blocks that didn't belong to his body.

But maybe he was safe.

The steps grew nearer, perhaps reaching the place he'd been when he was struck with the arrow. A man's voice sounded, too low for him to understand. The woman responded, her words also indecipherable.

Levi forced his breath to slow and quiet. His eyes struggled to focus, as though he were light-headed. He worked for deeper breaths, though still as silent as he could manage. Was this a side effect of so much exertion with his feet benumbed? He'd never felt this odd sensation, like he was both heavy and light at the same time. Of course, he'd never run through an icy creek then climbed a mountain before.

The footsteps came closer but didn't sound like they were on the same path as before. Had they gone farther up the mountain? Or down? Maybe the searchers had spread out.

His vision became even more blurry, and a fog descended in his mind, making it hard to think through the questions.

Had he grown too cold and his body was beginning to succumb to the elements? Surely not. The air held the sharp bite of winter, but many of the nights he'd endured on the ride north to this place had been more frigid.

His mind finally registered footsteps almost precisely above him. He had to move, had to shift down below the boulder. He might already be too late. With his vision so dim, he couldn't know for sure.

With as much effort as he could manage, he lifted the foreign blocks his feet had become high enough so they didn't scrape on the stone.

If he tucked down on his belly and curled his feet underneath him like a turtle, the light fur of his coat might blend into the rock. If they saw him, they may think him an animal and come to investigate.

Still, he bent low, tucking as close to the boulder as he could. Though his sight seemed to be growing darker, his ears picked out the sounds of footsteps above him still. Were they moving faster now? Past him? As he strained to focus his eyes, a yawn forced his mouth open. Why would his body not cooperate? The cold must have addled him completely. He'd heard that sleepiness could be one indicator that a man's body had grown so chilled that he risked freezing to death.

He had to stay awake. Had to make his eyes work again.

As best he could tell, his pursuers had moved past him. He needed to shift around to keep the stone positioned between him and them, but he didn't dare move when he couldn't see where he stepped. Only a faint light penetrated his vision now.

Fear shivered through him. Would the blindness leave when he got warm? How could he start a fire if he couldn't see to find the cave? Maybe it would help to take off these wet shoes and socks and wrap his feet. He'd have to move around a great deal to remove the coat and tug off both his tunic and undershirt. Perhaps he would wait for that part until he knew for sure his pursuers were out of sight.

Even now, strains of their voices drifted back to him.

Pressing close to the boulder, he shifted his back to the voices. His numb fingers struggled to pull off his boots. His legs moved when he told them to, but the sensation was so strange since he couldn't feel his feet. Another yawn forced its way out while he worked. His head felt impossibly heavy, yet fear gave him strength to finally tug off both boots, then the stockings.

If only he had something to wrap around them that wouldn't require removing clothing. The satchel of food seemed the only possibility. Made of leather, it might at least help keep in any warmth his icy feet created.

He fumbled with the opening, then lifted first one foot inside, then the other. He did his best to close the bag around his trousers. The effort seemed so paltry, but exhaustion pressed harder than he could withstand. He slumped closer to the boulder. His vision had grown completely black, maybe because his eyes wouldn't stay open. He could no longer hear the sound of voices.

He could hear . . . nothing.

8

Audrey paced by the gate, her coat pulled tight around her against the cold, hands fisted in her pockets. She would have to go inside the wall soon, but the sounds of village life increased her dread. What had she done? Why had she thought helping the prisoner escape was the right choice?

Brielle would find Levi and drag him back. Then the council would punish her and him both. What a foolish choice she'd made.

How much longer would it take Brielle and the men to return? They'd been gone at least an hour so far. Did Audrey dare stay out here and wait more? No matter what lay in store for her back in the village, returning alongside Brielle didn't intimidate her as much as returning by herself. Though Brielle would be as angry as a prodded mother bear, they'd been like sisters as far back as she could remember. She desperately needed a friend right now, even one furious with her.

She spun and paced back the other direction. Her tracks made a muddy mess of the snow out here. Surely whoever manned the gatehouse watched her. But as long as they left her alone, so be it.

Maybe she should have gone with Levi. She could have showed him the cave instead of letting him waste precious time searching for it. And she wouldn't have to endure the disappointment of all those she loved.

The weight on her chest pressed even harder. How could she face this?

The crackle of footsteps on leaves sounded, and she spun to scan the woods where Brielle last disappeared.

Her friend emerged from the trees, expression grim, her bow in hand. Evan strode just behind her, and Leonard brought up the rear. Where was Levi?

Her heart leapt in her chest. Maybe they hadn't caught him. But how could he have slipped away? Brielle was a master at tracking.

Audrey stepped toward them, then paused as she did her best to read what had happened on her friend's face. She looked angry, as would be expected. Frustrated.

Brielle finally glanced at her. "I hit him with an arrow, then we lost him. I'm getting more men and supplies for a full hunt."

As the three filed by her and proceeded through the gate, Audrey fell into step behind them. Her belly clenched with the thought of men spreading out for an expansive search. They would find him, surely.

And if Brielle had hit him with an arrow, he must be injured. How badly?

A new thought plunged through her. Brielle's arrow tips . . . she dipped them in a sleeping tonic Audrey had created. They'd mixed the substance so the prey she shot wouldn't wander away before she could catch up to it, and Evan was the only human who'd ever been pierced by the tonic-covered arrowhead. He'd slept for half an hour, then awakened groggy.

Was Levi lying out there asleep somewhere? *Lord, let him wake up and get to safety before all the men begin searching.*

When they'd trekked halfway across the courtyard, the door to the Durand family's apartment opened. Chief Durand stood in the opening, silent and watchful as they approached.

Brielle stopped in front of her father and spoke the same terse sentences she'd said to Audrey minutes before. The chief nodded and stepped back, allowing them entrance.

His gaze locked on Audrey as she brought up the rear of their group. She attempted a weak smile for him, doing her best to show her apology in her gaze.

"I wish to speak with you, Audrey, once the searchers have gone out." Though his voice stayed low and gentle, the burn of tears rose to her eyes. How much did he know? He couldn't yet be aware of everything she'd done, but he probably knew enough to realize she should be questioned.

She nodded, and they both shifted their attention to the people swarming Brielle, Evan, and Leonard.

Brielle took charge immediately, calling for every able-bodied man to take part in the search. She instructed which weapons and gear each should bring, then told them to meet her in the courtyard in a quarter hour.

As the group disseminated, Audrey craved the security and quiet of her own chamber next door. She slipped forward and murmured as she passed Brielle, "I'll prepare food to send with you all."

Her friend didn't stop her, but the weight of Brielle's gaze pressed heavily as Audrey stepped out the rear door.

She'd seen her father among those in the Durand home, so it didn't surprise her that he was also gathering weapons when she stepped into their quarters.

He glanced at her as she shut the door but kept at his work, so she strode across to her food supplies. Collecting three different satchels, she stuffed them with baked goods and dried meats. The act reminded her too much of the bag she'd packed for Levi that morning.

If the men of Laurent found him, what would they do to him? Brielle had already shot him once, which told her they might not hesitate to do something more drastic to stop him.

Lord, surely that's not your will. Surely you don't want his life taken so needlessly.

Grief welled up in her throat at such a thought. Was there any way she could stop this? She'd already made her belief in his innocence clear. Speaking again now wouldn't stop the search party being gathered.

Maybe it would be better to try to protect Levi. Could she find him and get him to the cave safely? She would have to leave right away to get there before the rest of the group left. With all the commotion, it was possible they may not discover she'd gone. She could take a few extra supplies, maybe a knife, too, for he'd need that for hunting and cutting wood. She should have thought to send it with him the first time. A hatchet would be easier to cut wood, but the handle on theirs had just broken and she'd not had a chance to have it repaired. She should also tuck her meat knife into her own moccasin, just in case she needed it.

If she could get Levi to the cave, she could give him medicine for his wound, then circle around the long way back to the village to avoid those out looking. Her pulse thundered through her. That might work.

Quickly, she filled the last pack with dried fruit and closed up the three bags, then stood and carried them over to her father. "This is food for everyone going out. Can you please take them with you?"

Papa glanced at the satchels and nodded, then returned his attention to lacing the sheath for his knife onto his belt.

Good. She focused now on a bag for Levi. Grabbing a fur blanket, she rolled it tightly, then tucked it in one of the only satchels she had left. Was it wrong that she aided both sides? Serving was her role here. She nurtured and cared for people, feeding and nursing when those around her had need. Could they really expect her to turn a blind eye when a man suffered unjustly? She'd simply be feeding and nursing him as she would anyone else.

After adding two more blankets, she moved to her medicinals and gathered the pouches that might be needed—a salve for healing wounds and two kinds of blood purifiers that could be steeped into a tea. When Evan had been shot with Brielle's potion-covered arrows, he'd experienced a stomach illness the following day. Audrey had never been sure whether it was a random ailment or an effect of the tonic, but if she worked to purify Levi's blood immediately, maybe he would be spared the same experience. Or at least not be afflicted so severely. Evan had been weak as a babe for days afterward.

Once she'd gathered everything she could think of, including one of her extra meat knives, a small kettle and cup, and needle and thread for stitching wounds, she glanced at Papa. He'd begun layering on the underclothes he wore when he went outside in the winter. He seemed intent on his own preparations, so it might be best not to draw attention to her leaving. And he would also be looking for his coat soon—the one she'd sent with Levi. Better she be gone before she had to explain its absence.

Slipping the satchel over her shoulder, she opened the door and stepped outside.

A cold breeze wrapped around her as she retraced her earlier steps, being careful to walk in existing footprints the entire way. Thankfully, no one seemed to be in the court-yard at the moment, except some children at the far end. The men must all be readying for the search, their women helping them.

She barely breathed until she stepped through the gate to exit the village walls. She didn't dare glance toward where a guard should be perched at the peephole from the guard-house. She just turned and strode toward the woods.

As soon as she stepped into the shadow of the trees, she broke into a run. She didn't worry as much about stepping in existing footprints now, only avoided the patches of snow that would make her tracks obvious.

Her breaths came thick and heavy the longer she ran, and a cramp bit into her side. She enjoyed regular walks to gather herbs and berries in their seasons, but she rarely ran at a pace like this. She hadn't trained as Brielle had for such a moment.

But the thought of Levi lying injured on the mountain drove her forward.

When she reached the far edge of the trees, an expanse of unbroken snow stretched out over the meadow before her. She scanned the right, then the left, for tracks. A faint line of darker snow lay to the left, and a glance at the ground beside her showed prints following the tree line in that direction.

She did the same.

When she stepped away from the woods into the tracks that must have been made by Brielle and the others, she moved into a run again. As she neared the mountain, she lifted her gaze to scan the slope. So many boulders littered the surface, offering hundreds of places a man could hide.

As soon as she stepped up on the stone, she lifted her voice in a half-whisper, half-call. "Levi, are you here? I've come to help you get to the cave. Monsieur Masters?" She'd begun thinking of him by his Christian name in her mind, but she shouldn't speak that aloud.

No return call sounded, so she pressed on, scampering over the stone in the most likely path around the mountain. It was impossible to know where the others had traveled before, since the stone showed no tracks.

As she went, she peered around every rock she passed. "Monsieur Masters? Are you here? I've come to help you get to safety. It's Audrey Moreau."

She kept her voice just loud enough that he would hear if he was nearby, but not so piercing that it would ring across the open area. How much time did she have left before the searchers came? Five minutes? Ten?

She had to move faster.

With fear pressing her forward, she trekked a quarter of the way around the slope, moving higher up the mountain as the terrain required her to.

"Levi Masters." She called a little louder this time. If he was asleep, perhaps hearing his given name would prod him awake.

A sound tickled her ear, bringing her up short. Was that the groan of a man or merely a trick of the wind?

She scanned around her, first downhill, then up. There were several large stones he might have hidden behind. Moving as quickly as she could, she started up the slope first.

"Levi?" She circled all three rocks that seemed likely hiding places, then moved down the mountain. "Levi Masters, it's Audrey Moreau. I've come to help you get to safety."

If Brielle or one of the other searchers heard her say those words, or knew she was out on this mission of mercy, there was no telling what would happen. Her heart hammered faster at the thought.

Then another groan stilled her. She paused mid-step to scan the area. He might be behind any of these boulders.

She shifted into action, scampering down to first one rock, then the next. "Make another sound." This felt a little like the games of all-hide she and Brielle played as young girls. When one of them would come near to giving up, the other would make a faint noise to point the seeker in the right direction.

This time, the groan was accompanied by the sound of something scraping across a rock. She homed in on a mid-sized stone farther down.

As she scrambled toward it, the slope propelled her body faster than her feet could keep up. Her hands slammed into the boulder just in time to keep her from sprawling headfirst. Using her palms to brace herself as she maneuvered around the rock, she jerked to a halt, nearly stumbling over Levi Masters's form.

He sat with his back against the boulder, one leg spread out in front of him with his foot in the food satchel she'd sent, and the other leg bent sideways. She focused on that leg long enough to decide the angle wasn't so odd as to be broken. At least she hoped not. It seemed more like he was simply too exhausted to straighten it.

She refocused on his face, his eyes barely open enough to

look up at her. She dropped to her knees by his side. "Are you hurt? Can you walk?"

"Cold. Can't keep my eyes open."

She scanned the length of him once more. He wore the coat still, though the buttons were unfastened. He would be chilled from sitting here but shouldn't be too miserable. Unless maybe the potion that had coated the arrow made his body more sensitive to the elements. A glimpse of a bare foot winked at her from where the bent leg was tucked under the trousers of his other leg.

She leaned forward to brush the material aside. Yes, the foot was completely bare. A glance around the area showed two shoes propped nearby. Stockings too.

"Why aren't your shoes on?" She started to lean over him to grab them, but they were too far away.

"Wet. Walked . . . through the creek." His voice sounded a little stronger now.

She sank back on her heels, then turned to the bag she'd brought. "I'll wrap your feet in these leather blankets. That should help until we get you to the cave."

Within moments, she had both limbs bundled. Seeing his bare skin and the long, angular, very masculine feet felt intimate. She did her best to remind herself he was simply a patient, but covering them with blankets was the only thing that took away the sensation.

Turning back to the man, she reached for his arm. "Can you stand? We have to hurry."

9

Audrey watched as Levi struggled to stand. He moved painstakingly slow, and his eyelids nearly closed. He didn't seem to have the strength to rise.

"Here, move onto your hands and knees first. That way you can hold on to the boulder until you get your balance." The blankets wrapped around his feet would make him unsteady, especially since it looked like the sleeping tonic still had a strong hold on him.

While he struggled into that position, she hurried to gather up his shoes, his stockings, and their two bags. She would likely need both hands to help Levi, so she tucked the shoes into his food bag, as separate from the snacks as she could manage so the baked goods didn't get soggy.

Levi had worked up to his knees and was using his hands to crawl up the side of the boulder to a standing position.

"Good. Now put your left arm around my shoulders. I'll help you balance with those blankets around your feet." She would be on the downhill side, so hopefully she could act as a brace to keep him from tumbling.

He didn't obey right away, and urgency pressed through her. "Hurry. They could be here any minute." She glanced back in the direction of Laurent. No movement appeared that she could see from this angle.

Her words seemed to prod him into moving a little faster, almost into a regular pace. She helped settle his arm around her shoulders and tugged him the direction they needed to go. He was so unsteady, but she wrapped her arm around his waist to help hold him secure.

Together, they moved around the mountain and up to a game trail that would make for easier walking. Levi didn't stumble as much now, but he seemed to require her help to support part of his weight. Was this all truly from the sleeping potion?

She needed to dilute the strength of that tonic. She'd been careful to use only ingredients that could be safely consumed by people, in case the tonic punctured areas of meat on the game Brielle shot with her arrows. But she'd had no idea how well the stuff would work.

They were moving at a medium pace now. Would this keep them far enough ahead of the search party for Levi to be safe? She tugged him a little faster, and he trudged along with her.

Her body was coiled too tightly to think overlong on the fact that this man was practically embracing her. This achingly handsome man, who currently staggered along as though he'd imbibed too much fermented drink. His unsteadiness certainly wasn't his fault, though.

At last, they reached the base of the mountain at its farthest side and began to scale the second slope. The cave would be partway up, but this was the hardest stretch because they climbed uphill. It was also the most dangerous, because they would be more visible at a distance.

As they ascended, Levi finally became better able to walk

on his own. He still kept his arm around her shoulders but didn't lean on her. The touch felt almost like he was helping *her* up the slope. Or maybe they were assisting each other.

She kept them moving around the mountain, while still climbing with each step. Only once did she dare glance back. Were those figures on the side of the other mountain? Her breath caught as she froze and studied the landscape.

Levi, too, turned to look. "Get down. Behind this rock." He dropped low, pulling her with him.

Audrey knelt beside him and peered around the stone. In the distance, a male figure moved up the slope, checking around every rock he passed. Monsieur Rochette. If she wasn't mistaken, he searched near the place Levi had been hiding.

Thank you, Lord. You got us away just in time.

Levi sent a look over his shoulder, farther up the path they'd been taking. "How far to the cave?"

She followed the line of his gaze. "If the opening weren't so well hidden, we could see it from here. Just above that cliff, behind the scrubby tree."

"We'll have to stay low. Better to go one at a time so there's not as much movement."

She gave him a quick glance. Was he well enough to duck and run by himself? He seemed alert enough to be capable now. "I'll go first since I'll be able to find the opening easier."

"Be careful. Stay behind rocks as much as you can." He reached for a satchel. "I'll carry one of those."

She shook her head. "I have them." He might be able to get himself there, but they had no reason to make his struggle harder.

Before he could protest, she ducked low and sprinted six strides toward the nearest rock large enough to provide cover. Once there, she took the opportunity to check the other mountain once again. Still only one figure visible. The searchers must have spread out.

She didn't allow herself to glance at Levi and instead turned back to map out the rest of her route to the cave. From boulder to boulder she ran, keeping as low as she could and stopping at each one so a person watching from a distance wouldn't see a steady stream of movement.

At last, she reached the path beside the cliff, and she was breathing hard as she ducked behind the scrawny tree with its sharp needles. The thin strip of darkness that marked the opening of the cave finally came into view. She let out a long breath. They'd almost made it.

Leaning around the tree so she could see Levi, she motioned for him to come. Another glance at the other mountain showed two figures now. They didn't seem to have spotted her movement.

Levi started along the same path she'd taken, although he ran slower. Maybe, in part, because of the blankets on his feet. As he bent low to move, he sometimes had to touch the ground with his hands for balance.

Don't let him fall, Lord. If he sustained another injury, his chances of getting away safely would be so much worse.

She needed to light a candle and check the cave to make sure there weren't any unwanted *guests* inside, but she couldn't tear her gaze away from Levi as he ran.

At last, he slipped between the tree and the rock as she had. He was breathing hard as he came to a stop beside her.

She dropped one of the satchels to the ground and fished inside it for a candle and tinderbox.

When she pulled out the flint and steel, Levi reached for

the tinder remaining in the dish. "I can hold that." Working together, they had a candle lit within moments.

Levi picked up the satchel from the ground, then started toward the cave opening.

She moved to step around him. "I can go first since I know a little of the layout."

He didn't step aside. "I'll go first. Might be better if I hold the candle, though."

Part of her was more than happy to hand over the light and let him be the first to step through spider webs and encounter any creatures within. But was he up to the strain? The heavy, dazed look had left his eyes, and he seemed much steadier on his feet. Far more like the capable man she'd met by the creek—was that only yesterday? It seemed like weeks had passed since then. Months, even.

She handed over the candle and its holder. She should have thought to bring one of the torches they used to light the hallway inside the caves. Maybe once Levi was settled inside, a small fire could be built. Not so large that the stream of smoke would be obvious from outside, just big enough to give a little light and warmth.

The thought of leaving Levi nestled beside that fire sent a pain to her chest. She'd planned to come only long enough to make sure he reached the cave, tend any wounds, and leave these additional supplies with him. But what if he needed more help?

❧

Levi stepped into the cave, doing his best to take in everything illuminated by the candle. His senses still weren't as sharp as they should be, but he'd certainly come back to life from the benumbed condition he'd been in.

Miss Moreau had brought him back to life. Somehow. Maybe simply by forcing him to keep moving.

The cave didn't extend very deep. Or maybe that was a turn instead of the rear wall. Yes, the path twisted to the right. "How far does it go?" Though he kept his voice quiet, the sound seemed to echo around them.

"I think it ends right there." Her voice sounded immediately behind him, and he glanced back to make sure she was maneuvering without trouble.

The thin smile she turned to him was still one of the prettiest things he'd seen in a long time. He couldn't fathom why she was helping him. Perhaps once they were settled, he could learn the reason from her.

Refocusing his attention on the path ahead, they only went a half-dozen steps before they reached a solid wall. Bits of leaves and twigs and dirt—some that likely hadn't always been dirt—littered the floor. There might be a few dead insects in there, but nothing alive.

He lifted the candle to see the ceiling. He'd heard that nocturnal flying creatures sometimes lived in caves, but there appeared to be nothing here. He eased out a breath. "Looks empty."

Beside him, Miss Moreau stepped into action. "We need to get you settled, then I want to look at your feet and where the arrow hit you." She used her shoe to sweep the debris on the floor to the side.

"You don't need to worry about me." He attempted to use his own foot to help clear a place on the stone floor, but the blanket wrap didn't slide easily.

She'd said, *"Get you settled,"* which meant she would be leaving him soon. Of course she would. She was merely helping him escape. She would go back to her people. Would she be punished?

No doubt she would. His arms ached to protect her. Was there anything he could do? He had to ask. Had to do everything in his power.

He really wanted a few minutes to talk with Miss Moreau. Should he invite her to sit? This wasn't quite like visiting over tea. That thought made the pinch in his belly twist. He'd not eaten anything today, and what time was it, anyway? He'd suspect shortly after noon, but with the thick gray clouds obscuring the sun, it was hard to tell.

He had the food Miss Moreau packed for him, but he'd need to ration it, especially until it was safe to leave the cave and hunt. But he could share some with her now.

She seemed finally satisfied that the floor was clean enough, and now she pulled a fur from her pack and spread it across the ground. She motioned to the pelt. "Sit."

Dropping to his knees on the fur, he opened his own pack. "Are you hungry?"

She had placed his boots in the satchel, so he pulled them out and set them aside. Hopefully, he could get a fire going soon so the leather could dry out.

He pulled out the first bundle of food he came to and unwrapped it. Strips of some kind of roasted or dried meat lay on the leather wrapping. He held them out to her. "Have some."

She was pulling things out of the bag she carried but paused long enough to glance at the offering, then up to his face. "You need to eat it."

He had a feeling this woman would do for others without a second thought for herself, all the way until she fell over from exhaustion or hunger. He extended the food closer to her. "You probably haven't eaten today, either. Please, have some."

She dropped her gaze back to the food, and as she took a strip of meat, the hungry glimmer in her eyes showed more than she probably meant to.

He bit into his own piece—smoked venison that tasted better than any venison he could remember. He couldn't recall being this hungry, either.

Miss Moreau munched daintily on her slice as she continued pulling containers from her bag. Most were pouches, but she added a round tin to the stack.

At last, she turned her focus to him. "Brielle said she hit you with an arrow. Where did it strike?"

With the question, the ache in his side made itself known, but he didn't reach for the spot. "It was only a graze. A flesh wound." That wasn't entirely true, but he could tend it himself.

Her gaze began at the top of his head and worked its way down, scouring every part of him. "I'm our village healer. Brielle's arrows are coated with a sleeping tonic I created that puts her prey in a deep sleep so she can find them. It was intended for animals but seems to be very effective on people as well."

He had to do his best to keep his jaw from dropping open. Sleeping tonic? Was that what had overtaken him? He'd thought he was freezing to death. But it had really been sleeping tonic?

She was still talking, so he did his best to focus on her

words. "The other time a man was shot with an arrowhead dipped in the sleeping tonic, he seemed fine after he awoke. Then a day or so later, he developed a violent stomach ailment. I'm not certain if that was caused by the tonic or an unrelated malady, but I'd like to make a tea to help purify your blood."

He could only stare at her as the facts lined up in his mind. "You poisoned me?"

10

Bile rose in Levi's throat. Were these people more savage than he realized?

Miss Moreau's brows drew together. "It's only a sleeping tonic. All four of the ingredients I put into it are perfectly edible. I don't know for sure if the mixture made Evan sick, but I'd rather not take chances with you." Now she raised those brows. "Besides, I'm not the one who shot you with the arrow. I'm only trying to help."

He blew out a breath. She was right. She'd sacrificed much to help him. "I'm sorry. I didn't mean that as an accusation. I was just . . . surprised."

She took up the tin and motioned down the length of him. "Show me the wound. I have a salve for it. After that, I'll make a fire and brew the tea."

This time he didn't argue, just pulled his coat aside. The arrow still dangled from where the fletching had caught in the garment. He worked it out gently, then held that side of his coat away from his body. "The head only went in partway here." He used two fingers to spread the tear in his shirt. The gash was small enough she shouldn't worry over it. "I'll put your salve on, then be as good as new."

He let his coat flap shut. "Better I start the fire first. That candle's burning low, and the wood will take a few minutes to create coals for heating." He nodded toward the small pot she'd produced. "Do you have water for the kettle?"

She nodded, though a line still creased her forehead, indicating she wasn't pleased with something. Probably the fact that he hadn't stretched out so she could tend his wound. Healers could be sensitive like that. If the gash had really required stitching, he would let her. But he'd handled more than one scrape like this on his own.

He turned toward the sticks and debris she'd swept to the edges of the cave. "This will make good kindling. I saw a few branches dropped from the tree outside. That should burn for a while, and maybe by then I can sneak out to get more wood."

Within minutes, he had a small, healthy flame burning. Miss Moreau snuffed out the candle, then placed his boots and stockings beside the fire to dry. She knelt beside him with the kettle, and he shifted the branches to form a nook for the container.

When she straightened and turned to him, she was so near, and when she turned that sweet smile on him, its power nearly overwhelmed him. His hands ached to brush back the stray wisps of her hair. Maybe see if her cheeks were really as soft as they looked.

She didn't appear affected by the closeness, only glanced down at his side. "Let's see what that arrow wound needs. Do you mind taking off your coat for a minute? At least pull that arm from the sleeve?"

There was no way he could deny her any request at this point, though having her working so close would test his self-control.

He would resist, though. Alone as they were, he had to do everything he could to maintain propriety.

Moving back to the center of the fur, he pulled off his coat and lifted his left arm so she could have access to the hole in his shirt. There wasn't an easy way for her to see the wound without him lifting the tail of his tunic and his undershirt. But revealing that much skin certainly didn't feel proper.

With the tin in her hands, she knelt beside him. "Can you lie on your side? I need better lighting to see." Her voice held the no-nonsense tone of a nurse focused on her work.

Yet even if *she* could ignore how close they were—how alone they were—*he* could not. He would be a gentleman, though. And an obedient patient.

Stretching out on his side, he moved his arm out of the way.

With a quick motion, she grabbed the hem of his tunic and slid it up his side. Then his undershirt.

He focused on the grain of the animal hair beneath him. How each strand contained two or more colors. What animal had it come from? Were there bobcats in this area? The fur looked too large for that creature, but the coloring was about right.

The cool softness of her fingers brushing his side made him suck in a breath. He tried to find the pain of the wound to distract himself, something to keep his body from tingling at her touch. But then she moved her hand away, and he finally eased out a breath.

Back to thinking of the bobcat. Or maybe . . . His mind could conjure no other possible animal. Not when his senses tracked every movement she made. The swish of her skirt as she shifted back to her pack. A rustling, then a scrape. Then that swish again as she returned to his side.

"I need to wash out any of the tonic that might remain in the wound. You're correct that the gash isn't deep. It didn't puncture an organ or break a rib, God be praised."

Yes, God be praised. His condition could be so much worse.

"This will be cold."

She didn't lie. He barely kept from sucking in a gulp of air as icy liquid burned inside his wound, then dribbled down his back. A cloth brushed the liquid away from his unmarred skin.

"This might sting a bit."

He prepared himself, and good thing, too. She seemed to be digging around inside the gash, loosing a fiery blaze in his side. He didn't move, didn't breathe. Could only hold himself in a constricted knot as he waited for her to finish her torture.

"There. It's as clean as I can manage with what I have. The salve should keep it from festering and aid healing. We'll wrap it to keep the medicine in place and the wound clean."

She dabbed a cold substance in the cut, then her fingers settled on the healthy skin beside his wound. The softness of her touch almost made up for the pain from moments before.

A shifting sounded, like she was reaching for something. "Do you think you could come up on your elbow so I can wrap this bandage fully around you?"

He did as she asked, keeping his attention on the fur. A glance at her now would be far too intimate, what with his shirt pulled halfway up. As a healer, she might be accustomed to this type of thing, but surely she always had a brother or father around in these situations.

"Perfect." Something in the tone of her voice drew his

notice as she began to wrap a bandage around his middle. She sounded almost breathy.

The thought distracted him so much that when her wrist brushed against his belly, his body flinched before he could stop it. This torture—the desire sluicing through him that he was doing his best to bind up with heavy chains—had to end soon. He'd always prided himself on his strength, but it turned out he was far weaker than he'd thought.

Finally, she gave a tug on the bandage. "There. That should stay put for a while." She worked the hems of his shirts down, her knuckles only brushing his skin twice in the process.

He sat up, keeping his back to her. "Thank you." So much energy coiled inside him, he had to do something to release it. Preferably something that gave him a bit of space from her. Maybe this would be a good time for him to peek outside the cave and see what was happening with their pursuers.

He started to push to his feet, but the action quickly reminded him of the confounded blankets wrapped around his feet. He eyed his shoes and stockings. They wouldn't be dry yet, and taking them away from the small fire would slow the process. But keeping these blankets on made him clumsy. He couldn't chance the possibility that he might stumble or accidentally do something else to draw attention.

Better to go barefoot for a while. He quickly cast off his footwear and stood. "I'm going to see what's happening outside."

"Be careful." Miss Moreau's tone sounded hesitant, maybe even a bit worried.

He sent her a confident smile. "I'm just going to the opening. I'll be back soon."

As Audrey waited for Levi to return, she had to do something to keep her worry at bay. She couldn't leave yet with all the searchers out there. She'd have to wait for the cover of night.

She removed the contents of the two satchels—food, doctoring supplies, blankets, candles, the knife. She sorted the food atop one of them, using the leather as a counter space. Animals didn't appear to be a concern inside this cave, so it might be fine to leave these rations out today to allow them to get what they needed easily. After all, each food item was still wrapped in leather.

She did the same with the rest of the gear, spreading it on the second satchel, including the blankets she'd wrapped around Levi's feet. When he came back, she would show him all the items so he would know what he had to work with.

But when she finished, he still hadn't returned. Maybe she should go ensure nothing had happened. Would he have been foolish enough to step out of the cave? Surely she would've heard sounds if he'd been caught.

First, she would check the tea, then if he still wasn't back, she would go make sure all was well. It was likely that he found watching the searchers more interesting than sitting in the faint light of this cave.

The water in the pot had grown hot but not yet boiling. The longer the tea ingredients steeped, the more potent they would be.

At last, a faint noise behind her made her spin. Levi padded forward, nearly soundless as he stepped onto the fur.

Her gaze dropped down to his bare feet, maybe because her kneeling position put her close to them already.

Once more, the sight of their angles and masculinity felt intimate—his feet, of all things.

She tore her gaze away, shifting her focus upward to his face to read from his expression if he'd seen anything of concern outside. He towered above her, but then he dropped to his haunches to bring them closer to eye level.

"I saw four people searching, two of them on this mountain but still farther back. One of those was the woman who dresses like a man."

The odd description nearly brought a smile through her worry. "Brielle. She's the leader of the guards and hunters. And my closest friend." She tried to make that last part sound casual, but it came out more yearning than anything.

His gaze softened, his brows tenting in an earnest expression. "I'm sorry I put you in this position." He looked as though he wanted to say more, but he didn't.

What was there to say, anyway? She'd made the decision. Put herself in this position of her own accord. She tried to summon a confident smile. "You have nothing to be sorry about."

His expression turned pained, but he didn't answer. Instead, he glanced around and dropped his voice to barely more than a whisper. "Is the tea ready enough? I think we'd better let the fire go out."

She nodded instead of speaking. Ready or not, he was right.

As she poured the drink into the only cup she'd brought, Levi lifted their fur mat and moved it beside one wall. He settled against the stone and took the cup she handed him, then tapped the pelt beside him. "Best to be still and wait."

Sit still? At his side? Her body was sprung so tightly, she wasn't sure she could sit and be quiet. Yet the chance to be near this man called to her.

She settled in where he'd motioned, the position nearest the fire and farthest from the cave opening. A place that felt safe and protected, as though no matter what entered the cave, he would act as a barrier between her and the danger.

If only she never had to face the repercussions that waited for her back in Laurent. She pushed the thought aside before it turned so strongly in her belly to call back what little food she'd eaten. She would worry about the consequences later.

As they sat, he took sips of the tea. She didn't dare look over to see if his expression showed how bitter it must taste. She'd not brought honey to sweeten the strong flavors.

Instead, she sent her gaze everywhere else, searching for something to occupy her mind. Her focus locked on the supplies, and she motioned toward her carefully organized piles, keeping her voice to a whisper. "I spread out everything we brought so you can see what you have. The food is over there. I should have sent more meat, but I'm afraid it's heavy on baked goods." She sent him an apologetic look.

His eyes creased in a smile that didn't cover his uneasiness. "I like baked goods. Yours especially."

Heat warmed her neck, so she turned her attention back to the provisions and motioned to the second bundle. "Everything else is sorted there. Blankets. Candles. A knife. It was my extra, so it's not as sharp as it could be, but I thought it better than nothing."

The breath he took in echoed in the quiet cave. For long

moments, he studied the supplies spread out. Then he turned to her, his gaze more sincere than on any man she'd seen. "Miss Moreau, I don't . . . know how to thank you. You've done so much. So much more than I could have dreamed."

Was that a catch in his voice? She had trouble holding his gaze with the intensity in his eyes. "It's—" She almost said *nothing,* but that wasn't true. They both knew it. Instead, she concentrated on the real reason she'd helped him. "It was the right thing to do, keeping you from punishment when you haven't committed a crime."

But had her method been the best one? Stealing him away when the guard trusted her?

Lord, let this all turn out well, even if I ran ahead of your plan. And if I did sin in my actions, please forgive me.

She had a feeling that if she really analyzed the situation through the lens of Scripture, what she'd done would definitely be labeled as sin. But she couldn't let herself examine it yet. Not when Levi's safety wasn't confirmed.

For long, long, *long* minutes, they sat in silence. Levi sipped from the cup until he'd drained it dry, then placed the empty container beside him. They needed to remain still and quiet in case the searchers neared the opening of the cave. The fire had faded to only a few glowing embers, but enough light still filtered from the opening around the corner.

How much time passed, she couldn't have said. It felt like hours. Felt like darkness should have set outside, but it might be no later than midafternoon.

At last, Levi stirred beside her and spoke in a whisper. "I'm going to see where they are."

She itched to stand and follow him, but two were more

likely to make noise than one. She settled for placing the cup with the other food supplies and checking his boots. Still damp. If they'd been able to keep the fire burning, the leather might be nearly dry by now. But letting it go out had been the wisest choice.

As the temperature dropped with darkness, Levi would need something to warm his feet. With the cold, neither these shoes nor stockings would be dry enough to help him.

A new thought slipped in. They had a blanket and a knife to cut with, and she'd brought needle and thread in case she needed to stitch his wound. With those supplies, stockings she made would be rough, but at least they would keep his feet warm and help him get around easier than when they were bundled in blankets.

She set to work, using his wet stockings as a pattern.

By the time she had the first piece cut and stitched halfway up, Levi still hadn't returned. She tried to keep her attention on her sewing, but the thought of what might be happening outside stole her focus far too much.

At last, she set down her work and rose, creeping as quietly as she could toward the mouth of the cave. When she peered around the bend in the hall, the brightness outside made her squint. The light outlined Levi's form as he knelt just inside the opening, peering out to the left.

She tiptoed forward, her feet only making an occasional whisper. Levi didn't give a sign that he heard her until she'd nearly reached him.

He glanced back, and though the light cast a shadow on his features, his expression seemed animated. He touched a finger to his lips as a reminder for silence, then motioned her forward and shifted to make space for her on his left.

Sidling forward, she slipped in beside him. He pointed where he'd been looking, and she followed the line of his finger.

She nearly gasped as, less than a stone's throw away and a bit farther down, a person appeared on the mountainside.

11

Leonard. Where had he come from?

When Audrey had first glanced that way, he'd not been there. Then he was, stepping from the stone itself. Maybe a bend in the rock gave the illusion.

"I think it's another cave." Levi's breath warmed her ear as he kept his whisper soft enough to barely reach her. "They've all gone in and out at least once."

His nearness sent a tingle all the way down her back, making it hard to focus on his words. But another cave? She'd never seen that particular one, though there were caves spread all through these mountains—some only small, shallow holes, and some much deeper and winding.

It seemed unusual to have two caverns so close together, and both with openings mostly hidden. The one she and Levi had taken refuge in was a bit higher up, and the cliff below made it appear as if nothing could reach this place. Not that anyone would see the opening with the juniper tree concealing it so well.

She'd never seen that other cave, yet the searchers had been diligent enough to find it. Would they also discover this one? Maybe that other cavern would be a distraction to them, keeping this opening hidden.

Let that be the case, Lord.

As they watched, two more men emerged, Philip and Evan. Then Brielle and Monsieur Rochette stepped out. The five gathered, and the latter spoke first, motioning back toward the cave, then in the direction of Audrey and Levi—though it appeared more of a general gesture, not a specific pointing.

Still, Audrey shrank back until she could barely see them.

Brielle responded to Monsieur Rochette, pointing several directions as she spoke. Probably giving orders. Where were the rest of the men from town? Brielle had been planning a large search party, but now there were only five.

Philip and Evan started toward the juniper tree hiding their cave, and Audrey's chest tightened. Levi's hand closed around her arm in a light touch, giving a tug to guide her backward.

She tiptoed behind him around the corner to their little campsite against the back wall. The fire no longer glowed, and no remnants of smoke wafted upward. The smoky scent did linger in the air, though. Would the searchers smell it outside?

She settled back into her seat beside the rock wall and took up her sewing. Levi sank down beside her, and the weight of his gaze watching her work made the skin on her arm tingle.

At last, she stretched out the stocking across her lap and whispered, "I thought these would help keep you warm until your shoes dry. I'm almost done with this one." Just a few more stitches, then she could tie off the thread and work on the second one.

She sent a quick glance to check his expression. With brows lifted, he stared at the garment in her hands as though he was still trying to decipher her meaning. He finally lifted his gaze to meet hers. Even in a whisper, his "thank you" rang thick with earnestness.

She sent him a quick smile to acknowledge the words, then refocused on her stitching. Within a minute, she finished the first stocking and laid it out to measure for the second. Cutting the material with the knife blade was the hardest part of the project.

Levi held the soft leather in place as she wielded the blade. He kept his fingers well out of the way, but still, their hands brushed several times in the process. Each time, heat swept up her arm as though she'd been licked by a flame. Why was she so aware of this man? So affected by him?

When she finished cutting, he moved back to his position by the wall, but she remained sitting in the center of the fur mat. If he commented on why she didn't sit beside him again, she could say the lighting was better here, which might be true. Though this entire end of the cave was dim enough to make her eyes ache from squinting over her needlework.

After securing the first few stitches, she proceeded quickly, finishing the last within minutes. She tied off the thread, then straightened her back and blinked, giving her eyes a chance to rest. She tucked her needle back in her kit of healing supplies, then took up both stockings and turned to Levi. "See how they fit."

He took them almost reverently, but as he lifted his foot to obey her command, she jerked her focus away. She daren't watch him dress. This man affected her far too much, even his feet.

Turning away, she busied herself with food for them to eat. They both needed sustenance to keep their strength up.

From the corner of her eye, she watched Levi's outline enough to know when he'd finished donning both stockings. She glanced back, just to make sure they fit.

He sat with his knees bent, soles of his feet resting on the floor. The stockings appeared to cradle his feet perfectly, the leather wrapping almost like moccasins.

She lifted her gaze to his face, and a grin flashed in his eyes. "Perfect. They're already warmer."

She tugged her attention away as heat swarmed up her neck. Gathering a packet of smoked caribou and a roll for each of them, she kept her gaze on the food as she crawled back to her seat beside him. They could both eat from the meat if she sat here. And this way, she didn't have to look at him.

After they'd eaten the meager meal, silence surrounded them. Then a noise sounded outside, like a shout. She cringed, and Levi stiffened too. When he looked her way, the shadows darkened his face, so it was hard to see the expression in his eyes.

But then he turned toward the cave opening, and they both sat in intense expectation.

Nothing happened. No one entered the cave. No more voices sounded outside.

They were simply cloaked in silence.

As more time passed, she almost reached for her needle and the leather again. She could make a pair of true moccasins, but this leather had been worked until it was thin and very pliable, so it wouldn't hold up well against the stony ground. And the darkness of the cave would make her head ache if she did precision work for a longer span of time.

After a while, her eyes grew heavy. She always rose early, and this morning had been no different. But she rarely sat still for so long. She blinked and straightened, stretching her back to reawaken her muscles. She had to keep herself ready for whatever might happen.

❦

Levi's neck and shoulders throbbed from holding himself so still. But the woman resting against him, head nestled on his shoulder, felt like a gift. He didn't dare do anything to wake her. She'd done so much for him. The least he could offer in return was to allow her a shoulder to lean against during her much-needed nap.

As dusk had fallen, he'd watched the search party turn with slumped shoulders back toward Laurent. They would surely be back tomorrow morning. Did that mean it was safe to venture out until then? He wasn't willing to risk a fire again.

He'd had hours to sit here and contemplate what they should do next—and he still wasn't certain. If he were the only person he had to consider, he would leave this place. Head back to Washington, gather his belongings, and board a ship to England. His work with the intelligence branch was over now. He could finally pursue the life he wanted.

What was that, exactly? In truth, Mum needed him more than anyone else did, so he should return to Kettlewell and see what he could do for her. Maybe the work he'd done during the war would finally be enough to earn his father's respect.

But he *wasn't* the only person he had to consider. What

would happen to Miss Moreau? Could she even return to her village? What kind of punishment would she suffer?

A new thought slipped in. She'd been alone with him for the better part of the day, and now night had fallen. In England, that would be enough to ruin a woman. Did her people hold the same standards? In such a small village, would their rules be more lenient—or even stricter?

Against his arm, she stirred. In the darkness of the cave, she might awake completely disoriented. Would she cry out? In the same situation, his sister would probably awaken with a scream, though he couldn't imagine innocent little Libby being alone with a strange man in a black-as-pitch cave.

She stiffened, then lifted her head. He kept his voice to a whisper. "Miss Moreau? Nothing to be alarmed about. The cave is a bit darker now, is all."

She was silent, save for the rustle of her clothing as she straightened. At last, she whispered, "Has anything happened?"

He shook his head, though she wouldn't see that in the darkness. "All has been quiet since the searchers left. I think I'll go to the cave opening and see what's happening out there."

"Can I come too?" Her whisper barely sounded as he prepared to move.

He stilled. "Of course." She didn't have to ask, but the fact that she had touched something deep inside him.

Miss Audrey Moreau was such a good, kind woman. The very last person he would expect to break a captive free from his jail cell. Yet the fact that she'd believed in him enough to risk so much made him ache inside. He owed her everything. What could he do to make her situation better?

110

He stood, and from the sounds of shifting, she must be doing the same. This utter darkness was uncanny, making his senses feel unreliable. Should he let her go first? He'd be more comfortable taking the lead, but he didn't want to lose her or cause her to trip.

He extended his hand. "Here. Take my hand so we don't run into each other." A heartbeat later, her fingers brushed his sleeve, then slid down his arm to fit into his palm.

He closed his hand around hers, the weight of the trust she offered pressing in his chest. Holding her grip secure, he started forward, small steps at a time. Thankfully, this cave had very few loose rocks littering its floor, so there wouldn't be much to stumble on or raise a clatter.

As they turned the corner, faint moonlight filtered through the opening. Miss Moreau moved up beside him and secured her hand more firmly in his. Almost as if they were out for an evening stroll. He'd never walked hand-in-hand with a lady under the stars. There'd never been a woman in Kettlewell he wished to do such with.

If Miss Moreau had been there . . .

He swiped the thought away before his mind could ponder it. They had to focus on discerning whether anyone was out there watching. Though it looked like all the searchers had left earlier, they had to be careful.

Settling into the same position as before, Levi scanned the landscape outside. The crescent moon shed a small amount of light, certainly more than they had inside the cave.

Somewhere in the distance, a horse whinnied. *Chaucer.*

Levi tensed, straining to hear more. He glanced at Audrey. She was staring at him, eyes wide with hope. He dared brave a low whisper. "Are there any other horses in the area?"

She shook her head, confirming what he'd suspected. That had to be his gelding.

He itched to go out and find Chaucer, but the risk might still be too great. "It sounds like the whinny came from over there." He motioned to the right, the opposite direction of Laurent. "Would they have taken him so far from the village?"

Her brows furrowed with deep shadows in the dim moonlight. "No. Maybe he got loose from where they tied him. There's a nice meadow there where he might have found good grazing."

Levi eased out a breath. If Chaucer broke loose and had found a hearty section of grass as near as that whinny sounded, he shouldn't wander far in the night. Tomorrow he would search for the gelding.

But there was also a chance the villagers might have moved him to that location as a trap to lure Levi there. He would have to be careful.

The animal didn't make the noise again, and quiet settled over the land. A breeze ruffled the needles on the juniper tree. They stood there for long minutes, taking in the stillness.

A new thought flickered in, one he should've considered long before now. What would Audrey's friends and family do when they realized she was missing? The ball of dread in his gut twisted tighter. They would send another search party tomorrow, and this time it might be the entire village. They would leave no stone unturned. As much as he worried about how they might punish her, everything within him knew beyond a doubt she was special to this community. How could she not be? And if they thought he'd kidnapped her or she was in danger, they would hunt until they found her.

He had to talk to Audrey. Had to convince her to go back. But he also had to be careful not to send her into danger or unnecessary risk.

Reaching for her hand, he signaled for them to return into the cave. She followed wordlessly, and he didn't dare speak even in a whisper until they reached their supplies.

With his eyes still adjusted to the moonlight, this area seemed even darker than before—if that were possible. "Do you think it's safe to light a candle? We need to talk about what happens next."

"I. . . suppose so. I'll light it." She likely knew better than he did where the candle and tinderbox were positioned.

She tugged her hand from his, and cold made his fingers tingle as rustling sounds drifted from the direction where she'd laid out the supplies. A moment or two passed before she whispered, "There."

The sound of metal clicking came next, probably her flint and steel. A spark illuminated the darkness but faded almost immediately. Another flashed, and this time the glimmer lasted long enough to cast light on her chin as she blew a gentle puff. The spark wasn't strong enough to survive, though.

The third flash bloomed brighter, illuminating her mouth as she sent a steady stream of air. The light grew brighter, revealing her cheeks and nose. Then a tiny flame sprung up in the tinder, casting a glow in her eyes, illuminating her smile, just like an angel's.

Within seconds, she lit the candle and snuffed out the flame in the tinderbox. She turned to him and held out the light. He took it, then motioned for her to be seated. Instead of sitting against the cave wall, she settled beside the supplies.

If he rested against the stone, they would be able to see each other as they spoke. That practical positioning would help with the conversation. Surely she hadn't moved simply to keep from sitting beside him.

He settled himself and positioned the candle, then did his best to gather his thoughts. Better to ask about her first. "What do you intend to do next?"

Her face appeared paler than before, though that might be an effect of the candlelight. She didn't speak for a long moment, then her shoulders dipped as she released the spent air she'd been holding. "I had planned to go back tonight. I'm sure once I explain why I released you, they'll understand."

Despite her words, her voice sounded like she most certainly *didn't* think they would understand.

He dipped his chin to meet her gaze. "Are you certain of that? That they'll understand?"

A sea of worry clouded her eyes. "I pray they will. They know my heart is to help people, not inflict pain. I hope they'll be lenient." She must hear how unlikely her line of reasoning was.

He leaned forward and propped his arms on his legs. "What can I do to make it easier for you? If I go back with you, would they pardon you?"

She jerked upright, her eyes widening and chin lifting. "I'm not taking you back to Laurent. That would defeat all our efforts so far. All of our risks would be for naught."

He inhaled a steadying breath, then released it. She spoke the truth there. He couldn't cast aside everything she'd done to help him, as if her sacrifices meant nothing.

But he also couldn't leave her to face the wrath of her people alone.

He leaned forward again as a new thought took hold. "Come with me, then. I have to go back to Washington to retrieve my belongings, then I'm going home to England. My family would welcome you. My sister would be overjoyed. Her dearest friend moved away last year, and she's been pining for neighbors who aren't in their dotage."

She tipped her chin, concern and hesitation marking her expression. "Travel with you? To England?"

As she said the words, the problem with his plan rose up like a mountain between them. She, an unmarried woman, could never travel with him, an unmarried man. The time they'd spent alone today was enough to ruin her. Anything more would be beyond recovery.

There was one way he could resolve the concern, though. "I'll marry you, if that would help."

12

The moment Levi spoke the words, Audrey jerked back, as though his offer had scalded her. In his mind, he scrambled back through his comments. Could he have found a clumsier way to offer for her hand?

His proposal hadn't been preplanned, but as the possibility took shape in his thoughts, desire slipped through him. She had shown herself to be kind beyond words and a woman who took action for what she believed to be right. A woman of faith . . . and her beauty spoke for itself.

What would she think of his little village if he took her home with him? Mum would love her, and so would Libby. Dad? He had never approved of anything Levi did. Would bringing Audrey be the first?

Yet she knew little about him. That, combined with his less-than-tactful proposal, *would* send her skittering away.

He did his best to apologize with his gaze as much as his words. "I'm sorry. That didn't come out as I meant it. You've done so much for me, and through it all I've seen what a fine woman you are. You've risked your standing, and even your life, to free me. If at all possible, I would like to do what I can for you. It would be my honor to take you as my wife. To provide for your needs and protection for the rest of our days."

There. Hopefully that came through a little better. He'd never planned how he would propose to a woman—had always thought he'd have a little time to consider it. But at least her eyes were no longer round as saucers.

She studied him, but her face gave no sign of her thoughts. No inkling of what her response would be.

At last, her shoulders eased as she released a breath. "Thank you for the offer. It proves once more that you're as good a man as I first believed. I need to return to my people, though. My father depends on me. And I can't disappear without even a farewell. My place is here."

The ache tightening his chest was probably from the rejection, though her reasons made sense. Had he really expected her to marry a man she'd only known two days, and run away with him to a land she'd never been to? She seemed to prefer to face the wrath of her people.

Perhaps he really had no say in her actions. This was her life. She'd chosen to sneak him out. He'd offered what he could to help her, but she'd made her decision.

Her expression shifted, turning determined. "I can't go back now, though, not until I know you've left here. Brielle will make me bring her to this cave to look for you. If I beg for the council's mercy, I'll have to tell them everything. I can't do that unless I know for certain you're far away."

His throat tightened at the thought of leaving this place completely. Of leaving her behind to become only a memory. A story he would tell Mum and Libby at the dinner table.

In these two very long days, Audrey Moreau had become a

friend. They may not know a great deal about each other, at least from a factual perspective. But they'd bonded through trial. Through shared fears and struggles. He would trust her with his life—indeed, he had done so several times already.

Only this one thing she asked of him. Surely he could do this single act. Even if it required leaving her behind.

He forced himself to nod. "I'll leave at first light."

"I will, too, then." But the relief that should sound in her voice wasn't there. Only a sadness that tightened the knot inside him.

The moment a hint of the sun's rays filtered from the curve in the cave's tunnel, Audrey allowed herself to sit up, though she kept the blankets tucked around her against the cold. She usually rose several hours before the sun, but with no clock here and a long restless night, she'd had no idea when her normal time came.

Levi also sat up in his bed pallet on the other side of the cave. He'd stirred several times in the night, though not nearly as much as she did. Was he worried as much about his journey south as she was about returning to Laurent?

He glanced her way, and the sleepy smile he offered made something flutter in her belly. How could a man be so appealing, even with tufts of hair sticking in all directions?

She shifted her focus toward the food. "Hungry?" She cleared her throat to force away the sleep gravel.

"I am." The morning rasp in his voice sounded so much better in his rich baritone.

With the food positioned beside her bed pallet, she didn't

have to stir from her warmth to prepare their morning fare. She gathered a substantial meal for him, since he would need a good start for a full day of travels. She had less than an hour's hike to Laurent, so she could make do with a small bit of meat.

His eyes creased in a thankful smile as she handed him the food. After setting aside her own fare, she wrapped everything back up so it would be safe for traveling.

"You're going to eat more than that, aren't you?"

She glanced at Levi as he motioned to the slice of meat she left out. "I can get extra when I reach Laurent."

"And I plan to hunt for my meals along the way. You barely ate more than a bird yesterday. Please, take more food." His tone left little room for argument.

Maybe one additional strip of meat. Especially if he planned to hunt. He should take all the bread and dried berries with him since he wouldn't be able to procure more along the way.

As she packed the food, he rolled the blankets they'd slept in. Once they had everything bundled in the two bags, Levi sat to put on his shoes and the cloth stockings he'd worn with them.

She let herself sit and watch him. This was the last time she would be able to, and there was nothing more for her to pack. "Are your shoes dry enough?" Though the worst of winter was behind them, the weather was still too cold for damp footwear. And walking all day in such gear would rub blisters.

He nodded, his mouth tipping in a weak smile. "I kept them in my blankets all night so they would dry."

A wise thought. The cold would have made them freeze

instead of drying, but the heat his body created would keep them warm.

At last, there was nothing more for them to do. No reason to delay.

He sent her a look that seemed to contain the same mix of wistful sadness that clogged her own chest. "I suppose I should leave now. I'm going to see if I can find my horse on my way out."

She nodded, then forced herself to stand as he did. "Be careful. The searchers shouldn't be out again yet, but take care just in case."

"I will." Levi hoisted both packs on his shoulders, lifting them as though they held only dried leaves. Then he fit the knife at his waist. A final glance around the place showed nothing left behind.

He ambled forward, and she fell into step behind him as they turned the corner in the cave. Dim morning light flooded through the opening before them. He paused before reaching the exit and turned to her. His eyes asked if she was certain of her decision. If he spoke the words, she might have trouble keeping firm to her plan.

Before he could voice the question, she fumbled for something to say. "I'll wait a while here before I return to Laurent. That should give you a head start."

He nodded. Then his throat worked, as if he was struggling for words. "Thank you. Those two words are insufficient to say how I feel about what you've done for me. If there's ever anything I can do to help you . . ."

She nodded. She would never be able to get word to him in England, but still, the sentiment was nice.

He reached out, as though he wanted to shake hands.

That wasn't a custom Laurent's women participated in, but maybe English women did.

She extended her hand, and he caught up her fingers, lifting them to press a kiss to their backs.

The gesture was so gentlemanly, so noble—just like the man she'd come to know. The burn in her chest rose up to the back of her throat, then crept higher into her eyes. She couldn't let the tears fall until he left.

Maybe he realized how close to the edge she was, for he released her hand and stepped the final distance to exit the cave. After pausing to peer out at the surroundings for a long moment, he slipped outside.

She moved to the opening as unruly drops slipped down her cheeks. She'd only known this man two days. How could she feel such an attachment to him already?

He maneuvered down the path to the side of the cliff, staying low and keeping his movements quiet. The searchers wouldn't have reached this place yet, even if they'd left Laurent at first light, but he was being careful, just like she'd asked.

In the distance, a whinny sounded. Levi paused and stared toward the right, where the sound had come from. Then he turned back to her and waved.

She returned the motion, even as a sob hiccuped from her throat. He wouldn't be able to see her tears from this distance, so she soaked in this final glimpse of him.

Lord, be with him. Keep him safe in his travels. Give him the happy life he deserves.

The words had barely winged from her thoughts when the whiz of an arrow hummed through the cold morning air.

The missile struck Levi in the back, pitching him forward.

A scream tore from Audrey's throat.

The blow came so unexpectedly, Levi barely kept his feet beneath him. Fortunately, whatever struck him hadn't penetrated his thick coat. As soon as he caught his balance, he spun to find his attacker.

His gaze shot to the cave first, but Audrey still stood in the opening, shock widening her features. He followed her line of sight down the slope.

A man stepped from behind a boulder. Leonard, the guard who'd been watching Levi when Audrey had sneaked him out.

"You're not going anywhere, Masters." The man held another arrow drawn tight in his bow.

Aimed at Levi.

About thirty strides separated them, and the man had already proved he could hit a target at that distance.

Levi eased his hands up, spreading them away from his body. "I mean no harm to you or to any of your people."

"You can come back and tell the council." Leonard's voice was hard, determined. How much had this man been punished for losing the prisoner on his watch?

"No!" Audrey's voice cut through the air, and Leonard jerked with the sound. Thankfully, he didn't release the arrow in the midst of his surprise.

The guard's voice rang high as he yelled, "Stay back, Audrey. This man has done enough damage. Stay out of this for your own good."

The words pinched in Levi's chest. He spoke truth. Audrey would be much better off if she'd stayed far away from him. He kept his voice level. "I'll return with you." Anything else would put Audrey in worse straits.

"No." This time Audrey's tone sounded more defeated than determined.

I'm sorry. He couldn't speak the words aloud, but maybe he would eventually be able to tell her. He hated that all her sacrifice would be for naught, yet what choice did he have? Especially with this guard pointing an arrow at him?

This must be God's hand guiding him, stopping him from running when he should stand and face his punishment. Not that he'd really done anything wrong, not intentionally. He'd not hurt anyone, nor had he planned to. He'd not lied. Maybe he should have refused when Audrey told him to escape.

He started toward Leonard, keeping his hands raised and away from his sides. He didn't dare glance at Audrey. He couldn't bear the sadness, or maybe even the anger, that would be in her beautiful green eyes.

As he neared Leonard, the man pulled the bowstring tighter. If he released the arrow at this distance, the shaft might penetrate halfway through Levi, depending on what it struck on its way in.

"Stop there."

Levi jerked to a halt, more than happy not to draw closer to this young guard whose eyes held a feral determination. Surely he didn't plan to kill Levi now, then drag his body back to the village.

"Drop those bags and the knife. Move slowly." Leonard's voice was as tight as his bowstring.

Levi eased the satchels from his shoulder and dropped them to the ground, then moved one hand down to grasp the knife handle. He kept his movements painfully slow so he didn't give this young guard a reason to release the arrow.

Leonard nodded to his left. "Toss it down the mountain."

Below the boulder the man had been hiding behind, the slope dropped off steeply, forming a vertical cliff farther down. Levi tossed the blade far enough that it skittered over that steep incline.

"Now your other weapons."

Levi met the man's gaze, returning both hands to the positions away from his sides. "That was all I had."

He was near enough to see the sweat glistening on Leonard's brow, despite the cold. It took a great deal of strength to keep a bow drawn as long as he had, but the man looked as cagey as a cornered bobcat. How old was he, anyway? He didn't look more than one- or two-and-twenty. The pressure to make up for letting his prisoner escape must be intense. Had Leonard spent the entire night out here, lying in wait, even when the rest of the searchers went home?

Levi kept his voice as steady as he could. "You don't have to worry, Leonard. I'll go back with you. I won't try to escape again."

"You won't get away. Not this time." The guard nearly snarled the words. Levi's meaning clearly hadn't penetrated.

The fellow stepped up the mountain and motioned for Levi to walk past him along the animal path. Finally, he eased a little of the tension on the bowstring, holding it only half drawn, and no longer pointed at Levi's chest.

As he passed the man, Levi kept an eye on him from the corner of his gaze. A man as nervous as this guard might do something dangerous—either intentionally or not.

When Levi had taken three steps past him, Leonard moved back down to the trail.

Something flashed in the corner of Levi's gaze, farther

off the mountain. He glanced back, more from instinct than conscious intention. Audrey stepped from behind the tree that guarded the cave, clattering down the mountain with no attempt to conceal her approach.

A yelp of frustration sounded just behind him. Levi turned to see Leonard's reaction to her approach. If he thought to hurt her or restrain her in any way . . .

The guard's vexation must have thrown him off balance, and he took a step backward to catch his footing. The movement took him off the path, his foot landing down the slope and sideways on a loose stone.

He twisted to right himself, and a grunt slipped out as he scrambled for purchase with his other foot. The slope was too steep, though, with too many fist-sized rocks.

Leonard stumbled forward, his upper body joining the battle to regain his balance. But the momentum forced by the incline sent him toppling downward. With the bow still in his arms, he tried to brace himself with his hands.

Levi lunged forward to help, sliding down the slope on the sides of his feet as he fought to keep himself from tumbling like Leonard.

The man was on his side now, so maybe he could use his hands to keep from rolling. But he still held the bow—was tangled in it, maybe. His body flipped over before Levi could reach him.

The fellow cried out, almost at the same moment as a scream echoed from behind them.

13

The descent was steeper now, and Levi had to drop to his knees as he moved. But he had to go faster. Had to stop Leonard before his tumbling picked up speed.

The guard had begun to howl. The rocks must be pounding his face and every other part of him. He didn't seem able to use his hands to stop himself. Though the bow rolled with him, he didn't look entangled anymore. Maybe he'd broken his wrists in the fall.

Levi had to move faster, or he'd never reach the man. Leonard was only a few rolls away from the drop-off that tumbled down in a sheer cliff.

A single scrubby tree caught his eye. The overgrown bush perched right at the top of the cliff and looked to be in line with where Leonard's feet would hit. Was the tree strong enough to stop the man? It had the same prickly needles as the one blocking the cave.

"Grab the tree!" Levi screamed to Leonard, even as he himself launched toward the plant.

The man might be too roughed up to hear and understand. If his wrists were broken, he wouldn't be able to obey. But if

Levi could reach him before he toppled over the precipice, he could use the tree to stop them both from tumbling over.

"No!" Audrey's scream barely penetrated his mind as he landed headfirst in the prickly branches.

Leonard's upper body had already begun to roll over the edge, but Levi grabbed his leg with one hand and the tree with the other.

His hold wasn't firm enough on the man, and he scrambled to wrap his arm around the tree's base so he could use both hands to grip Leonard.

The guard's bellow filled the air as every part of him from the knees up hung suspended over the cliff.

Levi fought for a better hold. He only had one of Leonard's legs, and one of his hands gripped mostly leather. He strained with everything in him to keep Leonard from falling farther. His awkward position kept him from using the strength in the core of his body, so he had to rely almost completely on the abilities of his arms. His fingers were the weak link.

With Leonard's entire bulk dangling over the edge, the grip Levi clung to relied heavily on the strength of the man's leather leggings.

His grip slipped. First a little, then an awful ripping sound rose even over Leonard's cries. Levi had to get a better hold on the man's leg. A firm grip with both hands on more than leather.

Stones skittered down beside him, then Audrey slid into view, barely stopping at his side. Levi's heartbeats stalled as panic washed through him. What if she hadn't halted before going over the edge? As much as he needed help getting Leonard up, he couldn't risk Audrey's safety.

But she was already reaching over the ledge. She dropped to her belly to stretch lower. Levi couldn't hold Leonard and Audrey both—he wasn't even certain how much longer he could hold the guard. He had to get a firmer grip.

"I have his trousers." Audrey's voice sounded strained.

Gritting his teeth and tightening his one good hold on Leonard's leg, Levi released his grip on the leather and grabbed for a firm clutch around the ankle.

He caught the joint, but the shift made Leonard drop even lower, stretching Levi's arms and stealing more of his strength.

Leonard screamed. Audrey slid forward, reaching farther over the cliff's edge.

No! Every bit of Levi's muscles strained to hold the man, so he couldn't even eke out the word.

Beneath him, Leonard began to writhe, twisting and kicking as though he wanted to be free. As though he were trying to plunge headfirst to the rocks below.

"Leonard, stop! Be still." Audrey yelled the words thundering through Levi's mind.

But the man didn't listen.

As Leonard jerked, Levi's hold slipped until he was barely grasping the man's foot. He clung with everything he had left.

But with another kick, the frantic guard broke loose.

Audrey screamed and jerked forward. Levi scrambled to reach her, but with his body leaning so far over the ledge and one arm wrapped around the tree, he couldn't grab her.

So, he twisted, half rolling so his legs could pin Audrey to the ground. He landed atop her, enough to keep her from sliding father over the cliff. His own head had snapped backward, the sharp stone of the ledge biting into the base of his skull.

He didn't dare move. Just sucked in deep breaths. Audrey was safe. He was alive, too, though his arms felt like they'd been stretched to twice the length of his body, and he might have a rib or two broken from his efforts.

But Leonard . . .

Dear Lord, take him to paradise with you today. He squeezed his eyes shut as the awful ordeal played back through his mind. He couldn't let the images fester, not now when he still had to get Audrey back up the mountain.

At last, he drew enough breath to speak. "Audrey."

"Yes?" Her voice was so soft he barely heard it. She was lying motionless, too, though part of that might be because of his weight. Yet surely she'd been affected by watching Leonard die.

He had to help her focus on their next tasks. "Can you crawl backward away from the edge?"

"You're on my legs." Her voice sounded stronger now, though still soft. Perhaps because she faced the ground.

"As I move, scoot back. All right?"

"All right." Something didn't sound normal in her voice, but he would find out more once they were back on solid ground.

He slid one leg off her, then the other, keeping his body twisted so he could see for sure that she moved away from danger. He clung to the tree with both hands now, though his grip trembled so much, he probably wouldn't be able to stop himself if he somehow slid over the ledge.

But that wouldn't happen. He wouldn't allow it.

Audrey finished crawling backward, then sat on the slope,

far enough away that his heart might finally return to its regular pace.

Now he had to get himself upright. Shifting his legs one over the other, he untwisted his body and did his best to roll onto his belly. His face pressed into the tree needles again, and he tried to get his hands underneath him to move into a crawling position.

But his arms wouldn't hold him.

His entire body was weak as a babe's. He lay there for a long time, gathering his strength.

"Levi?" Worry tinged Audrey's voice.

"I'm all right. Just need a minute." He should make another try now that his breath had mostly returned to him.

Using the strength of his legs more than anything, he managed to crawl backward from the ledge. His chest definitely ached, down near his lower ribs. Maybe he'd only bruised them as he'd pressed against the stony ground while he clung to Leonard. The ache in his side from yesterday's arrow wound had all but disappeared amid all the chaos. Every inhale pressed into his ribs like a knife, and he did his best to keep his breaths shallow.

At last, he struggled to a sitting position beside Audrey. She stared toward the edge of the cliff, as though remembering the moment Leonard tumbled over. As Levi settled beside her, she glanced his way, sending her gaze down the length of him. A frown drew her brows together, and her attention jerked up to his face. "You're hurt?"

He shook his head. "Probably just a bruise." His hand slid across his ribs, but the moment he neared the spot, the pain told him he'd better not touch.

"We should go back to the cave and let me check." There

was something distant in her voice, maybe simply the hollow tones of grief. She'd probably known Leonard his entire life. They'd likely played together as children. And now to see his life ended in such a violent way . . .

Her focus drifted forward again, back to whatever she'd been thinking or reliving before. "I need to go check on him. Just in case."

Levi's entire body tensed. That glimpse of Leonard sprawled out on the rocks below would stay with him for a long time. Audrey shouldn't see a death like that, especially someone she knew well. Besides, he couldn't imagine there was a chance the man still breathed.

"I'll do it." But with the way his body felt, even if he made it down the mountain, it might be a while before he found the strength to climb back up.

She turned to study him again, and after a long moment, she spoke once more in that hollow voice. "All right. I think you can get down over there." She pointed to the left, where the steepness of the mountain's base eased. It looked like goats or some other animal had pounded out a route through the stones.

He gave himself three more breaths to gather his strength and steel himself against the pain. When he attempted to stand, even using his hands to push off from the slope behind him, the knife in his ribs plunged deeper, twisting as though on fire.

He only made it partway to standing before his body forced him to stop. He froze in that position, not daring to breathe until the flames inside cooled. At last, he eased back down. He would have to roll over on his hands and knees and work up to standing that way.

By the time he turned over, Audrey was already on her feet and placed a staying hand on his shoulder. "Rest here. I'll go look."

Not as long as he had breath in his body. He clenched his jaw against the pain and finished standing. Audrey must have realized it wasn't worth the attempt to stop him, for she slid her hand down to his arm and helped with the last of his efforts.

After straightening, he took in steady, shallow breaths to let his insides settle. To cover his weakness, he used the time to map out the best path down the slope.

"I'll walk down with you." Without waiting for him to respond, Audrey turned and started toward the goat trail.

He let out a careful breath and followed. She could go to the bottom of the mountain, but he would be the one to approach Leonard.

Keeping his eyes on the next step ahead was the only way he managed to maneuver down the slope. Audrey easily out-distanced him, but she paused to wait for him several times on the descent before continuing on.

At last, they reached the area where the ground leveled off. Everything in him begged to stay here and rest. To catch his breath and let the burning in his ribs subside before he proceeded. But if he didn't move now, Audrey would start off without him again.

He stepped past her and held up a hand. "Wait here."

As he picked his way around a section of boulders that looked like they'd once come from a rockslide, he prepared himself for what he would find. Blood, undoubtedly. Limbs in unlikely positions from broken bones.

The life of a promising young man snuffed out.

After finally making his way around the rockslide, he reached the area where the cliff met the ground. Except it didn't meet the ground exactly. The base of the vertical slope joined a flat stone platform as tall as his shoulders that he would have to hoist himself up onto. His arms had regained some of their strength, but lifting his body like that would be a challenge.

He could see Leonard's form on the platform about fifteen strides away, but from this angle, he could only make out the top of the man's head and one arm. He'd have to climb up there and check Leonard's pulse to be sure no life remained.

By the time he managed to wriggle and groan his way up onto the stone platform, he was more than grateful Audrey hadn't watched his awkward, exhausted attempts. His ribs felt like they'd never heal, especially if he kept climbing up and down this mountain.

He lay on his back for a long moment to gather himself, then prepared for the arduous task of standing. When he gained his feet, the thought occurred that maybe he should have just crawled over to Leonard. He had to come back to his knees when he reached the man anyway. But his pain-numbed mind wasn't thinking quickly enough to save himself the effort.

He stilled himself as he approached the body, forcing his emotions back and letting his mind focus only on the facts.

Blood coated the man's face, streaking through his hair and pooling beneath his head. One arm lay twisted, the wrist bent down in a position that had to mean it was broken. The other hand lay under Leonard's body, so he couldn't tell for sure about that one. The legs weren't noticeably broken, but there might be damage not obvious.

As he dropped to his knees to check the man's pulse, he had to look away from Leonard's young face. The damage from the rocks marred his features, giving him a grotesque appearance.

Levi pressed fingers to his neck, searching in several places for sign of a heartbeat. Nothing. No rise and fall of his chest.

Just in case, Levi gripped the man's shoulder and gave a shake. "Leonard, can you hear me?" He knew the effort was wasted, but he had to be able to tell Audrey he'd checked thoroughly for any sign of life.

At last, Levi pulled his hands back and closed his eyes. *Lord, have mercy on his soul.* He had no idea if Leonard belonged to the heavenly Father. *And give his family peace.*

How would they tell the man's next of kin? Audrey would have to let them know when she returned. A new wave of pain crept through him. Her return would be hard in so many ways.

He finally stood and gave a final salute to the fallen guard. Then he turned his attention to getting back to Audrey.

Likely, searchers would come again today. There may even be people in the area now. He needed to get back to the cave and figure out the extent of his injuries, then determine what to do next.

He reached the edge of the platform and bent to sit on the ledge. Getting down might be almost as painful as climbing up. He could either jump or turn around and lower himself. The latter would be harder on his ribs, so he would do better to jump and brace himself for the pain that would ricochet through his body upon landing.

Inhaling a breath to prepare, he launched forward to land far enough away from the platform that he avoided the loose stones at its base.

When his feet hit the ground, something shifted under his boot. His left leg twisted inward, shifting his weight sideways. He couldn't catch his balance, and something seemed to buckle beneath the limb.

The ground rushed up to meet him, slamming hard into his shoulder. He squeezed his eyes shut as the pain blinded him.

14

Should she follow Levi around this pile of rocks or not? Audrey's body had begun to shake as she waited. The cold played a part, no doubt, but so did the layers of reality sinking through her shock.

Leonard was dead. She'd never known him well, as he'd been a year behind her in school and he had no sisters. He was a gangly lad with freckles covering his cheeks and nose. He'd always played with the adventurous boys, so it hadn't surprised her when she learned he was training to be a guard.

But now . . . how would she tell his mother? How would she tell anyone in Laurent? When she turned herself in, she would have to be the one to give the awful news.

Until now, her actions had resulted mostly in good. Levi was safe, and free to return to his home and family.

But Leonard . . . One of Laurent's own, who had taken an oath to protect and provide for the village, had died as part of this debacle.

She squeezed her eyes shut as the shivers grew stronger. Pressing her hands into her coat pockets, she pulled the covering tighter around her. *Lord, forgive me.*

A yell from the other side of the fallen rocks jerked her eyes open. She stepped forward, then paused to listen. Had that been a person? As she replayed the sound in her mind, it could have been made by a bird.

Still, she would go see what was happening with Levi.

As she strode around the rocks, her teeth began to chatter. Now that she was moving, she thought the shivers would fade. But they didn't.

When she rounded the boulders, a ledge appeared ahead, about level with her eyes. If she'd gauged the distance correctly, that should be where Leonard lay. She quickened her step, straining to hear any voices as she walked.

A movement on the ground shifted her focus to the left. Realization pressed a cry through her lips.

A body lay among the stones and half-melted snow.

She broke into a run. Had Leonard's fall knocked him all the way out here? Yet the body was moving. Could he still be alive?

Then the figure turned so she could see the face, and a jolt passed through her.

Levi.

She sprinted faster, then slowed as she neared him to take in what might be wrong. Panic tried to well, but she forced it back. He was moving. Maybe he'd only tripped and had the breath knocked from his chest.

He opened his eyes, and relief swept through her. She dropped to her knees by his side. "What happened?"

His eyelids dropped to half mast, pain cloaking his face. "My leg." He touched his right leg, near the hip.

Fear gripped her chest as she ran her gaze down the length of him. Nothing looked out of place.

"I fell. Or tripped. Can't move it." His words grated out through his clenched jaw.

She honed her focus on the limb, scanning from top to bottom. His leggings didn't show any sign of swelling. The knee and foot pointed inward, but not enough to be abnormal. She needed to feel the limb all the way up to learn what her eyes couldn't see. "I need to remove your boot and check for injuries." She worked to settle her insides as she glanced at his face for a response.

Pain twisted his expression. "Do it."

She worked as quickly as she could, forcing her mind to focus on all the possible injuries and symptoms she should watch for. Broken bones were most likely, and also easiest to discover, as there would be swelling and heat, and sometimes an awkward angle or protrusion.

After removing the boot, she used both hands to start with the toes. "Tell me if I touch the place that hurts."

"That's . . . numb. I only feel . . . a tingle."

She still had one hand gripped around his toes and the other around his heel, but she stilled, thinking through what numbness might be a symptom of. Only one type of injury sprang to mind, but surely there were others. With careful movements, she kept going. Down the foot. Over the ankle, pressing with all her fingers to touch each bone. Up the lower leg, over the knee.

He didn't alert her to new pain, and her fingers found nothing unusual. Except . . . the leg seemed to move so easily, any direction she prodded, though it always came back to rest pointed inward. She cocked her head. Perhaps leaning a bit too much to the inside? That would go along with the symptom of numbness in the toes. . . .

She pressed the thought away, focusing on finding heat or swelling or anything abnormal. She was working her way up his thigh bone now. How much farther did she dare go? When she'd checked halfway up that part of the limb, she pulled her hands away. She couldn't ignore what her instincts kept pointing her toward. Better to address that possibility head-on before making this inspection even more awkward than it was becoming.

She did her best to give her voice the tone of a healer working with a patient. "Can you point to the place where the pain is the worst?"

He pressed a hand to the outside of his hip. Her own stomach dipped. That would match everything else.

Inhaling a breath for courage, she focused on the area. "I'm going to touch it to feel if the joint might have come out of place."

He moved his hand away, giving space for her to do what she'd said. His eyes were closed, his breathing thick and labored. She couldn't delay any longer.

As her fingers worked over the outside of his leg, she probed for the knot that would tell her for certain. The entire joint seemed to be swelling, but there it was, the telltale sign she'd only felt once before. Madame Maiser had been white-haired and wrinkled when she began to teach Audrey some of the ways of a healer. Many of their ministrations stood out boldly in Audrey's memories, for she'd soaked in every tidbit the woman shared.

Even now, she could close her eyes and remember the time they'd worked the Vignette lad's hip joint back into place. He'd fallen from a cliff and had cried out in a steady stream of sobs and moans while they worked. It had taken both of them, Audrey and Madame Maiser, to leverage the joint back into place. That had been six or seven years ago, so perhaps Audrey was strong enough to manage it alone now.

She would have to. And the sooner she accomplished it, the sooner his pain would subside.

She shifted so she was facing his thigh bone, doing her best to recall everything she could about the maneuver. "Your hip joint is out of place, so I'm going to try to work it back in. This will hurt at first, but then you should feel much better." *If* she could get this done right. And if there wasn't an even greater problem, like broken bone fragments in the joint, or some other painful possibility.

She wouldn't know for sure until she tried.

If only she had some of Papa's drink to numb Levi's pain before she attempted this next step. Willow bark tea would be the next best thing. She had willow bark at the cave, but taking time to start a fire, heat water, and let the tea steep was too much delay. The sooner this joint was set, the less damage might be done inside the limb.

Lord, block the pain so he doesn't feel it. And guide my hands. Give me wisdom to know how to set this.

With one hand under his knee and the other supporting his lower leg, she lifted the limb and braced her own knee under his so his knee rested on her thigh. His limbs were so much larger than hers. So much heavier than the Vignette lad's had been. This brawny man needed her to be strong. No half-hearted attempt would do.

Settling herself in the right position so she could press down and inward on his lower leg, using her own raised knee as a lever, she began applying pressure. First a little, then more. Levi groaned, and she allowed herself a single glance at his face. The lines in his jaw pulled tight, his eyes squeezed shut.

She refocused on her work, feeling the strain in her arms through her core and through his leg. She pushed harder, leaning into the effort, listening for the pop and jerk that would signal the joint was back in place.

A grunt slipped from Levi, louder than the groan from before, but she stayed focused on every sensation, every bit of pressure that ebbed through her hands and down his hip to the joint.

Nothing was happening, save the torture she was inflicting on this strong man. She angled her knee to the left and pushed down harder on his foot. This had to work. *God, help it work. Move this joint back into place.*

As she clenched her jaw with the effort, she tipped his knee a bit inward. A jerk pulsed up from his hip, and a surge of relief washed through her stealing her strength.

She glanced at Levi's face. He lay still, his skin almost as pale as the snow. Had he lost consciousness from the pain?

"Levi." She barely spoke above a whisper.

"Hmm." He didn't open his eyes, and his voice sounded almost groggy. Maybe he was simply exhausted from fighting through the torture she'd just inflicted. Not to mention everything he'd endured before. His ribs had been injured, too, she was fairly certain.

Pulling her knee from under his, she gently laid out his leg. Getting the joint into place had been the hardest part, but what if bones had been broken as well?

The immensity of it all, the host of unknowns, threatened to overwhelm her. She rested both hands on Levi's leg, then bowed her head and laid out her heart before the Lord.

Heavenly Father, only you can heal this leg correctly. Place your divine hand around him so his body knits straight and true. Repair any bones or vessels that are damaged. And help us get him safely up to the cave.

She stayed in that place of reverence for another moment, soaking in the connection with the Father. The One who had promised to never leave or forsake her. Levi, too, was His child. And God was the One who knit each bone and joint and sinew in the first place. He could certainly put a few of them back together now.

"Thank you, Lord." She whispered the final words, then lifted her head and opened her eyes. A glance around helped return her to the present.

How late in the day was it? A glance at the gray sky showed the sun only an hour or two above the horizon. How could it still be early morning? A day seemed to have passed since she watched Levi leave the cave, bound for places she would never see. Brielle and the others would be back to begin searching again soon.

Now it would be weeks before he went anywhere. She would need to rethink their entire plan. This hip needed to be rested, and likely the ribs, too, so they didn't damage internal organs. Levi wouldn't be able to care for himself.

First things first, though. She had to focus on getting him to the cave.

If she found a pair of sticks to slip under his arms, would he be able to maneuver up the mountain? That might be the best option, but it would be a challenge on the path beside the cliff, just below the cave's entrance.

Her mind scrambled through other options. If she found his horse, would riding up the mountain be a better course?

Twisting his leg at that angle might pull the hip back out of joint again so soon after the first occurrence. The sinews around it hadn't had a chance to resecure themselves.

Staying down here wasn't an option. Not with the cold and remnants of snow, and with the searchers likely to return any moment.

Getting him up to the cave was her only chance to keep him safe.

15

Levi focused on steadily breathing, counting each inhale. His entire body felt numb in the aftermath of the agony in his hip. Audrey had taken away the burning flame inside him, dulling it to a weary throb.

And now she'd gone.

She'd said what she was going to retrieve, but his cloudy mind hadn't picked out the words. If he let himself, he could easily drift into oblivion as he lay here, mired in muddy snow.

A thumping registered, approaching from somewhere past his feet. He cracked his eyes open. Only a little, for the light made his head pound harder, but he could just make out Audrey walking toward him.

He let his eyes drift shut again. His mind didn't have the strength to decipher what she carried.

She dropped to her knees beside him. "I gathered the packs, then found two walking sticks that will help you get back up to the cave. I wish you could stay here and rest a while, but the searchers might be out any time, and we have to get you to shelter."

If he'd had the energy, he might have groaned at her suggestion. She was right, they weren't safe out here. But climb that mountain? Everything inside him revolted against the idea.

Then cool soft fingers brushed across his brow, sending tendrils of relief all the way through him. As her touch feathered down his temple, new life seemed to rise up everywhere her hand moved.

He focused on steadying his breathing as she stroked his other temple. She might really be an angel, as much power as her fingers possessed.

Then she pulled her hand away, and the ache resumed in his head.

"More." The word slipped out, a desperate attempt to restore the comfort of her touch.

Those gentle fingers settled on his brow again. "This?" Her voice sounded uncertain, tentative.

He leaned into the touch as she slid her hand down the side of his face. "Helps." If only he could tell her how much.

She continued to stroke his face—his brow, his temples, his cheeks. But when she ran the tips of her fingernails through his hair, he nearly groaned. He'd better get up now, before her fingers lulled him to sleep.

Forcing his eyes open, he saw her beautiful face. Even with worry lines fanning under her eyes, just the sight of her brought something alive inside him. She'd done so much for him. The least he could do was put forth whatever effort he had to so they could both get up to the cave. He couldn't let her be discovered helping him. When she was ready to return to her people, it had to be on her own terms.

Locking that determination inside to fuel him, he dropped his gaze to the bundles beside her. "Let me have the walking sticks."

Getting on his feet sent a new wave of pain through him. Not the all-consuming inferno engulfing his hip from before, but a smaller flame had definitely rekindled there. His ribs and head had resumed their pounding, too, making even shallow breaths a challenge.

As he gripped the poles, he worked to steady his breathing. That might take days, though, so he finally turned himself toward the mountain.

He managed the first few steps with a little of his dignity intact. But as they ascended, Audrey hovering on the side of his injured hip, the pain and exhaustion pressed him lower, stealing both breath and strength. Only his grip on the sticks kept him from crumpling onto the stones he stumbled over.

"You can do this. We're making good progress." Audrey kept up steady encouragement, her gentle tone nudging when he wasn't sure he could manage another step.

It might have taken all day to reach the trail beside the cliff where the path grew steepest. It certainly felt like hours had passed since they started out from the mountain's base. Audrey had grown tense beside him, probably worried about searchers appearing. He hadn't the strength to focus on anything other than the next movement.

"We're almost there." Her hand gripped his arm, pushing him up the last part of the slope.

The green of juniper needles appeared in his blurry vision. A few more steps. Once he reached the darkness of the cave, he could give in to the fathomless exhaustion that was desperate to overwhelm him.

The moment the shadow of the cave covered him, his arms slackened like custard, and his knees buckled. His ribs screamed, but they could hardly grow louder than when they'd screeched as he struggled to climb.

Audrey's arms were at his back, easing him to a sitting position, then helping him lie back. Laying his legs out straight to soften the pounding in his hip.

Without her, he might have died down in the muddy snow—a slow, torturous end. He had so much to thank her for. And he would make sure he said the words . . . as soon as his body found the strength.

Audrey finally let herself pause to breathe. As they'd climbed the last few steps to duck behind the juniper tree, she'd glimpsed people on the mountain beside theirs. Brielle had been one of the figures, but Audrey hadn't waited to determine who was with her. She could only pray they hadn't looked to this spot before she tugged Levi to safety.

There was nothing she could do about the muddy footprints marring the ground where Levi fell. At least their tracks disappeared on the stone mountainside.

Levi needed to be moved deeper into the cave where they'd camped before, but that could wait a little while for him to regain some strength after the climb. She should bring a few blankets to keep him warm and provide a softer pillow than the hard stone. She also needed to wrap the hip to support the joint as it healed. And the arrow wound on his side should be re-tended. That bandage could also help wrap his injured ribs. She should do a full check for other injuries, though the thought of that sent heat swarming up her neck.

But all that could wait a few minutes. Levi needed rest,

and her own mind needed a moment to clear. This was a good time to see how many searchers had come out today.

When she peered out the cave opening, people had already moved onto their mountain, so she stayed well within the shadows of the cave, leaning out only enough to see them. Two of the men entered the nearby cave they'd found yesterday. They brought a torch this time, which they lit just before entering with knives drawn. Within less than a minute, they reemerged. That cave must be as small as this one.

As the search party spread wide, fanning both higher up the mountain and down near its base, Audrey's middle churned. They would find Leonard soon. Two older men from the village traipsed toward the cluster of trees where she'd procured a brace for Levi's leg. They would probably be the ones to discover the blood and footprints, which would lead them to Leonard's body.

Within a few minutes, the cry sounded. Searchers from all over swarmed down to the base of the mountain—at least fifteen people. Brielle was among them, of course, but Evan didn't seem to be with them this time. The sound of voices drifted up to her, but she couldn't make out any words.

Then a hush settled over the area. They must have found Leonard's body. Tears burned her eyes, swelling her throat. He hadn't deserved to die this way. No man did, but Leonard was so young. So much of his life lay ahead.

And what of Gina? The two had been betrothed, though she'd recently broken it off. She would be devastated to learn the news. The two had known each other since infancy and been sweethearts these past two years. Audrey had always suspected that Leonard had harbored affection long before that.

A shout drifted from below—angry, as though vowing to take revenge on the man who did this to one of their own.

Another voice sounded, Brielle's this time, using the official tone she took on when speaking as Le Commandant. For a few minutes, Brielle's voice was interspersed with the deeper tones of men. Then the sounds ceased.

A moment later, a handful of men—four of them—appeared through a gap in the rocks. They seemed to be marching with purpose in the direction of Laurent. Maybe returning to let the rest of the village know what had happened. She could imagine the grief that would well up. Would this cause the people to revert fully to their former fear of strangers? With Evan's coming, they'd made such great strides in considering the good of opening trade with the outside world. She had a feeling much of that progress would be undone now.

The four men could be seen clearly traipsing across the base of the other mountain. Four men wouldn't be needed simply to spread the news. They must be planning something else as well.

She waited a few more minutes, and as some of the searchers seemed to resume looking for Levi near the base of the mountain, she retreated back into the cave.

At least Leonard's body had distracted the search party. Her focus now had to be on the man who desperately needed help for his injuries.

He needs your healing touch, Lord. Now more than ever.

16

Audrey didn't dare start a fire until night fell and she was certain the searchers were long gone. She'd used a candle when she needed light to tend Levi, but otherwise, she sat in the curve of the cave where she could see both the opening blocked by the juniper tree and Levi's sleeping body. She'd done everything she could for him, except brew the tea that would help cleanse his blood and ease his pain. That required a fire.

When darkness spread over the mountain and she was sure the last of the searchers had gone, she reached for the tinderbox. She managed to start a small blaze with the kindling left from before, then moved to Levi's side. "Levi, are you awake?" She kept her voice to a whisper. She didn't actually want to wake him, only let him know where she was going if he was already conscious.

His eyelids flicked open, and after a moment, his gaze honed on her. Even through the tension that had hovered in the cave all day, a smile tugged at her mouth. He was so handsome, and when he turned those intense eyes on her . . . the rest of their troubles faded. At least for a moment.

She forced her mind to what she needed to tell him. "It's dark now, so I'm going out to get firewood. I'll prepare a meal for us when I return." He'd only eaten a few bites of meat at midday, so he should be hungry.

His eyes opened more fully, then he lifted his head. "I can help."

She pressed a hand to his shoulder. "No. You need to keep that hip still at least another day so the joint can set. After that, you can sit up, but I still don't want you walking." His face took on a look of horror, so she softened both her voice and her touch, smoothing her fingers over his coat. "Stay here. I'll be back soon."

She didn't give him a chance to argue, just stood and turned toward the cave entrance. Using the easier trail down the mountain, she crept in the darkness to the trees where she'd have the best chance of finding firewood. She needed to make several trips to stock up, just in case she wasn't able to leave the cave later.

By the time she hauled her third armload of sticks and logs up the mountain, she struggled to catch her breath. The stitch in her side told her she'd better rest awhile before making a fourth trip.

Levi was obeying her order to remain still, but his mouth formed a thin line as he watched her each time she brought in a load. After adding another log to the fire and adjusting the kettle she'd placed to warm, she glanced around the room. She needed to bring up a pot of snow to melt. She could make a broth for Levi from the smoked meat, which might settle better than solid food in his weakened condition.

At last, she turned to the man. She'd done her best to keep her attentions clinical, to think of him as only a patient—

not the handsome man who stirred her longings in a way no one else ever had.

He'd closed his eyes, and for just a moment, she let her gaze roam his face. Pain still etched lines across his brow and around his eyes. The scruff that had grown over his jaw defined his strong features and gave him a bit of a roguish look. In so many ways it didn't match his character, as he'd proven to be a gentleman. But the look added to his appeal. In truth, could anything detract from the masterpiece God created in him?

He shifted, and his eyelids parted to thin cracks.

She worked for a smile. "Does light hurt your eyes?"

"Some."

She scooted close enough to touch his face. "You must have bumped your head when you fell. Is there a place that hurts, maybe tender to the touch?"

She reached out but hesitated before her fingers brushed his thick hair. *Clinical.* She had to shift her thinking back to that of a healer working with her patient, discerning injuries.

Levi must have thought she paused to wait for his answer, for he parted his lips and seemed to struggle to speak. "I don't know." His entire head must ache, then.

She forced her hands to do their work, slipping her fingers through his hair and moving methodically around his head, seeking out bumps or scratches.

"Helps."

The word Levi murmured made her pause. Maybe she hadn't heard him right. But when he cracked one eyelid open and asked in pleading tone, "More?" she barely bit back a smile. Yes, she could apply this treatment as long as he needed.

She let her fingers enjoy the sensations, but when she brushed a spot behind his left ear, he flinched. Easing back over the area, she found what she'd been looking for—a small bump, at least part of the cause for his aching head.

"Hurts." The pain lines on his face deepened again, and she moved away from the knot.

"I'll avoid that area." As she resumed running her fingers through his hair, brushing her nails across his scalp in a soothing rhythm, his features softened again. Within a few minutes, his breathing deepened. Maybe he would finally get the sleep his body needed so much.

At last, she eased away, stood, and headed back out into the night. She had much to do before she could sleep. She had to gather everything they would need tonight, for who knew what tomorrow would bring?

⁂

When Levi awoke, a dim light filled the cave. Daylight.

His eyelids cracked open easier than they had before. The pain still gnawed at him, but his mind felt a little clearer. Not as clouded by numbness.

Audrey sat across the cave, her back to him as she worked on something. A faint glow from the fire illuminated her side. Waking to her nearby seemed natural, as though they'd always lived like this.

Yet what of her people? Her father? He must be frantic to find her.

She must've sensed him watching, for she glanced back, and a gentle smile warmed her face, even in the shadows. Turning partly to see him better, her gaze lingered on his face. Maybe checking for pain, or awareness, or who knew what. "You're feeling better?" She was learning to read him. That thought brought a mixture of pleasure and worry.

"I think so. How late is it?"

She reached for something near the fire, then shifted to face him fully, a cup in her hand. "Around midday, I think."

He'd slept all night and through the morning, too?

She slipped her hand under his head to lift it as she placed the cup at his mouth. He drank obediently. Broth this time, with chunks of meat floating in the liquid. His belly said he needed more sustenance.

When she pulled the cup back, he swallowed the liquid in his mouth. "Is there any meat left? Or a roll?"

The shadows on her face deepened as her cheeks rounded in a smile. "You *are* feeling better." She reached behind her, then turned back with a chunk of bread in her hand. "This is getting crusty. We need to finish off the baked goods in the next day or two. I wish I had ingredients to make more."

He took the food and bit into it. It was a little on the tough side, and the bite made his head ache again. He broke off smaller pieces, and after a few minutes, his belly relaxed as it began to fill.

When he finished the bread, Audrey was ready with another cup. "Here's tea that will help with the pain and keep your wounds from festering."

He eyed the brew. "Is that what made me sleep so long?"

Her smile turned indulgent. "It helped you rest, but only because your body needs sleep to recover."

He couldn't deny that, but before he faded into that mindless place, they needed to talk. She moved closer with the cup, but he raised a staying hand. "In a minute."

She paused, and her brows lowered as she studied him. She pulled the cup back to hold it in both hands, as though she needed something to occupy them.

"Your people must be worried about you. Your father."

With her eyes shadowed, he couldn't read her thoughts, but her lips pursed. Then finally they parted, but another moment passed before she spoke. "I think they believe I'm gone."

A jolt shook him. "Dead?" Like Leonard?

She shook her head. "Left with you. Only a few people were out searching yesterday. I think they might have sent a group southward to try to catch up with us."

As that thought worked through his mind, he did his best to examine the idea from every perspective, even though his wits weren't nearly as sharp as they should be.

If the people of Laurent thought he'd left the area, they should be safe here in this cave. Unless someone accidentally spotted smoke from their fire or glimpsed Audrey when she was out gathering firewood.

But if they thought she'd run away with him, her reputation was permanently besmirched. Would it help to send her back now? It would prove that she hadn't left with him, but it also might bring suspicion about whether he still hid nearby.

But that didn't change the fact that she must miss her father. Her friends. Even if most of the village would really believe that she'd run away with a man, those who loved her best must know the purity of her heart.

He shifted his focus to her face, the faint glow of daylight illuminating her cheeks. "Do you think you should go back?"

She hesitated only a heartbeat before shaking her head. "I can't leave you. Not when you can't get around for days. If you move too soon, your hip joint could move out of place again and cause permanent damage."

Heaviness pressed down on him. She was staying here—had thrown her reputation aside—solely for him. And he needed her. She was probably right about his hip, especially the part about permanent damage if he mangled it again right away.

So, what should he do? Insist she return, despite his need of her? That's what any decent man should do. But what if he was sending her back to dire punishment? Or, at the very least, a miserable life as an outcast? He wasn't a good judge of how her people would respond, but in England, her lot in life would be hard with such a reputation.

In the end, this had to be her choice. But he needed to make sure she was making the decision based on what *she* wanted and what would be best for *her*, not him.

Shifting his head so he could better face her, he met her gaze. "Please don't stay away from your people on my account. If you want to return, I want you to go. I'm more grateful than I can say for everything you've done for me. But I don't want you to give up your life and happiness because of me."

She shifted her hands on the cup in her lap, then dropped her gaze to stare at it. If only he could tell what she was thinking. Part of him—the very selfish part—feared she might pack up and leave him here, right now. What would he do then?

That question didn't bear pondering, for a greater part of him knew she wouldn't go. Though he didn't know why it was that she stayed.

Finally, she lifted her face to him. "I want to stay here. I want to help."

She spoke plainly, and her tone gave no insight as to her reason. Perhaps he was overthinking this. He should simply take Audrey at her word and let his weary mind rest.

He tried to nod, but the movement sent a pain through his head. "I want it always to be your choice, and please know how grateful I am for you. Anything I can do in return, tell me."

Her glance flicked down the length of him, then back up, and the firelight deepened the shadows as her mouth tugged in a grin. Clearly, they both knew he was in no condition to do anything for her. He'd have to make sure he repeated the offer later, when he could follow through.

She lifted the cup. "Are you ready for this now?"

"Very." His body was already drawing him into the abyss, but hopefully the drink would dampen the pain radiating throughout him.

17

Audrey eyed the dark clouds pressing low in the morning sky as she stepped from the trees with an armload of wood. The air felt much thicker than the usual winter morning. Snow would fall sometime today. She'd fully stocked their woodpile the night before, mostly because there was little else to do. Perhaps she should still bring up a few extra loads this morning.

For the last three days, the weather had been tolerable, but she'd stayed tucked in the cave during daylight hours. The searchers hadn't been back for two days now, but she still tried to stay in the cave during the brighter hours of each day, saving her outings for wood or water for the dusky light of morning or evening.

The long daylight hours sitting across the cave from Levi had been a treasure, getting to know him and hearing stories of his family, especially his baby sister, who was only a year younger than he was. Hearing their escapades as they grew up in the countryside made her chest ache with laughter. She'd never had the chance for a younger brother or sister. Not when her own mother died during her birth.

The low chattering of a bird brought her back to the present. She needed to focus on what should be done to prepare them in case they were snowed in for several days.

Food. She'd been rationing what little they had left, but soon there would be only berries remaining. Could she hunt with only a knife? The thought of killing an animal soured her stomach. She'd dressed hundreds of carcasses brought to her by the village hunters, but she'd never had to look in the eyes of a creature and take its life. Could she do it, knowing the alternative was to starve?

Maybe she should return to Laurent for food. But once she made it through the gates, they would never allow her to return to Levi. That wasn't an option.

Perhaps she could set a snare. That would be an easier way to hunt. She would only have to skin and cook the animal, both things she was very accustomed to.

When Levi awoke, she could ask him if he knew much about trapping. With the snow coming, today wouldn't be a good day to set the snare, but they could prepare.

By the time she carried three more loads of wood up to the cave, Levi had awakened. Anytime she glanced over and saw his dark brown eyes watching her, shivers of pleasure swept through her. She could imagine them as an old married couple, her keeping house for him and cooking his meals. Reveling in the warmth of his gaze and snuggling in the strength of his arms.

She pushed the daydream aside, a task getting harder and harder as the days passed. In many ways, it felt like this world they created had always been.

But she *wasn't* his wife—she was his nurse. Here to tend his injuries and see that he stayed warm and received the nourishment he needed to recover.

Fortified with that reminder, she brushed the wood residue from her hands, then moved to the fire to pour a cup of the broth she'd kept warming. "Are you hungry?"

"Very." His voice rumbled in that way it always did first thing in the morning. There was a brightness in his eyes today that hadn't been there in a while.

She approached with the cup, but he raised a hand to pause her. "I'll sit up."

After helping him to an upright position, she shifted his injured leg while he turned so his back could rest against the cave wall. "There. You look ready for some breakfast." She handed him the cup and a chunk of bread. She'd save the last pastry for his evening meal. "This bread is so hard you'll need to dunk it in the broth to keep from choking."

He took the food with a grateful smile. "Anything that fills the empty places will be perfect. It would be nice to have some snow to melt for wash water today, too."

That was a need she could take care of now. As he started into his meal, she took the pot outside, cleaned the inside with snow, then refilled it and returned to the cave. As she placed the container near the fire for the snow to melt, she kept her tone casual. "I've been contemplating how to get fresh meat, and I thought it might be best to set snares. Have you any experience there?"

He studied her as he chewed a bite. "Some when I was a boy, but not since then. Do you have string to use?"

She'd not gotten that far in her thinking. "I can cut strips of leather. Would that work?"

His brows dipped in thought. "The trick is to make it blend into its surroundings, so you'd have to set the snare in an area with brown branches or grass."

She glanced toward the cave opening, though she couldn't see around the curve in the stone. "I think it will snow today. The ground will likely have a fresh coating of white by the time I set the snares." A new thought slipped in. "What of Leonard's bow? If I could find it, maybe we could use the string from that."

His expression lifted. "If you can find the bow and an arrow or two, I could sit at the cave opening and hunt from there. Surely if I wait long enough, prey will come by."

New hope tried to burgeon within her. "You're competent with a bow and arrow?" He'd carried a gun and knife, so she didn't want to assume.

His nose scrunched. "I have plenty of time to practice, if you wouldn't mind retrieving the arrow for me each time."

She blew out a breath. She'd seen how many months— even years—it took to develop accuracy with a bow, but perhaps Levi could do well enough to bring down an animal or two.

Either way, if she could find the bow and any arrows, they would be of benefit. "I'll see if I can locate them."

A few minutes later, she crept down the mountain toward where Leonard fell. She'd avoided this path, not only because it was steeper and harder to travel, but also because the memories still brought the sting of tears.

Yet she had to relive those moments in order to remember what might have happened to the bow and arrows. Leonard had kept the arrow notched in the string all the way until the moment he stumbled. As he rolled down the hill, it seemed the bow had become entangled in his arms. He must have dropped the arrow before that.

She found the area where he tripped easily enough, but

as she worked her way down the slope, her heart quickened. The ground grew steep so quickly that her feet threatened to slip down the incline. She dropped to a sitting position, then crept farther down.

At last, she saw one end of the bow poking out from behind a rock on her left. She scooted that way and grasped the wood. *Thank you, Lord.*

As she extracted the piece from where it lay caught under a stone, it looked like the wood part of the bow was mostly intact. Closer inspection revealed that part of the notch on one end had cracked, allowing the string to slip free. She or Levi should be able to repair that, at least to make it usable for now.

Finding arrows proved trickier. She scoured the slope in both directions, even moving up above the trail in case one had been thrown that direction. Finally, she traipsed down to the base of the mountain and around to the platform that had been Leonard's final demise. Almost Levi's, too.

She hated this area, had stayed far away from it once she'd gotten Levi up the mountain. But she had to face the place. Just this once.

With a prayer for strength, she steeled herself against what she might see, then rounded the base of the rockslide. Much of the snow had melted, and Leonard's blood had seeped into the ground, though she could still see staining. She focused on searching for the arrow, or even a straight stick that could be whittled into a decent projectile.

Nothing presented itself, so she attempted to climb up onto the platform. The ledge was too high, so she painstakingly hauled over several rocks until she could climb up enough to hoist herself the rest of the way.

At last, she stood on the platform and stared around the

area. Leonard's blood still darkened the stone where he'd lain. She avoided that spot as she focused her attention on finding arrows.

There. Near the base of the cliff lay a perfectly preserved arrow. It sat tucked behind a rock, which must be why the men from the village hadn't seen it and brought it back with Leonard's body.

She carried it with both hands, a treasure she would safeguard on her climb back up the mountain.

After leaving the platform, she carried the bow and arrow to the copse of trees. Maybe she could find a straight pine branch that could be whittled into a second arrow. That might give Levi a task to keep busy as the snow fell.

She finally located one that might work, and as she was cutting the piece from the tree, the first flakes began to fall. On her way back up the mountain, an icy wind crept beneath the edges of her coat, numbing her face and making her nose run. How wonderful it would be to sit tucked inside a warm apartment with a fire blazing and a steaming bowl of hearty soup.

At least they had the cave for protection. She could add enough wood to the fire for a roaring blaze and heat water for a soothing tea. She might not be experienced at hunting for meat, but she could find bark or leaves to make tea almost anywhere.

Levi still sat upright when she entered the cave.

"Look what I found." She held up the bow in one hand and the arrow and stick in the other, though the dying fire cast such a dim light he wouldn't see them well.

He reached out, and she handed the weapons over, then moved to add more logs to the fire.

"Well done. The bow should be easy to repair."

"I thought that pine branch might make a decent arrow with some whittling. I haven't looked for a stone to use as an arrowhead."

"It's a wonder you found as much as you did."

She glanced down the length of him. "Before you get to work, I'd like to check your injuries."

A sigh slipped from him, then a nod. Her poking and prodding probably brought extra pain, though he'd never said so. He rarely talked about his distress at all. Never complained, only helped where she'd allow. Just one of the many qualities she was coming to admire more with each passing day.

18

Once Audrey finished her ministrations, she positioned Levi's leg straight in front of him. He sank back against the stone wall as before, though he looked more exhausted now.

He reached for the bow and examined the end. "Is the knife nearby?"

She extracted it from her moccasin and handed the tool over.

For a while, he worked at preparing the weapon, and she busied herself adding another log to the fire, warming more tea, and checking the weather outside.

"The snow is really coming down now." She settled herself across the cave from him, where she usually worked by the fire. When he sat upright, the space at his side seemed too near. Her awareness of his attraction too strong.

He looked up from the bow long enough to send her a weary smile. "It's time you sit and rest. You've been working yourself ragged while I lie here abed."

A snort slipped out with her laugh, a completely unlady-like sound. "Hardly. I've been struggling to find things to keep myself busy."

He raised his brows. "Talk to me then."

She rested her hands in her lap. "Anything particular you'd like to talk about?"

"Tell me about your people. How did you come to live so far away from the rest of the world? And why caves instead of building homes? How long has your village been here?"

A smile curved her lips as she leaned back and thought through the stories she'd heard so many times. "Our forefathers first came west about a century ago. Louis Curtois was the leader of the group, and all of them were frustrated with the turmoil back in New France. The Canadas, I guess they call it these days." She glanced at his face. "A part of your country now, I hear?"

He nodded. "Do you know which part they came from? Upper or Lower Canada?"

She searched the recesses of her memory. "I'd never heard the name *Canada* until Evan first told us of the changes there. I believe our people came from somewhere near Alberta."

Understanding settled across his features, and she shifted back into her memories. "Our people wanted to live simple, peaceful lives, where they could serve God and work together to prosper. I think Curtois and those other forefathers must have had an adventurous streak, too."

"It sounds as though they did." Humor touched Levi's voice.

She settled into the words she'd heard recited so many times. "They traveled four weeks through several different landscapes. They almost settled in the prairie, but the mountains in the distance beckoned them. The beauty and grandeur of the peaks was hard to resist, so they kept going until they found a mountain with a giant cavern inside. Several smaller tunnels split off from it, and the shape of the mountain formed an *L*. There were several valleys around with plentiful game. It seemed the perfect place to settle."

She glanced at him again to check his expression. He'd stopped working on the bow and sat listening, watching her.

"They lived in the cavern that winter and cut apartments out of the other tunnels. Much of the stone they removed was used to form the walls of the remaining two sides of our courtyard. As families have grown through the years, we've added more rooms and dwellings. And we have a garden area where we grow food and herbs that wouldn't survive in the cold. We keep fires burning there day and night to warm the ground so the plants can thrive."

"Really? That's quite a creative solution." He appeared to be thinking for a moment. "And other than what you grow in the garden, you eat . . . ?"

"Meat, for one. Brielle is in charge of the hunters, so she makes sure there's fresh game on every table in the village. We also harvest a great deal of berries and other fruits, and some roots through the summer. We trade with two of the native villages, too, although not as much for food as for other supplies."

"Other supplies?"

She nodded. "We taught them to make parchment for paper and torches to light our homes and hallways. They bring extra roots and berries to tide us through the winter. Sometimes we also trade medicinals. Our women make an effective cough syrup."

"Sounds like you have a thriving industry." He seemed to think for a moment. "It's remarkable how your people have stayed hidden for so many years, and not only survived but thrived. Do you mind if I ask how MacManus came to learn of your village?"

Audrey hesitated. Was he fishing for secrets to help his country? Whatever she said about Evan wouldn't reveal anything. And he really did sound simply curious. She would be interested, too, if she were in his place. "I believe he came upon us by chance. I don't think he even knew he was approaching our gate, but he came too close and Brielle shot him with an arrow." She couldn't help a grin. "One of those arrows dipped in sleeping tonic. He didn't have time to put up much of a fight before he collapsed at her feet."

Levi's face contorted into a grimace, and he pressed a hand to his side. "I know that feeling well."

But something in his tone—something guarded—piqued her curiosity. He'd asked about Evan, so surely she could do the same. "Do you mind if *I* ask how you know him?" Evan had shared a few details with the council, but Levi would likely tell a very different side of the story.

He stilled, and silence lengthened between them as he stared ahead. What memories played through his mind? The thrill of overhearing valuable war intelligence? His rush to get the information into the hands of the commanding officers?

At last, he spoke, his voice distant enough to be still lost in memories. "War is an awful thing." He looked over at her, and the sadness in his eyes pressed into her chest. "So many lives needlessly taken."

She nodded. They were blessed to be protected from such atrocities in Laurent.

"I think Evan and I both did things during the war that we regret now. Most men probably do, if they let themselves stop and think about it. But you can't stop. Not in the midst of an assignment. It's only later that the memories haunt you."

She could see the haunting in his eyes, and her hand itched to reach out and comfort him. But he spoke again before she could work up the courage.

"I overheard battle secrets MacManus was relaying to an officer. When I passed those on, they saved British lives. I think he saw me that day, and he likely holds a grudge." Levi paused, then his throat worked, as though preparing for what he had to say next. "I saw him a few months later entering a fort in Canada. Less than a half hour later, the entire fort went up in flames, killing not only British soldiers, but civilian women and children."

His voice cracked on the last words, and his mouth sealed shut, his throat working once more. The import of what he'd said finally slipped through her. Levi likely had a very good reason to be angry with Evan, just as Evan did with Levi. As he'd said, it seemed no one could escape war unsullied. The lines grew too muddy, right and wrong too gray, depending on which side one fought for.

Levi tipped his head sideways to meet her gaze. "I don't really blame him for what happened anymore. There are times when I feel sorry for him. He must have been only following orders, and he has to live with what happened." He stared forward again, and a long sigh eased out of him. "I'm more thankful than I can say that the war is behind us."

Silence settled around them again as she sorted through all the new details she'd just learned. She just prayed that, one day, both Evan and Levi would be freed from the horror of the war and find peace within themselves and with each other.

Levi was the first to break the quiet. "So . . . it seems like your friend and MacManus get along much better now than their first meeting." A weak grin played at the corners of his mouth.

The weight of war talk slid away as memories arose of Evan and Brielle's unlikely courtship. Audrey should have seen it sooner, but Brielle usually kept herself so distant from the men. She was Le Commandant, fearsome warrior. But a few days in Evan's company had slain her pretenses like no one else ever had.

She raised her brows. "They do. They're to be married now that he's returned." A new pain sliced through Audrey's chest. She would miss the wedding. Brielle had been counting on her to help with decorations for the assembly room and to organize food for the feast. In this, too, she was failing her friend. The sting of tears threatened again.

Levi seemed to sense her pain, even though he surely couldn't see any redness in her eyes in this dim light. His brows drew together. "Do you think they'll wait to see if you return?"

Audrey inhaled a breath to settle herself. "I'm sure they think I'm far away by now. It might take Brielle longer to ready things without me there."

Silence settled between them. Not a comfortable quiet, but not awkward either. Mostly, the air around them felt tainted by her grief.

"You need to go back, Audrey." Levi's voice filled the cave with quiet certainty. "You need to be there with your friend for the day you've probably both been planning a long time."

Emotions turned inside her, clogging her thoughts and

burning her throat. "I want to be in both places—there for Brielle and here with you."

He leveled a long look at her. "I don't want you to stay here out of a sense of duty. And I greatly dislike the fact that I'm the cause for you to miss the special day with your best friend."

He was so noble, this Levi Masters. One of the most caring men she'd ever met. And if she returned to Laurent, she might be sealing his fate here in this cave. She couldn't do that—not to anyone, but especially not to him. Did he have any idea how quickly he was winning her heart?

She had to say something to put his mind at ease over this matter. "It's Brielle's special day with her *groom*. Others from the village will help with decorations and food. Her sister, too, I'm sure."

Levi didn't seem convinced, but he let the matter rest. He'd set the bow and arrow aside, though the string still hung loose on the bow. Perhaps he was too tired to finish the repair now.

She studied his face, and the exhaustion in his eyes nudged her. "Are you ready to rest?"

"I think so."

"Let's lay you down. Then I'll pour you some tea." She maneuvered his leg as he rested back on the fur. When he finally nestled in the softness, the last of his strength seemed to ebb out of him. She had let him stay up talking for too long. It took too much of the strength his body needed for healing.

She helped him drink the full cup of tea, rich with herbs that would help purify his blood and ease the pain. *Thank you, Lord, for helping me remember to pack these.*

As she set the cup aside, Levi looked half-asleep already,

his eyelids drooping. But as she prepared to scoot away from him so he could rest, he caught her arm.

"Audrey."

She stilled. "What is it? What can I get you?"

"Just . . . will you stay with me? Will you rub my face and hair like you did before? Just for a minute."

Her heart pumped faster. Was it only the relief of the gentle touch he sought? Did her presence ease his pain? Either way, she would gladly comply. "Of course."

His hand slid off her arm, and she began a gentle caress, first over the sun-darkened skin of his face, then through his thick hair.

The time would come soon when Levi would be well enough to manage on his own. Then she'd have to face the people and repercussions she'd been doing her best to ignore.

For now, though, she could simply enjoy these moments to caress him as much as she pleased.

19

As the falling snow outside thickened to a snowstorm that was almost as dark as night, Levi slept. When there was nothing else to do but wait, Audrey sat across from his still form and took up the bow. He'd formed a new notch at the broken end, and it looked like all that remained was to reattach the string. She had to work at the task for a while, pulling and adjusting the bow at different angles to get more tension. At last, the string seemed tight enough, but it took three tries to tie the end without releasing the tension she'd worked so hard to gain. Levi might want to work more on the bow, so she left the string tied in such a way that he could unfasten it if he wished.

Whittling an arrow from the branch proved to be much more satisfying work. Even after she'd scraped away as much of the outer coating as she dared, Levi still hadn't awakened. She searched the loose stones in the cave for something that could be formed into an arrowhead, but nothing promising presented itself. If only she had a Bible here to help pass the hours. But when she'd packed the hasty bag of supplies for Levi, she'd not thought she'd be waiting out a snowstorm in the cave, desperate for something to occupy her.

She focused on reciting all the Scripture she'd committed to memory, sometimes only bits of sentences. She really needed to be more intentional about memorizing the Lord's words. Though she kept her voice quiet, speaking these comforting words aloud soothed her spirit.

She was reciting from Psalm 37 when a stirring from Levi's pallet drew her focus. His eyes were open, watching her. He must have heard her words.

Doing her best to ignore the heat climbing into her neck, she moved toward the fire. "Are you hungry? I have broth ready."

While she poured a cup, he shifted his elbows underneath him and sat upright by himself. "Your ribs must be feeling much better." All this rest had probably quickened their healing.

He took the cup she handed him, holding it in both hands as his gaze regarded her. His intensity made her want to look away. Yet his eyes held her.

Finally, he spoke, his voice softer than before. "It still doesn't quite seem real that you could be so wonderful. How God could have placed the perfect person in Laurent to get me out safely and bring me to this hiding place."

The kindness in his words sent a flush to her cheeks. She didn't deserve such a high opinion. "You think I got you out safely?" She sent a pointed look down the length of him.

"That wasn't your doing, nor anything you could control. But God has given you the talents and knowledge of a healer. I suspect there's not another woman within two weeks' ride with your abilities. God knew what would happen and placed you here just when I needed you." His eyes darkened with emotion. "It's humbling to realize how richly He provides. I'm more than grateful to you both."

As much as she wanted to sink into his regard, to see if there was any sentiment deeper than appreciation, she couldn't. She pulled her gaze away and sat beside the fire. Not as far away from him as her usual place across the cave. "I was only doing what felt right. I couldn't let you be punished for something you didn't do."

Silence settled for a moment, save for the crackling of the fire. Then Levi's quiet words filled the space. "Are you always so good at reading people? Always the protector of the wrongfully condemned?"

She chanced another look at his face. She'd never spoken of her mother to others, none except her father and Brielle. The older villagers knew the story too well, and though the matrons had always been kind to her, she'd heard the whispers that lingered even when she was old enough to understand and question Papa. She'd hated hearing that story and had never thought she would willingly bring it up. Yet part of her wanted Levi to understand. To see why it was so important to her to give people the benefit of the doubt.

Would he think less of her once he knew her history? If he did, that might be for the best. His opinion now was far higher than she deserved. It took a moment to find the best way to relate the sordid details.

"My . . . mother died giving birth to me. But before that, she hadn't been faithful to my father. She regretted what she'd done and was honest with him. I was a product of her unfaithfulness, and after several of the matrons learned of the affair, the scandal spread quickly. The man who sired me wanted nothing to do with me or my mother, and he died of sickness a few months after I was born." She inhaled a steadying breath. "Despite everything, my parents made amends before I was born. But then I took her life. My father was left with a babe not his own, and even worse than that, a child who was a constant reminder of his wife's unfaithfulness and the disgrace she brought on him."

That first part was easier to speak without emotion, for she'd not been there for most of the turmoil. But this next . . .

"Yet, from the very beginning, my papa cared for me and loved me like I was his own flesh and blood. He never ever made me feel unwanted or unloved, either through his words or actions. I always felt treasured, always appreciated, even for the little things." Her voice broke, but she swallowed and pressed on. "He didn't count my past against me. He looked for the good in me and loved me for it, even when I surely disappointed him and brought even more disgrace on him at times."

Passion slipped into her words as she continued. "My father struggles with melancholy, and, some days, with too much strong drink. Being around people can be hard for him, and some of the others look down on him for these tendencies. But I know who my father is deep inside." She pressed a fist to her chest. "What a good, loyal, caring man he is. With the same measure he accepted me, I want to accept others. Find the good in them, and treat them with kindness."

As she waited for Levi to respond to her story, she studied his eyes for a sign of his thoughts. They glistened, and she might've thought that was from pain or fever if not for the warmth simmering in his gaze.

At last, his mouth parted to speak, even as his eyes still held her. "Your father sounds like a good man, and I'm grateful he did the right thing. That he raised you in a home filled with love." Something in his voice hitched with those words, but he kept speaking, so she marked the thought to consider later. "I can understand why you feel the way you do."

He leaned forward, and she almost moved closer to better hear what he would say next. "You know, though, that you're not responsible for the actions of your parents, either good or bad. It doesn't matter how you were conceived. You were perfectly formed by God. He loves you as His daughter, no matter what you do or don't do."

A sting of tears made her eyes ache with his words. As much as she wanted to take them in, part of her couldn't stand the thought of opening herself again to the pain. Papa's love was a refuge, something solid. If she truly absorbed what Levi said, she would have to fully shift her refuge to God's love. She knew it was real. Knew in her head God created every person and cared for each unconditionally. That knowledge helped her reach out to others in that same way. But accepting that love for herself . . . Trusting in it and allowing that certainty to be her strength . . . She wasn't ready to face the shift that would require.

But still, the fact that Levi would say such a kind thing stirred in her chest. She placed her hand on his and smiled. "Thank you. I needed that reminder."

Something in his gaze deepened, and an awareness rose up between them. Not that she hadn't been incredibly aware of him before—his strength, his good looks, and so many other qualities that had come to mean so much to her.

But this awareness felt mutual. And their touch seemed to seal the connection.

Before she could pull her hand away, he turned his wrist and closed his fingers around hers. The warmth of his hand, the intimacy of the contact slid a tingle all the way up her arm.

His gaze searched hers, drawing her in, tugging her toward him with a heady feeling that she didn't want to fight. He moved in to meet her, and his other hand brushed her cheek. Fingers strong and callused, a strength she wanted to lean into.

And then his breath warmed her face and her heart ceased beating. She'd never realized how perfect his mouth was, not until his lips brushed hers.

Another shiver slipped through her, and when his lips swept over hers again, they moved with certainty. The strength he wore in every action now wrapped around her, stealing every thought and drawing her deeper into the kiss.

Deeper and deeper, until nothing inside her wanted to stop.

Levi had to stop. But even as the thought flickered through him, he drew Audrey closer. Her back arched under his palm, and the fingers of his other hand tunneled through her hair, weaving through its softness.

This woman. As much as he'd come to regard her, he'd never imagined her kiss would be so . . . intoxicating. She stirred every part of him, yet she was so fragile. So . . . He didn't know the word, but he did know everything inside him wanted to protect her. Even from himself.

Especially from himself.

He eased the kiss, dwelling on the last tender caress of her mouth. Then once more. At last, he drew back, only enough to give them both air. She seemed to be struggling to catch her breath as much as he was, though her heart couldn't be racing nearly as fast.

She stayed where he left her, her lips swollen and apple red. But her gaze didn't meet his, her lashes lowered to conceal her thoughts.

Pain speared his chest. The last thing he wanted was for her to be embarrassed or sorry about what had just passed between them. Nor did he want her to regret what had happened. But they could never go back to before, and he was pretty sure he would never wish to.

Reaching for her hand, he took it and pressed a kiss to her fingers. Her gaze finally lifted to meet his, tentative and searching.

This was the time that he should say something charming and witty, a comment to defuse her embarrassment and break down the wall she was building between them. Nothing sprang to mind, so he searched for what he'd committed to speaking—the truth.

"Audrey, I didn't plan that, but I can't say I haven't wanted to kiss you." He swallowed. That hardly made him sound like a gentleman, and it didn't pay her the respect she deserved, either. "I . . . realize such a thing isn't done without an agreement. And I don't want you to think that just because we're alone and hidden like this, propriety no longer matters. In truth, it matters even more."

He was making a mess of this. He needed to get to the point. "You're a remarkable woman, Audrey Moreau. Your heart, your kindness, the way you use your talents to help those around you . . . they all enhance your beauty in ways that captured me from the first time I met you." And now the hard part of this honesty business. "I don't know what will happen with you, and with me."

A flicker of common sense pressed. He'd been trying to

send her back to Laurent. How could he now confess his growing feelings for her? It wasn't as if they lived on neighboring farms outside of Kettlewell.

Yet he had to finish what he'd begun. And he owed her untainted candor.

He squeezed her hand. "I want what's best for you, Audrey. If you lived in England with me, I would ask to court you properly. But I realize that may not happen in our situation. Either way, I want you to know that I won't do anything untoward. I won't take advantage of our . . . remoteness."

He raised her hand to his lips for a final kiss, then lowered it and released her.

She let out a long, shuddering breath, as though she'd been holding in the air the entire time he spoke. A sadness touched her gaze, even as her mouth curved in a smile. "Thank you."

As her voice lingered in the air between them, something about her expression made him think she meant her words to mean more than his promise to be a gentleman.

20

Audrey stared out into the white world the next morning, as snow still fell in a heavy blanket. Wind howled through the peaks around them and whipped the flakes in gusts. If she was home in the warmth of their apartment, she would hate the thought of going out in such weather.

But after tossing on her pallet all night and staying cooped up in the small cave most of the days before, even the icy haze outside looked appealing. When the snow finally stopped, it would be unwise to venture out where she would leave footprints, in case anyone from Laurent happened this way. But the falling snow would cover every track she left now.

Besides, with Levi still sleeping, this might be her best chance to stretch her legs before she needed to prepare food for him. The thought of being so near him, of meeting his gaze and carrying on a casual conversation, stirred the same tingle of emotions that had churned inside her all night. Not just because of that kiss, but also because of his words after.

If he were free . . . if their situations were different . . . his intentions toward her would be serious.

But their situations *hadn't* changed. So, did that mean

these feelings for him she couldn't seem to squelch had to be ignored? When he recovered, would she be willing to leave everything she knew and loved to go with him? Leave Papa? Brielle? Her home?

Tucking her coat and hood tighter around her neck, she stepped out, abandoning the turmoil of thoughts behind her. Snow rose up above her knees, and the moment she left the protection of the juniper tree guarding the front of the cave, the wind gusted around her. Icy crystals stung her face, and she pulled her coat up higher over her mouth and nose.

Finding the trail she usually took down the mountain proved harder with it covered in snow, but if she veered off the path, the thick white padding softened her landing. She aimed toward the cluster of trees, if for no other reason than for a moment of protection against the wind.

She should gather a load of firewood while she was out, but she'd have to go farther for that, as she'd exhausted everything easily obtained from this copse. A few more groupings of trees could be found past this area, along the base of the mountain, where they'd heard Levi's horse that first night in the cave.

Would he still be there? If he'd found good grazing and water, he might be. Levi had spoken of the animal as an old friend, naming him Chaucer after one of his favorite authors. She should have ventured out to look for the gelding before now. Had he found shelter from the storm? She had nothing to feed him, but if he'd be willing to come under the cave's low ceiling, she could at least provide protection from the elements.

She headed toward the only place she knew to look for him. By the time she'd followed the line of rocks into the open area, her legs were exhausted from hiking through the high snow. Snowshoes would be so much easier for traveling out here, but she didn't have that luxury. As soon as she searched the area for the horse, she would head straight back to the cave and spend the rest of the day by the warm fire.

She continued around the base of the mountain that flanked one side of the meadow, tucking as far as she could into her coat to combat the wind. Still, the gusts seemed to blow right through her.

At last, through the swirling flakes, a brown animal appeared beside a boulder in the distance.

The closer she approached, the more the form took the shape of a horse, head tucked low against this vicious wind. Her insides clenched. Was this the best shelter he could find? She renewed her stride, plunging forward as quickly as she could.

Chaucer didn't even lift his head as she approached. He looked miserable. Though he was standing beside a large stone on his right, the wind whipped from his left, with no barrier to ease its fierceness.

She reached the gelding and pulled her hand from her coat pocket to stroke his neck. He was soaked through and shivered violently beneath her touch. Her hand grew numb in less than a minute, so she slipped her icy fingers back into her coat pocket, letting her eyes take in Chaucer's condition instead.

With his long winter coat so wet, the hair crinkled over each rib. How much weight had the gelding lost since coming to this area and being required to fend for himself? He'd been in prime condition when she'd first seen Levi mounted on him. She'd assumed he'd been able to forage enough, despite the partially snow-covered ground. But she had such little experience with horses, and clearly she'd been wrong.

Her heart ached at the sight of him, almost lifeless except for the violent shivering. She had to get the horse to shelter, out of the wind and swirling snow. To a place where there would be fodder, though likely not enough to restore him to full vitality, but at least to get him through the storm until better grazing could be found.

Moving to his head, she slipped her right hand out of her coat pocket, then tucked the fingers into her sleeve. She would never survive the walk all the way back to the cave with her skin exposed.

With a tug on his halter, she turned back toward the cave. "Come, boy. Let's get you help."

The horse didn't step willingly, but she finally coaxed him into following. Once they were moving in a steady rhythm, walking seemed easier for him, though he wobbled at times. Surely once she got him to a better place, away from the wind and frigid moisture, he would be steadier.

Would the shelter of the trees be enough? *Lord, help me find a good place for him.* This horse had served Levi so faithfully. She couldn't allow him to die at the mercy of this weather. Nor from starvation.

What could she find for him to eat? One of the tribes they traded with had a few ponies, and they'd mentioned feeding the animals bark through the winter. They also brought the horses into their homes during colder times. Could she get Chaucer to enter the cave? He walked beside her with his head dipped low, no longer the grand mount from only a few days ago. It seemed a greater question of whether the horse could climb the hill.

If she couldn't find decent shelter for him in the trees, she would attempt to bring him into the cave. If he wouldn't enter where she and Levi were staying, perhaps the other cave the searchers had discovered would work better for him.

It seemed to take three times as long to reach the grove of trees, and while the branches overhead sheltered them from some of the snow, wind still whipped fiercely. When she allowed Chaucer to stop beside a grouping of three trunks close together, the horse dropped his head again, nose nearly bowing to the ground. Within moments, his shaking had resumed.

Even if he was no longer pelted by constant moisture, the icy wind wouldn't allow him to dry or warm very quickly. The poor gelding didn't have any excess flesh to help insulate against the elements. If she left him here, she wouldn't be able to rest for worry.

"Come, boy. Let's find a better place." This time when she took up his halter, he followed without hesitation.

Climbing the mountain proved harder for the gelding, but together they maneuvered the slope. Several times, she had to brace her feet and pull with both hands to encourage him to expend the effort necessary for the climb.

At last, they reached the juniper tree marking the entrance to the cave. Audrey patted the horse's neck for encouragement but kept him moving past the branches. He'd already stepped into the cave before he seemed to realize his surroundings were different.

He stopped, nostrils flaring, though his head stayed low.

"Thatta boy." She stroked his neck again, then tugged him forward.

Finally away from the piercing wind, her body began to

relax, as though she could breathe for the first time since leaving the cave. The warmth flowing from the fire around the corner eased the strain in her muscles.

She focused her attention on the horse again and tugged his halter. "Come, boy."

He took a tentative step forward, and with her next pull, he moved again. But after two more steps, he halted, nose flaring once more. They'd almost reached the curve in the stone that would reveal Levi and their fire. Its glow already lit the cavern around them, and the heat felt glorious. But that scent of smoke might be what worried the horse.

She stroked his neck over and over, speaking calming words until the horse no longer snorted his apprehension. If he would go no farther, this would still be a safe place for him to wait out the storm.

She needed to rub Chaucer dry and find something to feed him. Water too. Even with the abundance of snow, he probably hadn't been able to drink for a while. If he had tasted the snow, that might have contributed to his cold. She could warm water over the fire to help bring his temperature up.

When the horse stood quietly, his head lowered in rest, she gave him a final stroke. "Stay here while I get something to help you feel better." Surely the gelding wouldn't go back out into the weather on his own. Maybe she should find a way to tie him, just in case.

Leaving the horse, she turned the corner in the cave to gather what she could to help him. Levi had likely heard her speaking and wondered who she'd brought.

But a glance at him showed him still asleep. Or . . . perhaps just waking up.

As his eyelids opened and his gaze landed on her, his focus

sharpened. The corners of his mouth curved in the hint of a smile, springing up memories of their kiss with a heat that wound through every part of her.

This man affected her like no one ever had. Soon, she would have to decide exactly what she planned to do about that.

⟨ⰔⰇⰉⰃⰉⰔⰃⰉⰆⰉⰃⰉⰆ⟩

Levi would never tire of waking up to Audrey Moreau's beautiful face. If only these perfect days would never have to end. He would gladly do without the pain, but he'd endure a lifetime of it if that meant having Audrey by his side.

She might not think this time in the cave was perfect, with all the extra work she'd had to do for them both. Signs of that toil showed on her face now, with her wind-reddened cheeks and nose. He was becoming a sluggard, sleeping till all hours of the morning while she had clearly been out gathering wood or other supplies.

He worked to sit upright, a task much harder than it should be, but growing easier each day.

"Good morning." Audrey's sweet voice drew near as she approached the fire. "I have a surprise for you."

"Morning." His voice came out raspy and gruff, weighed down by remnants of sleep. He did his best to clear the slough from his throat, then tried again. "A surprise?"

She lifted the kettle from the fire and turned a smile on him. "I found your horse." Hesitation checked the pleasure in her grin. "He's cold and hungry, but hopefully we can nurse him back to health soon enough."

Pleasure slipped through him, but something about the

forced lightness in her tone with those last words brought with it a thread of worry. "Where is he?" Levi pushed the fur coverings off his legs. He needed to see Chaucer, to confirm the animal was fine. And he certainly didn't need to lay the brunt of the animal's care on Audrey.

It was high time he got up and accomplished something himself.

He'd barely gotten his legs beneath him when Audrey was by his side. "I'm not sure you should stand yet."

He didn't let her words slow him, just turned onto his hands and knees. That position would give his hip a chance to grow accustomed to bearing weight again, and he could use the cave wall to help rise to his feet. "It's definitely time." He had to work hard to keep the pain out of his voice. That deep ache was surely only because his muscles had weakened from disuse.

Audrey fluttered around the cave, then returned to his side with the two poles he'd used to haul himself back up to the cave after his fall.

Inhaling a breath for fortification, he planted one hand on the wall and one on the cave floor, using both surfaces to push himself upright. Audrey gripped his upper arm and aided his efforts, though she didn't let go when he'd worked to standing. He kept the hand braced on the stone wall, and with her so near, his body itched to wrap the other around her. He could pretend it was for support.

But he couldn't. He'd promised he wouldn't take advantage of their remoteness in this cave, of her nearness, no matter how much she tempted him.

He had to force away the sensations that thought conjured, and he turned toward the cave entrance. The movement succeeded in dropping her hand from his arm, and she reached down to pick up the walking sticks.

"Use these to help bear your weight." She held them both out.

He took one of the poles. "This should be all I need."

The frustration on her face was clear, but she didn't push for him to comply. He didn't allow himself to look at her again. He had to strengthen himself again, take on some of the burden she'd been shouldering for a week now.

Audrey followed him as he rounded the curve in the cave. There, in profile against the white of the snow outside, stood Chaucer.

Levi hobbled forward to greet his old friend, but the horse didn't even raise his head. "Hello there, fellow." As he reached the gelding's side, he stroked a hand over his shoulder. Thick wet hair met his touch, but beneath that, the sharp outline of bone made him suck in a breath.

He moved his hand over Chaucer's withers, then down his back and side. With Levi's eyes still adjusting to the light, he had to rely on what his hand told him about the horse's condition. And that news made his belly churn. Had Chaucer eaten at all in the past week?

Levi moved back to his neck and stroked with a gentle touch. "You hungry, old man? We need to find you some food, don't we?"

The horse tipped his nose toward Levi, but didn't lift his head from his position dropped nearly to the cave floor. He didn't seem to have the strength.

With fresh worry rising up into his throat, Levi turned to Audrey, who'd stood waiting. "Do we have anything to feed him? I don't know how much longer he'll last."

"I'm not sure we can find grass with the storm still blowing, but I've heard that the Dinee feed their horses bark through the winter. We can pull some from the firewood here, and I can go back out to strip more from the trees."

That suggestion only eased a tiny bit of the tension building in his chest. He'd never heard of horses living off bark. Had never attempted to feed the stuff to Chaucer. But if it was their only option, they should try it.

With a nod, he turned back toward the cave. "I'll start pulling the bark off the firewood."

Finally, a job he could do himself. And the sooner he accomplished the task, the more chance they had to revive his old friend.

21

Audrey stroked the horse a final time, then pulled her coat tighter around her as she turned to face Levi. "I shouldn't be gone long." She made the mistake of meeting his gaze, those dark eyes that always pulled her in.

"I should be going out there. Not you." He stood an arm's length away, yet his voice wrapped around her like an embrace.

She smiled as she shook her head. "I know all the places to look. Now that we know which barks he'll eat, gathering them won't take any time at all."

Levi's brow furrowed, and her fingers itched to reach up and smooth the skin there. She'd stroked his face often when the pain was bad. But now, with him standing and looking at her that way . . . and after that kiss . . .

Her body nearly stepped forward of its own accord, desperate for another kiss like the first. She inhaled a deep breath, then forced herself to step back. Levi didn't move, but his gaze stayed on hers, a sadness seeming to slip through him. Maybe he was remembering his words after the kiss.

The distance between their worlds. Could that distance ever be overcome?

Doing her best to force another smile, she turned away from him. "I'll be back shortly."

"I'll watch at the entrance. If you need anything at all, either call or signal me."

She nodded to acknowledge his words, though she didn't glance back at him. As she stepped from the cave, a gust of wind pummeled her, its howling blocking out all other sound. Ice crystals stung the uncovered areas on her face. The storm seemed to be growing worse, not better.

She half walked, half slid down much of the mountain. The cold had already sunk into her bones, stealing her strength. She could probably find enough bark in the nearby copse of trees, so it wouldn't be long before she'd be back in the cave. Back by the warm fire.

Back with Levi.

Tucking herself as deeply as she could into her hood and wrap, she trudged toward the trees. There were plenty of pines in the cluster, but Chaucer seemed to especially like bark from the poplar logs they'd found, so she would search for those.

As soon as she stepped among the trunks, the bite of the wind eased. The dimness under the trees compared to the blinding white outside made her blink. At last, she could see well enough to focus on the trees around her.

A figure stepped from behind a trunk, not two strides away.

A squeal slipped out before Audrey could contain it, and she stepped back. *Who . . . ?*

But the familiar outline, that wolf fur coat she'd seen thousands of times . . . she'd know anywhere that strong yet feminine face outlined by the hood.

Brielle.

Audrey's chest clenched even tighter than it had at the initial shock of seeing a person where she'd expected only trees. Her belly roiled as the full reality of this meeting sank in.

Brielle now knew she'd not left the area. Brielle would march her back to Laurent, and she would have to face the chief, the council, her own father. Leonard's mother.

The pain of that final thought constricted her throat, raising tears to her eyes as Leonard's face appeared in her memory. She pressed the thought away. One step at a time.

Audrey worked for a smile for her dearest friend. "Brielle. How are you?"

Brielle's face didn't shift from her warrior façade, though a familiar twitch at her eyes gave evidence of deeper emotion. Sadness? Mostly anger, no doubt. Audrey had helped a prisoner escape, run away from the village before she could face punishment, put countless searchers in danger, been the cause of Leonard's death, and probably brought an immeasurable amount of sadness to her father. In many ways, Audrey had become Brielle's chief adversary, the primary threat against Laurent. And Brielle had sworn to protect Laurent at any cost—even her life.

"Where have you been?" Brielle's voice bit sharply above the wind still whipping beyond the trees.

Audrey swallowed, but the icy air had dried out her throat so much and the act only brought more pain. She couldn't lie. Her other sins were awful enough. She wouldn't compound them by speaking an intentional falsehood. "A cave."

Brielle's gaze lifted to the mountainside. "I saw you come out of it."

A jolt pressed through her. She'd never imagined Brielle—or anyone—would be out in this storm. Watching. Waiting for her to reveal herself. And Levi . . . He hadn't left the cave, so Brielle wouldn't have seen him. But she would suspect he was there, wouldn't she?

"Why haven't you come home?" Though Brielle's tone still held accusation, there was a hint of pain there, too.

Audrey met her gaze, as hard as that was. But Brielle still had her warrior mask firmly in place. Her expression gave away nothing.

Audrey laced as much gentleness as she could through her voice. "I couldn't. Not yet." Did she dare say anything about Levi? Perhaps it would be better to wait and see what her friend did.

Brielle's face only hardened. "You're going home now." She motioned for Audrey to turn. "You know the way."

Audrey hesitated. She couldn't leave Levi without telling him where she was going. But if he was watching from the cave, as he said he would be doing, he would see her leave with Brielle. He would know she went back to the village.

Would he leave the area as soon as he was recovered? Of course, he would. He needed to return to his family. To England. She could only pray he didn't rush his departure and reinjure the hip before it fully healed.

But that wasn't the only reason she didn't want him to leave right away.

Once Brielle brought her within Laurent's walls, she'd be watched every minute—maybe even kept under guard until the council decided her punishment. She wouldn't have another chance to sneak out. To say good-bye.

Even as tears stung her eyes, she turned toward Laurent.

With Brielle close behind her, she had no choice. But that didn't change the fact she was leaving her heart in a cave on the mountain.

⚬⚭⚬

The snow still whipped around Audrey as she and Brielle approached the gate of the only home she'd ever known. Brielle sounded the call to alert the guards of their approach.

The churning inside Audrey grew stronger with every step. She couldn't seem to stop herself from imagining what it would be like to see the villagers again, the people she'd known her entire life.

And Papa. Would disappointment dim his eyes when he looked at her? Would he understand when she told him why she left and stayed away so long?

And what of Chief Durand? She couldn't bring herself to think of him as Papa Durand any longer. He likely didn't possess many tender feelings for her now. Hesitation—or maybe worry—tried to slow her steps, but she pushed herself forward.

Voices sounded from inside the wall. Male voices.

She gripped the inside of her pockets and kept herself moving. When she and Brielle stepped inside the gate, two men were sprinting toward them, within ten strides of reaching them.

Both slowed when they saw her, and the familiar faces of Wesley and Philip seemed surreal as shock morphed their features.

Philip recovered first and strode forward, his steps determined. "Audrey. You're the last person we expected." His expression was hard to read.

She sent both men what would hopefully pass for a pleasant look. "Hello, Philip. Wesley."

When both men came alongside her, their intentions grew plain. She was flanked on three sides by guards, giving her no chance to run again. Panic tried to well at the thought of being escorted through the village like a criminal.

She glanced back at Brielle. "Could I speak with you and Chief Durand? And maybe my father, too, if he can." She wasn't sure she could manage the disappointment—or worse yet, anger—from the three people who meant most to her, all at the same time. But it would be better to tell the whole story to them at once.

And the Lord would sustain her. No matter what came, He would be her strength. She simply had to make sure she followed His promptings.

A glance passed between Brielle and Wesley, and he jogged forward, probably to alert the others and hopefully coordinate the meeting she'd requested.

Even with the loud sound of the wind, the silence from Brielle and Philip weighed heavy. Philip had been like a mentor for Leonard. Did he think she had something to do with the young guard's death? At the very least, Leonard never would have been out there if it hadn't been for her actions.

Grief tightened her chest, stinging her eyes. She couldn't think about that now. The meeting ahead required her to be strong.

When they reached the outer door of the Durands' quarters, Philip rapped once with his knuckle, then pulled the latch string and opened the door. He motioned for Audrey to enter first, and the rush of warmth that wrapped around her as she stepped inside nearly made her light-headed.

Or maybe it was the dimness of the candlelit room compared with the bright white swirling outside. Or simply the fact that she was entering a chamber she knew so well. Stepping back into her old life.

But she wasn't.

It might be a long time before the people of Laurent allowed her to slip back into her old life. And did she really want to? The thought of day after day without Levi felt unbearable. He'd become so much more to her than any patient. More than any man she'd ever known. If she allowed herself to face it, she'd been coming to love the man more each day, with every conversation, every peek into his life and his character and his integrity. The way he sought to live out his faith had claimed her. And every look into his eyes certainly sealed her desire.

Could she really live without him?

But that was a fate she would have to contemplate later, for motion across the room snagged her gaze. The sight of the man who'd just entered the door made her breath cease.

Time slowed to a crawl as her father lifted his eyes to hers. The sagging lines of his face dipped lower as his mouth opened in disbelief. Had he not been told she was here? Or maybe he'd not believed it.

His expression gradually lifted, his eyes lighting with more joy than she'd seen on him in . . . so long.

A sob caught in her throat, and she took a step forward as he began striding toward her. Papa's arms spread just before he reached her, and just like when she was a girl, he enveloped her, squeezing her tight and rocking back and forth.

She soaked in the feel of him, the familiar scent that was his alone, though a little stronger than she remembered. Had he not been taking care of himself properly while she was gone? With her arms around him, his body felt as slender as it always did. Had someone been bringing him meals in her absence? She'd not allowed herself to think much about Papa's care.

But now, the ache of leaving him to fend for himself, of abandoning this man who'd poured his life into helping her from the moment she was born, brought a rush of shame. How could she have set aside her responsibilities so easily? She'd not *intended* to desert him. She'd planned to return to Papa as soon as Levi set out. But then Levi's injuries . . .

The reminder gave her the strength she needed to hold back the tears—most of them, anyway. She straightened but didn't pull out of her father's arms as his hands shifted to grip her elbows. His gaze roamed her face, as though hungry for details.

She worked for a smile. "I've missed you. Are you well? Eating enough?" Those last words weren't what she meant to say, but they simply slipped out.

His face wreathed in a smile and tears moistened his eyes even as he chuckled. "My Audrey."

Motion behind him forced her to turn away as Chief Durand stepped to her father's side. She made herself meet his gaze, though the churning in her middle attempted to rise up into her throat.

The look he gave her seemed to be a mixture of relief and sadness. "Audrey. We didn't think we would see you again."

Her father shifted to stand at her side, holding her arm with one hand and slipping his other around her waist. "Come and sit. Tell us what's happened." Papa's voice graveled more than she remembered. It felt as though she'd been gone for months, not less than two weeks.

198

Chief Durand stepped to her other side as the three of them moved toward the chairs around the hearth. Brielle's quiet tread barely sounded behind them, but her presence weighed like a stone in Audrey's chest.

Even though her father seemed relieved that she'd returned, she still had much to answer for to the entire village.

22

When they'd taken seats in a semicircle around the fire, Audrey glanced from her father to Brielle, then finally to Chief Durand. "I know you have lots of questions. Be assured, I'll tell you everything."

All three were silent as she relayed the events of the morning she'd helped Levi escape. How she'd known in her soul he was innocent of any evil intent, how she'd feared what the council might do to him, how the chance to free him had seemed almost God given.

"I may have acted too rashly. I'm sorry I broke your trust." She met the gaze of each person as she spoke. "I'm sorry I went against our laws and the decision of the council. I was only trying to protect an innocent man, but I'm sorry I took the decision into my own hands."

She looked at Chief Durand with those final words, but his only response was a nod. So she dove into the rest of her story. How when she heard that Levi had been shot by Brielle's arrow, she knew she had to treat the wound and make sure he reached safety. How she planned to return to the village as soon as she'd accomplished that. And then the awful events of the next morning with Leonard.

"I never ever meant for my actions to cause such a horrible thing. Watching Leonard tumble down that slope . . . then seeing Levi cling to him with every shred of his strength as Leonard dangled over the edge . . . It was awful. I've relived it so many times in my dreams." More than one tear had slipped down her cheeks while she spoke, and Papa gave her hand a gentle squeeze.

She turned to Brielle. "He's been given burial?"

Brielle's face had taken on a grimness as Audrey relayed the tale, but now she nodded. "In the graveyard. It's good that we know how it happened."

Audrey's throat ached. "I imagine you thought Levi did it. In reality, he did everything he could to save Leonard—much more than I was able to do."

She inhaled a breath for strength. "Levi was exhausted from his efforts to save Leonard, but I wanted to know for sure there was nothing more we could do, so I insisted one of us go down and check to see if he might still be breathing." This last part of the story came easier than the other, maybe because it didn't involve someone from the village.

Yet the emotion welled stronger within her as she told of Levi's dislocated hip, how he had to stay still until the joint healed, and even how she'd found the horse nearly frozen and starving. She glanced at Brielle. "That's why I came down to the trees again, to gather more bark for him to eat."

A line creased her friend's brow—whether from anger or simply depth of thought, she couldn't tell. Brielle gave a short nod. "Something kept telling me to go out and search that area once more, even in the storm. I didn't really expect to find you, though."

The dreaded silence settled as she waited for the others to

respond. Her father squeezed her hand again, and the support helped. But she kept her focus on Chief Durand and Brielle. The chief was well-known for being fair and taking all sides into consideration before making a decision. She'd always appreciated that quality in him and could only pray he would do the same now.

At last, he spoke, drawing everyone's attention. "This situation grieves me in so many ways. Not the least of which is that it all could have been avoided." His gaze turned sad as it locked on her, and his voice softened. "I had spent that first morning of the fast in long hours of prayer and felt the Lord telling me this man was no threat to us."

Shame slid over her as his words registered. Had she really gotten it so wrong? When the chance presented itself to free Levi, she'd assumed that was God's provision. She should have asked Him instead of jumping to the conclusion. *Lord, redeem this situation. And help Levi.* What would he think when she didn't return? Would he try to return home before his body had sufficiently healed?

The thought of him leaving the area, of never seeing him again, rose up to swell her throat and sting her eyes. His safe departure had been her goal from the very beginning, to allow him to return to his people. Yet the thought of living without him felt nearly unbearable.

Chief Durand spoke again, saving her from trying to form a response. "We need to deal with matters as they are now." He leaned forward a little, moving into his chiefly demeanor. "I'll call the council to discuss what should be done next. I'm sure news of your return has already spread."

As she'd expected.

The tears ran down her face, and Audrey didn't attempt

to stop them. Yet they didn't stem as much from facing the council's punishment as from the thought of never seeing Levi again.

❦

He had to help Audrey.

Levi held in a grunt as he dropped to his knees to gather their supplies into the satchels. He'd been watching from the cave entrance as Audrey stepped from the woods with Brielle close behind her. He couldn't tell if Brielle had been forcing Audrey toward Laurent at the end of a weapon, but either way, he had no doubt she wasn't given the choice about whether she wished to return to the village or not.

She *had* planned to return to her people. But on her own terms, not by capture.

And from the moment he watched the two of them disappear around the base of the first mountain, a certainty had become plain inside him.

He wanted to return with Audrey.

Leaving this land—at least, leaving without Audrey—was no longer an option. Whether he stayed here or returned to England, he wanted her by his side. He would do whatever it took to make her happy.

Even if that meant facing the council and villagers to prove himself honorable and work to earn their good opinion. Even if it meant facing Evan MacManus.

After filling the satchels and spreading the logs so the fire would burn out, he hoisted the packs on his back and gripped his walking stick. His hip ached from so much activity, but that couldn't stop him. He needed to get to Laurent to speak up for Audrey. Maybe his return would make the council more lenient with her.

As he limped around the curve in the cave, Chaucer lifted his head in greeting. A new pang pressed in Levi's chest. He'd been so worried about Audrey, he'd not thought what to do with the horse. Warm water and bark seemed to have given him a fresh burst of energy. He no longer shivered, and he seemed much more aware of his surroundings.

Could the gelding manage the trip to Laurent? Leaving him here might be a death sentence since the snowstorm still blew outside. He'd eaten all the bark they found on the firewood, but Audrey hadn't been able to return with more, so Chaucer would have nothing to eat until the storm lessened enough for him to venture out. But even then, he wouldn't find grass for a while.

Levi couldn't leave his old friend to that fate. He approached the gelding and rubbed his forehead. "Are you up to returning to the village with me? They're likely to take more pity on you than me."

Chaucer blew out a long breath, as though reluctantly agreeing.

"Let's be off, then." He took up the piece of rope that dangled from the halter, then hobbled forward so the horse could turn in the small space.

Maneuvering down the steep trail just outside the cave proved as hard as he expected, requiring him to almost sit in the snow and half slide, half crawl down. Every moment he expected the searing pain in his hip that meant the joint had moved out of place again. But only the ache made itself known, and the icy wind and snow nearly numbed that feeling.

He tried to follow the route down the mountain that Audrey had taken when she left in search of bark, for she'd been up and down this mountain so often, she surely knew the best paths.

At last, they reached somewhat level ground, and he stopped the horse for them both to rest. Levi's hip burned so much, he could barely stand to put weight on it, so he rested a hand on Chaucer's shoulders for support. The horse seemed to be managing the storm and travel so far. If only Levi could fare as well.

The wind bit too fiercely to stand still for long, so they started northward, following the same path Audrey and Brielle had taken not long before. He and Chaucer moved much slower than the women had, but at least they were moving.

Finally, they reached the end of the second mountain, and the open area spread before them, split by the small creek where he'd gotten his feet wet during that first fateful escape. He'd have to cross that stream of water, but that shouldn't be a problem. The snow had piled higher on either side than that other day, but surely he could find a place where he could easily step from one bank to the other.

About halfway across the open area, he found the perfect place to cross. The hint of footprints still in the snow showed this was probably the route the women had taken, as well.

Placing his walking stick on the opposite bank, he stepped with his good leg first. But when he tried to shift his weight forward and drag his weak limb across, a knife of pain plunged through his left hip.

A cry escaped his lips as his knees nearly gave way from the agony. He barely managed to pull himself across the water to safety before tumbling forward, first onto his elbows, then face down on the snow. His weak leg wouldn't move, and he could feel nothing through the limb except the torture radiating through his hip.

He could barely breathe through the pain. Could barely think.

But he had to. What could he do now? He was stranded out here, without Audrey. Completely alone with a debilitating injury.

Yet not alone. *Lord* . . . His spirit groaned out a desperate cry for help, though his mind couldn't manage words.

The frigid snow had begun to numb his face, but he still felt the nudge of something on the top of his head. Chaucer?

The horse pushed again, harder this time.

Levi forced himself to turn his face from the snow to see the animal. Chaucer nudged his forehead, an insistent push. Maybe if he could manage to stand, he could use the horse and his walking stick to make it the rest of the way to Laurent.

Just the thought of how hard that would be, of the piercing torture each step would require, made his belly wrench. But that was his only option. Unless God sent someone out to look for him, he'd die here in the snow.

Perhaps the Lord had led Audrey to find the gelding exactly for this purpose.

After fumbling in the snow for his walking stick, he worked himself up so that he knelt on his good knee. The position made his dislocated hip howl with agony, so he used the walking stick on one side and Chaucer's neck on the other to pull himself up to standing. With the two supports, he could keep his balance on the one foot. His injured leg would have to drag behind, which would be agonizing, but the limb would do nothing he asked of it.

The first few steps were even clumsier than he'd expected. Chaucer seemed to understand he wanted him to step forward, but Levi had to nearly lay on the horse's back to free his good leg to take a step.

Perhaps it would be better if he could push himself up onto the gelding completely. Maybe not sit upright, but at least lie on his belly and let his legs hang down.

Chaucer stood mercifully still while Levi used what little strength he had left to pull himself over the horse's back. The sharp outline of the horse's backbone pressed into his belly, but that pain barely registered compared to the stabbing in his hip.

As he nudged Chaucer forward, he barely kept a grip on the stub of rope he had to use to guide the horse. From this position, he'd have so little control.

Lord, it's up to you. Take us where you would have us go. And he meant that more than just in the final stretch of this journey to Laurent.

A rustling crept into Levi's awareness. Audrey must be moving around the cave. He forced his eyes open, but the brightness that met his gaze made him squint. She must have built the fire larger than usual. No wonder the cave finally felt warm.

"Levi." Her voice washed over him with its soothing comfort.

His eyes drifted shut as relief enveloped him. Then her hand brushed across his forehead. One day, if he ever had strength to manage a conversation again, he would tell her how much her gentle touches meant to him. The care wrapped in the act soothed something much deeper within him. Lord willing, he would have the chance to thank her.

Forcing his eyes open, he did his best to focus. The faint firelight illuminated Audrey so she shone just like the angel she was.

She began speaking, but he couldn't take in the words. Not when her beauty overwhelmed him. He'd been afraid he might never see her again, but God had granted him one more blessing.

"Levi, can you hear me?" She brushed her thumb across his cheek.

He tried to manage a word, but his throat ached too much to allow sound. His chest felt as though a bear sat atop him, burning with every breath. He struggled to nod. Her words were registering now, though he couldn't bring forth anything she'd said before.

"Can you lift your head to drink this?" Her hand slipped behind his head and raised him as she held a cup to his lips. Though her movements stayed slow and gentle, the shift sent a searing burn through his chest. A cough rose up, forcing its way up his throat and leaving a path of fire in its wake.

His entire body shook with the spasms racking through him. He leaned away from Audrey as they continued, and her small hands gripped his shoulder as though to keep him from tumbling over.

When the final cough ended, he sank back against the fur, his body completely spent. He didn't even have the strength to open his eyes.

"I'm going to spoon the tea into you. It will help clear your lungs. I'm not sure how long you were out there in the storm, but you were nearly frozen when Wesley found you and the horse."

When Wesley found . . . ? His mind ached as he tried to bring up a memory of what she described . . . *you and the horse.*

The image finally formed. A new throbbing made itself known in his hip, but it was not the same searing pain as before. Audrey must have worked the joint back into place.

Thank you, Lord, for Audrey.

With that final prayer taking root in his heart, he let himself succumb to the darkness.

23

Audrey poured another spoonful of the new tea she'd brewed into Levi's parted mouth. His throat worked in a swallow, but it seemed more reflex than intentional action. He'd only regained consciousness once since he'd been discovered slumped over Chaucer's back outside the gates of Laurent.

Chief Durand had allowed Levi to be placed in her apartment so she could offer the nursing care he needed. In addition to his hip being out of joint, the cold had taken root in his lungs, and he'd been locked in a feverish haze for over a day now.

She'd not left his side except to make a few quick trips to the necessary, but nothing she'd done seemed to allay the fever or the racking cough that shook his entire body. She'd used every herb she knew of. Surely something would take effect soon.

Lord, heal his body. Remove the poison in his lungs and heal the hip so thoroughly it can't dislocate again. Show me what to do to help him.

Though she'd prayed the prayer more times than she could

count, her spirit lifted up the words in earnest beseeching. *Give me wisdom and understanding.*

After three more spoonfuls, she'd emptied the cup, so she dipped the rags in cool water, wrung out most of the liquid, then placed them on his head and neck.

What else could be done to lower the fever?

In the distance, the sound of hammer on chisel drummed a steady beat, as had been the case during most of the waking hours since she'd returned. Evan was building a new apartment for Brielle for the start of their married life. Audrey hadn't been to see it yet, but from the sound of things, they must be making progress. The pounding seemed to be beating a rhythm in her head. Might it be hindering Levi's healing?

During a rare lull in the noise, the creaking of her father's chair lifted her focus as he shuffled toward her. He'd remained in their apartment most of the time since she'd arrived home, though staying in this room wasn't unusual for him.

He'd stayed mostly quiet, too—which also wasn't unusual. But his gaze had been ever watchful while she worked. At first, the constant scrutiny had unnerved her. Did Papa wonder if more existed between her and Levi than the relationship between healer and patient? She always poured her heart into caring for those who were sick or injured, and she did no less with Levi now.

Yet she couldn't deny him the gentle touches that might be more than she offered others—combing her fingers through his hair or massaging his face—for she knew how much relief those acts had given him before. Any relief she could offer, he desperately needed.

Now, as Papa came to stand over the man, he kept his silence for long minutes.

She needed to move back to the fire and start broth heating to provide Levi some sustenance, but curiosity over what her father might be thinking won out. She glanced up at him and waited expectantly.

At last, his gruff voice broke the quiet. "They're taking good care of the horse." Those words were the last thing she'd expected from him, but they almost pulled forth a weary smile. Her father would know she'd been worried about Chaucer. At least, when she could pull her mind from fretting over Levi's condition. In his usual halting way, he was doing his best to set her mind at ease about what he could.

He cleared his throat before speaking again. "Brielle. She's having her hunters bring back bark and other things it can eat. Wesley says it's perking up fine."

Audrey reached up to take his hand and gave a gentle squeeze, the first bit of contact they'd had since the conversation with the Durands yesterday. "Thank you. I'm relieved to hear it."

Papa gripped her palm and patted her hand with his other one. "Can I help you here?" His gaze slipped to the man lying on the bed. Thankfully, he didn't speak of Levi's condition.

She allowed herself only a glance at the handsome face that had grown so pale, then shook her head. "Pray for him. I'm doing everything else I know to do."

Papa squeezed her hand again. "If there's anyone who can bring him back, it's my girl."

The sweet words *my girl* always brought a rush of warmth in her chest, but this time the warmth crept up to sting her eyes. She was so grateful she'd not lost her father's love. If only she possessed the skill he credited to her. Even now, the reality tried to press in that she might lose Levi—today, even. But she forced the thought away.

She wouldn't give up on Levi. Wouldn't stop petitioning for the miracle they needed to save this man she'd come to love far more than she'd ever dreamed.

Silence hovered as Audrey sat beside Levi's still form. The weight of the third person in the room only thickened the quiet. For once, the hammering across the hall had ceased.

She glanced over at Brielle and searched for something to say. There should be much to catch up on, but the fear churning inside her for Levi overwhelmed every other thought.

Her gaze wandered down to the man, her eyes searching for any sign of change. Beads of sweat dotted his nose and cheeks. She'd just refreshed the cool damp cloth draping his brow and neck, but they seemed to help little.

Nothing helped.

Levi had been restless all morning, tossing his head and arms and coughing so hard it seemed his insides would spew out. Yet this last hour he'd grown still. Eerily still.

The fear roiling in her belly had nearly turned to panic. *Don't let this be the end, Lord. Please don't take him.*

She could barely recall life before she met this man, though that had been a little more than two weeks ago. He'd come in and overwhelmed her world, opening her mind to the fact that people beyond their walls were real, not just distant stories. God had created each one, each with their own struggles and talents and dreams. Lives that interwove in a myriad of ways, lives that could bring new hope and good to the people she loved so well, this village that had sheltered her all these years.

He'd brought color to her world, despite the turmoil that had come with him. His faith, his determination to do right, his integrity—they inspired her to be better. To make wiser choices. To love more fully.

Everything in her wanted the chance to be with him. Yet that chance seemed to be slipping away. She wrestled that thought from her mind as she had every time before. She couldn't face the possibility of losing him yet. Her hand craved to reach out and take Levi's, but she couldn't do that in Brielle's presence.

"I wish you'd come to me. Told me." Brielle's voice broke through the churning in her thoughts, and Audrey glanced over at the tight lines of her friend's face.

She didn't need to ask what Brielle meant, and frustration welled up in her chest. "I did come to you, Brielle. You said you'd talk with him, then cast your vote with the others. I was asking you to speak up for him, and you told me to be careful. I knew Evan had a run-in with him, but they were on opposite sides of the war, so of course he wouldn't trust Levi."

Audrey forced herself to calm, to slow her words, with a deep breath. "No one seemed to be listening to me. I couldn't let him be judged and punished for his family or birthplace. But everyone seemed so focused on that, they didn't hear his words. His earnest desire to do right."

Brielle studied her for a long moment, but her expression was hard to read. Audrey held her gaze. She was usually the one to back down when Brielle's ire rose, to reach out and smooth things over. But not this time.

At last, the hint of a sheen coated Brielle's eyes, and her gaze softened. "I'm sorry, Audrey. I'm sorry I didn't realize how important this was to you. I'm sorry I didn't listen better."

The words soaked through her like a balm, but the release of her anger allowed tears to crowd her vision. She looked away, her eyes coming to rest on Levi's still form. If Brielle could be strong enough to speak the truth, she had to also. "And I'm sorry I undermined your leadership. I'm sorry I took such drastic steps." *Actions that ended up stealing Leonard's life.* She couldn't bring herself to speak that last bit.

Silence settled between them, leaving only the rasping of Levi's breath. The quiet didn't hold the same weight as before, though.

"Evan's struggling with his presence here." Brielle's quiet words barely broke the silence. "He's not sure we can trust the man after what he did during the Battle of Stoney Creek."

Audrey turned to her, seeking from her expression what Brielle might not be saying. "They were on opposite sides of the war. Levi didn't do anything unethical. He performed his duties well. Saved the lives of his countrymen."

Brielle's mouth turned grim, and though she nodded, she didn't look Audrey's way. "I know. He did probably the same thing Evan would have done were the situation reversed. It's just hard . . ." Now she did meet Audrey's gaze, and her throat worked. "It's hard for a soldier to forget what he worked so hard for."

Audrey could only nod. Brielle would understand that feeling better than either of them. She sacrificed daily to keep Laurent safe and provided with fresh meat.

A small smile touched Brielle's mouth. "Just give Evan some time. He's praying about it. We both are."

Again, Audrey nodded. That was the most she could wish for. She'd be more diligent in her own prayers on that topic. For now, though, her beseeching to heaven was focused on begging for Levi's health to be returned.

She couldn't lose him.

Before that worry could consume her again, she sought out a new topic. "Have you set a day yet? For your ceremony?" Her voice cracked on the last words, turning them into something like a sob. Even that question reminded her of Levi, of the way he'd encouraged her to come back for her friend's wedding.

It turned out she would be here after all.

Brielle offered a sad smile. "As soon as our home is finished."

Audrey nodded, but words to answer wouldn't surface.

Maybe Brielle understood, for she supplied the lack. "They're making steady progress, but I think it will be another couple of weeks before they finish. If Evan doesn't work himself sick before then." A smile lifted her voice, matching the expression that always shone in her eyes when she spoke of her beloved. "He's determined the work won't take one day longer than it has to."

Audrey looked away as fresh burning stung her eyes and nose. She was so glad Brielle had found this man, this love that lit her from the inside. But hearing of it as Audrey's own love barely clung to life in front of her brought the tears too close. She struggled to regain control, to gather her raw emotions and press them down where they couldn't take over.

"He means a great deal to you, doesn't he?" Brielle's soft question slipped through before Audrey had finished pulling herself together.

A sob slipped out as she nodded.

Levi meant so much more than *a great deal* to her. She couldn't even put into words how much she cared for him.

Silence settled again, but need rose up inside Audrey. A desperate urge to explain the depth of character inside Levi Masters.

"He's a good man, Brielle. Respectful and kind. God honoring. He wanted me to come back, didn't want me to be estranged from our people." A half laugh, half sob broke through. "When he found out I might be missing your wedding day, I thought he would force me to leave, even though he would have been stranded in the cave until his leg healed."

She turned to fully face her friend. "I couldn't leave him. It would have meant possible death with his injuries. I had planned only to show him the cave and give him the supplies. But then just as I was going to return to Laurent, Leonard showed up. And then . . ." She couldn't speak again of that awful ordeal. "With Levi so hurt, I couldn't leave him. And the more I've come to know him . . ."

She let the words linger. There was nothing else to say. She could only pray Brielle understood. Maybe there was one more thing that would help her. She locked Brielle's gaze with her own. "Would you have been able to leave Evan if he'd been injured like that?"

Brielle flinched but didn't break their gaze. Her eyes had widened, though, as if she finally understood how deeply Audrey felt for this man.

Brielle didn't respond with words, but as her expression shifted from surprise to understanding to sadness, no spoken response was needed. She finally shifted her focus to Levi, that sadness deepening. "We'll be praying for him."

Audrey nodded her thanks. She should find a new topic for them. She cleared her throat. "Please tell Charlotte thank you for bringing meals for my father. He actually seems better these days. I know the changes have thrown off his routine, but still . . ."

Brielle's gaze warmed. "Papa says he hasn't overindulged since the day you left. We've all noticed how different he seems."

That news should fill Audrey with relief. She'd been praying for this for years. And these past few days, she'd wondered. Yet how could anything lighten the weight on her chest when Levi was barely clinging to life?

Brielle glanced down at the bed, and a frown pressed her brow. "Is he . . . ?"

Audrey jerked her gaze to Levi, panic coiling her insides. Surely he hadn't . . .

But the pallor and stillness she expected to see weren't what she found. His eyes . . . Had they cracked open?

She leaned over him and pressed a hand to his cheek, brushing the hair from his temple. "Levi? Are you awake?"

His eyelids parted even more, revealing the beautiful brown beneath. Her heart leapt, stretching her chest so tight she could barely breathe for the joy.

His mouth opened—at least it tried to. His chapped lips didn't seem able to separate.

She reached for the cup. "Here. Take a few sips."

As she poured in three spoonfuls, he swallowed after each one. He only coughed once, and just a slight sound, not the body-wrenching shudders of before. His eyes remained only half-opened but wide enough that she could see his gaze tracking her.

The fact that he'd awakened meant he might be turning the corner. Especially since his fever seemed a little lower than before.

God was answering her prayers, whether he used the herbs or only His divine hand. *Thank you, Father.*

She paused from spooning liquid into his mouth to give him a chance to rest. And to speak, if he wanted to.

First, she should tell him what had happened since their return. "We were so worried about you. You've been asleep with a high fever for days now." It felt like months. She glanced at Brielle. From her position behind his head, Levi probably hadn't seen her. Best to let him know of her presence.

She returned her focus to him. "I don't think you've officially met Brielle."

Brielle scooted her chair and leaned in where Levi could better see her. Her face certainly didn't match the joy radiating inside Audrey, but at least it was showing deep consideration instead of anger. "Welcome back, Monsieur Masters."

Levi glanced at her but couldn't seem to hold the gaze since it required his eyes opening wider. "Levi . . . call me." Even those few words seemed to exhaust him, and his eyelids drooped shut.

Audrey's need to touch him, to soothe him with what little relief she could, overwhelmed the restraint she'd been trying to show in Brielle's presence. She reached up and stroked the hair from his brow, running her fingernails through the locks the way he liked. She didn't continue the motion after that first time but did let her fingertips trail down the side of his face. "Sleep a little more so you can regain your strength. I'll be here if you need anything."

A small bob of his chin was Levi's only response, but the tension on his face eased.

After a long moment, Brielle rose from her chair and laid a hand on Audrey's shoulder. "My sister made a pot of stew big enough to feed three families. She'll bring some for your evening meal."

Audrey nodded. "I'll have a chance to thank her myself, then."

Brielle held her gaze with another sad smile. "I'm glad he's awakened."

Though the words were right, something in her friend's tone made Audrey's middle tighten.

When Levi recovered, they would both have to face the council—and accept whatever punishment they set.

24

Levi couldn't summon strength to do more than lift the spoon to his mouth, but at least he could do that much now. The day before, he'd barely been able to crack his eyes open, so this was progress. Achingly slow progress, but according to Audrey, he should be thankful he could still draw breath.

He'd never seen her so giddy, even with the constant hammering in the background. She flitted from her cookstove to her shelves to his bedside, always with a smile brightening her expression. Sometimes he even caught a soft humming as she worked by the fire—only when the hammers ceased, of course. Watching her for hours on end, joy lighting her sweet face . . . there could be no stronger inducement to regain his strength.

And to do so, he had to swallow more of this broth. His belly grumbled against the endless liquid. What he wouldn't do for a meat pie, or something else he could sink his teeth into. But Audrey insisted he needed to work up to heartier foods, and the fact that he still possessed a slight fever seemed to be holding him back.

She turned to him with another of those sweet smiles as

she stepped toward his bed. She paused to glance toward the rear door as it opened, her expression turning to a question. Her smile reappeared. "Papa. You're just in time. I've a meat stew simmering and pastry almost ready to come out of the oven."

Levi tried to shift his head to see the man, but the adjustment sent a shock of pain through the base of his skull. He squeezed his eyes shut to quiet his body, then reopened them slowly. He hated being this weak, this fragile. Especially in front of others.

He wanted to meet Audrey's father man-to-man, to clasp his hand and say how well he'd done raising such a remarkable woman. As it was, he could barely manage to string a few sentences together before his body wore out.

Monsieur Moreau shuffled into Levi's view, approaching to stand by his bedside. The man studied Levi's face for a long moment without speaking. His expression held the same gentleness Audrey's did, yet there was a guardedness in her father. A tension that seemed almost hostile at times.

Levi struggled to find something to say, but could only manage, "Hello, sir."

Moreau nodded in acknowledgment. "You're feeling better?"

"I am. Trying to get my strength back."

Audrey moved around her father and picked up the cup of water from the table she'd placed beside his bed. "He still has a bit of fever, but he's been awake for a while now."

She took the cup of broth from his hands and replaced it with the water. He gripped the container with both palms, so he didn't drop it as his shaky hands lifted the vessel to his mouth.

Audrey kept her fingers on the mug's base as he lifted, and good thing, or his trembles might have sloshed the water all over his face.

After a few sips, he lowered the cup, and she took it. "I think it's time for you to rest again. Let me get some tea to help you sleep."

The thought of more tea and more sleep made him want to groan, but his eyes were already drooping. He was weaker than a newborn babe.

Though the weight of Audrey's father's gaze still pressed upon him heavily, Levi could do nothing but fade into the darkness.

Audrey did her best to stay busy so she didn't appear to be listening in on the conversation behind her, though they clearly weren't trying to keep things private. Especially since they had to raise their voices over the background hammering.

Erik was the third council member who'd come to visit Levi over these last four days since his fever had faded completely and he was able to sit up for longer stretches. Chief Durand had been the first, and he'd worn his chief-of-Laurent expression throughout the conversation, making his thoughts hard to read. After inquiring about Levi's family back in England, he'd seemed sincere when expressing his sympathy about Levi's father's disabilities, even speaking for several minutes about how their own Louis Bureau had struggled with the same paralysis and sharing ways they'd helped him become more mobile.

Despite the chief's guardedness, Levi had been respectful and open throughout the conversation, sharing freely of his life and even what he planned for his next steps.

She couldn't help but notice the glance he sent her way when he used the words "What I *had* planned to do after leaving here . . ."

Had his plans changed? The reaggravated injury and sickness had surely altered the timing, but he would heal, as long as he gave the leg sufficient time to recover. He might always be prone to pain in that hip, and maybe even further injury, but he should eventually be able to walk and ride as he had before.

When Monsieur Gaume came two days after the chief, his questions were more heated and layered with accusation and insinuation, though he never voiced a specific charge against Levi.

Thankfully, the talk with Erik now stayed more subdued. As the keeper of the lawbooks and second-in-command to the chief, Erik usually held in his reactions in much the same way his mentor did. But his mind also tended to see things in black or white. Lawful or unlawful. Harmful or healthy. How would he view Levi's actions so far? She didn't have to ask how he would view her own.

At least it seemed the council members were doing their due diligence to learn more about him. Did that mean their opinions were still undecided? *Lord, help them see the real Levi Masters, not the version they fabricated from circumstances.*

Her own fate also remained undecided. No one from the council had even commented on her actions to free Levi, not since the day she returned and told the chief the full story. Their silence kept a bundle of nerves churning in her middle.

At last, Erik concluded his questioning and spoke his farewell. As the door shut behind him, Audrey filled a plate with the foods she'd kept warming for Levi. She'd finally been offering him fare with a little more substance than broth and soft soups.

She turned with the plate and couldn't help but smile at the sight of him alive and well. *Lord, no matter what the council's verdict, thank you for keeping him alive.* She'd said the same praise more times than she could count over the last days, but the pure joy that had accompanied the first thankful prayers now twinged with longing.

Having Levi alive should be enough, but she couldn't stop wishing he could also be hers. That he would be willing to adjust his plans to include her. But she could understand that his mother needed him, even with his sister there to assist with their family business.

Would she be willing to leave her village—her family and friends—for such a faraway land, if he asked again? As much as she'd sometimes longed to see such places, she couldn't imagine never coming back to Laurent again. Never seeing her father or Brielle or any of the others. She wouldn't get to play auntie to Brielle's future children. Who would care for her father as he aged? The thoughts made her chest ache.

But she kept her smile as she settled into the chair beside Levi. It certainly wasn't his fault that she couldn't bear to move away from her people. If she couldn't do it herself, it would be unfair to ask the same of him. And being sad about the state of things wouldn't help him recover. *A merry heart doeth good like a medicine.* She'd always firmly believed that Scripture, and now was the time to live it out.

Levi's eyes settled on the food as she placed the plate in his lap. "Is that a meat pie?" The reverence in his tone was a great deal more than the fare deserved, but it made her smile come easier.

"Breton galette, we call it, but I suppose the English version is meat pie." She stayed by his side and allowed herself a moment to watch as he savored his first bite. This was what she loved about cooking—seeing the enjoyment her efforts brought to others.

When Papa had praised her early attempts as a girl, she'd worked harder and sought out more recipes from the matrons, doing everything she could to earn his pleasure again. He'd complimented every effort, helping her build confidence to stretch her abilities even further.

Now, seeing Levi enjoy the results of her work made her want to find other foods that would produce that smile. "What are some of the meals you enjoyed in England?"

His gaze turned thoughtful as he chewed the last of his bite. "We eat a great many of these." He lifted the galette. "Though I like the way you season yours better."

She tried not to show too much pleasure at the compliment, just waited for him to continue.

"Lots of mutton and potatoes. And of course a great deal of tea." His expression turned wry with that last comment.

This time she had to bite back the width of her grin. She'd plied the poor man with more tea than any person should have to drink. But it was the best way to spread the herbs through his body.

When he finished his food, his head sank back against the

rolled furs she'd used to prop him up. His eyes relaxed with a satisfied grin as he met her gaze. "Thank you, Audrey. That was exactly what I needed."

His eyes . . . She could stare into them for the rest of her days. Their rich, earthy tones drew her, making her long to sink into his arms. To let his strength wrap around her and push away all the questions and challenges of family and distance.

His hand reached for hers, his thumb caressing the top. There was a great deal to say between them, yet where to start? He'd been so ill and weak, they'd not spoken since returning to Laurent—not of the important things. Not of what had passed between them in the cave, nor of his plans. Not of what the council might plan for both of them. Not knowing what the punishment would be tightened her insides more with every passing day.

Would he voice any of these now?

The corners of his mouth tipped a little. "I like your people."

Of everything he might've said, that was furthest from what she'd expected. She raised her brows at him. "Even with all the questioning?"

His smile grew a little stronger. "They really seem to care. They're not apathetic, not too wrapped up in their own lives to do what's necessary for the good of all."

She tilted her head as his description gave her a new perspective both on the villagers of Laurent and also on the place he came from. Laurent had only survived all these years because the people worked together—for safety, for provisions, and even for celebrations. "The people of Kettlewell aren't like that?"

His brows drew together in a thoughtful frown. "Not as much, though I don't mean that in a bad way. It's just different there. Maybe because the homes are more spread out, lives aren't as intertwined."

Levi's thumb stroked the back of her hand again, and his gaze caught hers with a serious expression. "I like your people. But the question is, what do they think of me?"

Audrey swallowed the thickening in her throat. If only she had the answer. "I . . . don't know. No one has spoken to me about what might be the penalty for either of us. The fact that the council members are visiting you to learn more about you bodes well, I think." *Lord, please let that be a good sign.*

He gave her hand a squeeze as he nodded. "Do you think it would help if I spoke to someone? The chief, maybe?"

A ripple of unease spread through her. "What would you say?"

Again that thoughtful frown and a moment of silence. "Maybe apologize for anything I did that contributed to Leonard's death. I didn't get a chance to tell him how sorry I was in our previous conversation. I'd like to tell him it was never my intention to hurt the people of Laurent in any way." His face cleared as he studied her with expectancy.

He'd not said anything about telling the chief he wished to leave. Was that simply because they didn't know how long it would take him to heal suitably? Probably so.

She forced her thoughts back to his question. Would raising the topic of Leonard's demise help ease the tension between Levi and the council? Or would it simply bring up wounds that might be struggling to heal?

"I . . ." She tried to picture Chief Durand's reaction to the conversation Levi proposed. He was such a thoughtful man, never responding rashly. Perhaps Levi could start there and see how much more would be wise to say.

She finally focused on him. "If you feel the Lord leading you to speak on the topic, Chief Durand would be the best to begin with. Even if it's hard for him to hear your words, I think he might appreciate your speaking them. I'm not sure how the others would feel, but his response might tell us."

Lord, don't let me be leading him astray. The Bible said to settle a dispute with a brother quietly, right? This wasn't a dispute, but the concept still seemed to apply.

Levi nodded. "If you have a way to invite him to come visit me when he has a free minute, I would appreciate it."

"All right." As she met the warmth of his eyes, she once more fell headlong into them. He seemed to have more to say, and she waited, captured.

"I'll do everything I can to earn your people's trust, Audrey. It's important to me. I want—"

The rear door opened with a *whoosh*, stealing his words as his gaze flicked up to see who was entering.

Disappointment slipped through her at the interruption. It felt like Levi was about to say something important. *I want—* What? To leave without having to sneak out in the wee hours of morning? To keep from being bound and held under guard as soon as he felt better?

. . . to stay here with you.

. . . to be accepted by the village and to make you my wife.

No matter how much she craved those words, the chances of them ever being spoken felt so slim.

25

Levi couldn't seem to help fidgeting as he waited for Chief Durand. Audrey had said the man would come by after he finished his noon meal, and that should be any minute. The workers across the hall must also be eating, for the sounds had just ceased.

Audrey had gone to visit some of her infirm patients around the village, so that must mean she thought his conversation with the chief might go better if she wasn't present. Did she realize her father would be here, though?

He sent a glance toward Monsieur Moreau, who sat in a chair by the fire. He didn't look at all like he planned to leave the apartment soon, for he was rubbing down a long wooden rod almost as thick as his wrist. The man so rarely spoke, it was hard to know what he might be thinking. His only comments had to do with daily living. *"I'm going to bring in more wood." "Charlotte sent over food for the evening meal."*

Those were usually aimed toward Audrey, and occasionally, when father and daughter were sitting at the table or taking in a meal together, he caught a gentle expression when the older man looked at Audrey. In those moments, the man seemed real, not the stranger who hobbled around like a wooden doll.

Did the distance he keep stem from Levi being in their home, invading their usual rhythm? The thought pinched in his belly. He didn't want his presence to be hard on them. And he hated the thought that the father of the woman he loved felt so ill at ease around him. Levi had tried to be friendly, but his efforts didn't seem to make a difference.

Maybe the only way to set things right between them was to have a candid conversation about what had happened, just like he was about to do with Chief Durand. That reminder renewed the roiling in his belly.

The click of the latch finally signaled the back door opening, and a man's head appeared first. Chief Durand glanced around the room, his gaze pausing on Levi, then a smile formed on his face as it settled on Audrey's father.

"Come in." Monsieur Moreau's expression also seemed to gain a bit of life at sight of the other man, though he didn't stand or set aside his work.

As the chief entered, he glanced toward Levi again with a nod of greeting but aimed his steps toward Monsieur Moreau. The two shared a handshake and a few words, then the chief finally turned his full attention to Levi as he moved to his bedside.

"How are you feeling these days?" His gaze slid down to the blanket covering Levi's leg, then back up to his face. "You look a lot better than the last time I saw you."

Levi nodded. "Yes, sir. Getting my strength back now. Audrey says the joint seems to be healing, though she won't let me test any weight on it." The moment he spoke Audrey's

Christian name, he nearly winced. Perhaps he should've called her Miss Moreau, but it had been a long time since he'd even thought of her that way.

The other man didn't appear put off by his slip. "Audrey has a lot of wisdom when it comes to wounds and injuries. I would do what she says without question."

The warm words caused pride to bloom deep inside him. If the chief still felt that way about her, surely that boded well for what the council might decide to do about her disobedience.

"Yes, sir." He nodded.

The chief glanced around and scooted a chair to where they could easily see each other as they talked, then settled onto the seat. "Speaking of Audrey, she said you have some things you wish to speak to me about."

Once more, Levi nodded. That seemed the only thing he could do around this man. He'd wanted to be the one to broach the topic first, but he'd missed his opportunity.

Now he had to make sure he did the next part right. "Sir, I wanted the chance to clear the air. We haven't spoken of . . . the details of what happened when Audrey and I left." He barely kept himself from wincing. Why couldn't he keep her name out of this? Still, he pressed on. "I want you to know that never at any point have I meant harm to your people— not any of them. I regret what happened to Leonard more than I can say."

Audrey had said she'd told the chief, Brielle, and her father the exact events of that day, so he wouldn't go into any details that might tarnish their memories of the young guard. Still, he wanted to be honest. "I've replayed that fall so many times in my mind. If I'd reached to steady him sooner or moved faster down the mountain, perhaps I could've grabbed him before he reached the ledge."

The chief's face had taken on a sadness that seemed to rise from deep inside. "Audrey said you did everything you could to save him. Thank you for that." The words were those of understanding and gratitude, but the man's tone came out stilted, as though he didn't fully believe what he said. Or maybe gratitude was too hard to find in the face of the grief this entire village must still be feeling.

Silence settled over them for a long moment as Levi searched for what he should say next. At this point, all he could do was put to words what had been building within him. "I know nothing I say can change what's happened. But if there's anything you think will help—anything I could say or do—please tell me."

The chief nodded, his throat working. His eyes were glazed. He stood and moved the chair back to where he'd secured it from. Then he turned back to Levi, his expression making it clear he had more to say. "The council will meet soon to make decisions about how we should move forward. I know we've been silent since your return, but there's been much we've been thinking and praying about."

Levi nodded. "If you have any questions for me, anything you're not certain of, you know where to find me." He worked for something like a wry grin, but it felt more like a grimace.

The chief offered a nod, then turned back to Audrey's father. "Martin, that design we discussed is coming along. Carter said to come by the workshop when you have a minute and he'll show you."

Monsieur Moreau finally set aside his project and rose, his

slow movements reflecting pain in the action. The two men shuffled toward the door, speaking in low voices of whatever design the Carter fellow was working on. Levi didn't strain to hear. The conversation was meant to be private, and he had no need to listen.

Besides, his own discussion with the chief had left much to ponder. The council would meet soon—he'd not said an exact day, had he?

A sense of urgency pressed through him. If they sent him away, he needed to make sure he'd said everything that needed to be spoken aloud. He longed to tell Audrey how he felt, to make his love clear to her. But if he was never allowed back in Laurent, speaking of those things would only make the parting harder. As painful as it would be to keep his love bottled inside, that would be best for her.

But there was one other conversation that was needed.

After Monsieur Moreau closed the door behind the chief, he turned and shuffled back toward his chair, and Levi's pulse picked up speed. "Sir, do you think we could talk for a minute, too?" He could speak with the older fellow in his chair by the fire, but the space separating them would feel awkward. One of the things he hoped to accomplish with this conversation was to clear away the distance between them.

Moreau paused in his trek, and his gaze slid from Levi to the chair by the fire, then back to Levi. He seemed to shore up something within himself, then he straightened and moved toward Levi with a surer step.

After shifting the chair and settling into it, Monsieur Moreau addressed him with a more serious—and a clearer—expression than Levi had seen on him. "It's time we talk."

After those ominous words, he folded his arms, then waited for Levi to speak first. Was the man trying to unbalance him for the conversation?

Levi recentered his thoughts on what he needed to tell him. "I want you to know that nothing untoward happened between Audrey and me in that cave." He tried to meet the man's gaze, but even though Monsieur Moreau was staring at him, his focus seemed impossible to penetrate. "I wouldn't take advantage of any woman, though I know so many days alone with a man can't have been good for her reputation. If you think there's anything I can do to repair her good name, I'll gladly accomplish it."

Even marry her. *Especially* marry her. But he had to keep those thoughts to himself until the council spoke its verdict.

Before he gave Monsieur Moreau a chance to speak, there was one more thing he needed to say. "I'm grateful for everything Audrey did to help me recover. Without her, I would have died out there on the mountain. She's a remarkable woman with an amazing spirit. I'm sure you're very proud of her."

At those words, Monsieur Moreau's expression shifted. The barrier in his gaze eased, revealing a light there. The glimmer was small, but real. Hope dared to rise within Levi.

Monsieur Moreau still had his arms crossed over his chest, but he nodded. "I am proud of her." His voice held something like a wistful tone, but then he straightened. He finally looked into Levi's eyes. "I trust my daughter, but that doesn't mean I won't do whatever is necessary to protect her. She seems to see something different in you, but I'm still very aware you're a man. One who has experienced a great many more things in the world than my Audrey. I've allowed you to stay in our home because of your injury, but I'm not easy about it."

The candor in the man's words was almost a relief. At least they were speaking openly now. "I understand your concern, and I'm grateful Audrey has you."

He paused. Should he speak of the future? He'd not planned to in this conversation, but maybe doing so would help Monsieur Moreau. At least it would be nothing less than the truth. "Sir, I've not said anything of my next words to Audrey. I don't plan to until after the council's decision is announced, and even then, I'll only say them if I'm free to plan such things. But my intentions toward Audrey are honorable. She's won my heart in more ways than I can list. I don't know if it will be possible for me to ever live in Laurent, but if the Lord makes a way, my hope is to ask you for your blessing and her for her hand."

As the words sounded in his ears, their unflagging optimism seemed to hang in the quiet of the room. Levi inhaled a breath. "I understand how unlikely it might be that I'm allowed to stay here, though. I wouldn't ask Audrey to leave her family and friends, so that's why I've not spoken of this to her."

Monsieur Moreau's brows had drawn together as he took in everything Levi said. Maybe it was too much. This conversation had been meant as an apology and a way to clear the air, not a declaration and a request for his daughter's hand. "I'm not asking for an answer or even a reply. I just wanted to let you know that my intentions toward Audrey are for her best, no matter the outcome of the council's vote."

Another long moment passed, a frown of concentration still gathering on the older man's face. At last, he nodded. "Good to know."

As he stood and shuffled toward his chair by the fire, Levi finally eased out a long breath. Would these hard conversations do any good, or would all the trouble be for naught?

⚬⚭⚬

Three days had passed since Chief Durand told Levi the council would meet soon, and Audrey was fairly certain today was that day. Tension seemed to hang thicker in the air the longer the morning progressed.

The few times she'd ventured out of their quarters, the people she met in the hallway or the courtyard seemed unable to meet her gaze. And she'd not been able to locate any of the council members. She tried to question Brielle, but her friend had been on her way out for a hunt, too occupied to answer.

All she could do was try to busy her hands until word came to them. She'd run out of things to do around the apartment—tasks she could accomplish with her mind in such a muddle, anyway—so she'd sat to finish the new coat for her father, since she'd given his old one to Levi for the escape.

Lord, give us favor with each person on the council. Give them wisdom to make the choice that aligns with your will.

Something shook inside her, and a full moment passed before she realized the tremor was outside her body, too. A glance at her pans hanging on the wall showed them swaying.

She tensed. "Is that . . . ?"

A look at Levi showed that he was waking from a doze. He wouldn't be aware enough to know what was happening.

Papa met her gaze with his brows lifted. "An earth tremor."

That's what she'd suspected, but the shaking had stopped

now. It hadn't been strong, more like a fluttering. She exhaled a breath to ease her insides. "We haven't had anything like that happen in several years."

A knock on their rear door cut off her father's response, and she sprang from the chair, dropping her project to the floor beside her. "I'll see who it is." Maybe someone had been hurt during the shaking. Even a weak tremor like that could knock someone off balance.

Papa returned his focus to the project he was working on. One thing about her father, when he finally set his mind to a task, he was meticulous in its completion.

When she opened the door, Brielle's younger brother, Andre, stood in the hallway. "Papa says for you to come to the council meeting as soon as you can."

Not an injury, then. For a moment, she'd been distracted from this particular worry. Her insides clenched again, and as much as she wanted to question him, she didn't. He likely wouldn't know why they summoned her, and even if he did, it wasn't his place to tell.

She brushed one hand over her hair and the other down her skirt. She looked like this most days, but maybe she should have dressed up in preparation to hear from the council. Too late to worry over that now.

She sent a glance behind her, first to her father, then to Levi. The latter caught her gaze and placed his hands together as if in prayer. The reminder eased a bit of tension from her shoulders. The Lord had control here. Nothing the council said would be a surprise to Him.

Turning back to Andre, she pulled the door open wider and stepped through. "I'm ready."

26

As Audrey moved through the large double doors into the assembly room, it felt as though she were stepping into another world. How many times in her life had she entered this giant chamber? Usually, she was carrying baskets of food and eagerly anticipating special time with her neighbors.

That life seemed distant from the somber mood cloaking the room now as she strode forward to where the council members sat in a circle. Chief Durand stood and motioned for her to come beside him. His expression did nothing to relieve the knots coiling tighter throughout her body. *Lord . . .*

She made the mistake of sending her glance around the dozen or so faces in the circle. Not one encouraging smile, not even an understanding look. Just sober expressions.

"Audrey." At Chief Durand's voice, she turned to him and steeled herself for what would come. His gaze, usually so kind, held only seriousness now. "We've had much to discuss and have delayed this final meeting so we could spend time in prayer and full investigation of the situation. But the time has come where we must make a decision—both about whether

Levi Masters is welcome in our village, and regarding what should be done for your part in his escape."

Her knees began to sway. This was really happening. The moment of judgment.

Maybe the chief saw her distress, for he motioned to a chair. "Sit."

As she sank down, he also took a seat, then returned his full focus to her. "Regarding Monsieur Masters. As you know, the way he came to our village—secretly following Evan—did not make us think positively toward the man. We understand he was doing what he felt was in the best interest of Britain, but the fact that he was working for an enemy of the country that we've vowed to support is another concern."

The chief hadn't mentioned the history between Evan and Levi. Did that mean it hadn't entered into the council's decision? She couldn't imagine that being the case.

But the chief continued, "His honesty during our questioning, both before and after his escape, has aided his cause. But the fact that he escaped before we'd even made a decision about his outcome is a strong mark against him."

This concern she could refute, for *she'd* been the one to initiate the escape and practically force him into it. But as she opened her mouth to say so, the chief raised a staying hand.

"Whether the escape was planned, and by whom, is not what I'm speaking of. He walked out of Laurent under his own power, knowing that our governing body intended for him to stay under guard until a decision was made. A decision, I'll add, that we were very clear would be accompanied by prayer and fasting so we might understand God's will in the situation."

The intentional look he gave her with those last words

made her want to curl into a ball and cry. How wrong her rash actions had been. She should have trusted better, thought twice before doing something her conscience tried to warn her about.

"Regarding *your* actions, our decision has been even harder."

She couldn't breathe, could barely think as numbness took over her mind. It felt as though she were watching the scene from a distance, absorbing the chief's words from far outside the circle.

"I believe I understand why you helped the prisoner escape. But that doesn't change the reality of your actions. You deliberately went against the council's order, releasing a prisoner we'd not yet deemed safe. I understand you felt differently, but that doesn't change the magnitude of your disobedience. That's something we can't take lightly, not when we're tasked with protecting and maintaining order in the village."

The words penetrated her mind, but the shell around her heart protected her from feeling their pain. The chief hadn't yet spoken the council's verdict, so she didn't have to respond.

"Because both of these matters affect the entire village, we've decided to allow the people to vote. They will choose your punishment and also determine what should be done with Levi." He paused, but a hesitation in his expression said he might have more to say.

Sadness slipped into his gaze. "Based on your testimony, we understand Monsieur Masters had no intentional part in Leonard's death, however I think it likely that event may play a role in the people's decision. We'll hold the vote at noon two days from now. That will give the entire village time to seek God's will through fervent prayer."

⌘

The numbness had finally cracked in the night, exposing Audrey's heart and emotions to the reality of what would come.

Tears slid down her cheeks, soaking her bedding as the pain of what might have been mixed with the fear of what might be. The chief was right; Levi had too many marks against him in the eyes of the people. They would insist he leave—or worse. What would they do to her? In the darkness of her apartment, with her father's snores filling the air, she let the weakness come. Let herself give in to the pain.

The whisper came so softly, the sound barely broke through the chaos in her mind. But she held herself motionless to listen, as a lingering tear traced down the side of her nose.

"Audrey." Even in a whisper, the way Levi spoke her name drew her. She'd not felt his presence through the pain and turmoil inside her, but awareness of him in the room surrounded her now.

She sat up in bed, wiping her nose and cheeks. He'd surely heard her, but she didn't want to make her crying obvious by sniffing. If she spoke, he would hear it in her voice, so she stayed quiet.

"I can't come to you." Regret filled his tone. Meaning he wanted to be there for her, but to accept the solace he offered, she would have to be the one to close the distance.

Every part of her wanted his strength to shore up her

weakness. Just this once. Just tonight. In the light of day, she would be strong again.

Slipping from her bed, she padded to his cot and sank down on the edge. His hand found hers, closing over it with his warmth. But that touch felt so small compared to the expanse of her pain. She wanted his arms around her, wanted someone else to carry the load for a while.

Maybe he read her thoughts, for when his soft "Come here" sounded, she didn't wait for a second invitation. She curled up beside him, her head on his shoulder.

He wrapped both arms around her, tucking her close and cradling her against him. One of his hands stroked her hair, like a mother would a child. She'd never felt so cared for, so sheltered.

The tears slipped down again, dampening his shirt. This time she didn't cry from desperation. Grief, yes, but also relief. She couldn't stay in the shelter of Levi's arms for long, but she would relish the moment while she could.

When the drops finally dried on her cheeks, and her body fully relaxed in the cradle of Levi's strength, he moved the hand that had been stroking her hair around to cup her cheek. His thumb brushed the tear-salted skin there, and he pressed a kiss in her hair.

"I'm praying, Audrey. The Lord has a plan in this, though I don't know what it is. He'll carry us through." His warm whisper caressed her forehead, and she squeezed her eyes shut as his words soaked through her. She'd lost sight of God's power in this situation, had focused on her own human capabilities. No wonder the weakness had overwhelmed her.

She lay there for long moments, her eyes closed as her spirit reached out to the Father. *I'm sorry, Lord. Work your plan in this situation. And please, if it's not too much to ask, don't take this man away from me.*

Finally, with new strength shoring her insides, she sat up on the edge of the bed. She couldn't help brushing her hand along Levi's temple, down the side of the beard that had grown thicker each week.

He kept his hand over hers, holding her there. "I need to shave. I haven't been this long in a while."

She brushed her thumb through the coarse hairs along his jaw. "I can help you with that. Maybe tomorrow."

He slid her hand down and pressed a kiss to her palm. "Tomorrow."

Before the tingle spreading up her arm could draw her back down to him, she stood and pulled her hand away. Better to find her own bed now.

Tomorrow would come sooner than she wanted.

Levi awoke to the pounding of metal on stone, as had happened so many times before. The apartment held no windows to see whether daylight lit the outside, but if men were already working across the hall, he must have slept late.

A glance around the room showed Audrey's father sitting at the table, a mug in his hands. He met Levi's gaze with a nod. Though he still wasn't talkative, at least he interacted more than before.

After sitting up, Levi propped the rolled furs behind him. If only he could get out of bed for himself—shave and wash and get his own food. How much longer until he could at least move to a chair?

Monsieur Moreau scooted his seat back from the table and rose slowly. He shuffled toward his seat by the fire, but instead of settling in, he leaned down and picked up the stick he'd been working on these past days. Two sticks, actually. He turned toward Levi, his steps slow, as though the cool morning air made his joints ache.

The man only glanced at Levi once as he approached, but there was a hint of a smile that brightened his expression as he halted at Levi's side. He separated the poles, one into each hand, and held them up. "Thought these might help you when Audrey lets you up from there." As the man shifted his hands, the work he'd done at the tops became evident. He'd fastened a short crossbar to form a *T* and wrapped it in leather, probably to be softer as Levi leaned on them.

The thought of standing on his own power, using these to bear his weight, brought a grin. "Walking sticks. Thank you."

He reached for them, but Moreau pulled them back. "You can't get up and try them until Audrey gives leave. She said your hip will need longer to recover this time, and if you put weight on it too soon, she'll have my head."

Levi worked to school his excitement. "I'll wait until I can ask her." He reached out again, and the man placed the sticks against his bed. "Has she gone visiting patients?" That seemed to be her habit most mornings, and sometimes she would be gone for an hour or two.

Memories from the night before were fresh in his thoughts. She'd been so fragile, her pain nearly overpowering her. He could only hope something he'd done or said had helped. She'd seemed better—stronger—by the time she left him.

Moreau glanced at the back door, as though checking to see if Audrey stood there. "I think so. When she left, I was across the hall, looking at the progress they're making."

The hammering seemed to grow louder with the man's words. "That's the apartment Evan MacManus is building?"

He nodded. "They're working hard on it. Trying to finish quickly so they can have the wedding."

They certainly were putting in long hours of pounding. He glanced around the stone chamber surrounding him. It would take hundreds of hours to cut something like this from the center of the mountain.

He sent his gaze back to Moreau. "How much progress have they made so far? Will it be as big as this room?"

Moreau shook his head. "Not at first, though I hear Evan plans to expand after a while. He said they're about halfway done cutting out the rock."

Something inside Levi trembled. Or maybe not *inside* . . .

The walking sticks leaning against his bed shook, then fell to the floor with a clatter. Across the room, a pot hanging over the fire swayed violently.

Another earth tremor? This felt much stronger than before. Like a full-sized quake.

Moreau stumbled, then grabbed a chair. Levi reached out to help steady him, but the man sank down into the seat.

The hammering across the hall silenced, even as another tremor seemed to vibrate the air. Levi clutched the mattress beneath him to find something solid. Even the walls seemed to shake. Somewhere outside their room, a man shouted. A child cried, then was joined by a second.

As quickly as it began, the room stopped trembling. The earthquake hadn't made a sound, but a hush now spread around them, though a baby still cried somewhere in the distance.

Then a new rumble broke through the quiet. Levi gripped the mattress again, preparing for the room to shake once more.

But all remained still, even as the noise grew in intensity. Another man's shout sounded from outside, this time tipping high with either surprise or fear. Then he yelled again as the rumble turned into thunder.

Levi strained forward on his bed. Something was happening out there. Something instigated by the earthquake, most likely.

Then, like a squeaky cart creaking to a stop, the rumble faded to silence.

Footsteps thundered in the corridor, and more shouts. Frantic calls, though he could only make out a few words of panicked French.

"Lots . . . they . . . trapped."

Moreau jumped to his feet and shuffled to the back door faster than Levi had ever seen him move. Everything within Levi wanted to grab the walking sticks and follow him out. But Moreau had left the door open, and Levi could now hear the voices better as he saw people sprinting past the doorway.

Dust clouded in the hallway, spreading into the room and stirring his itch to get up and see with his own eyes what was happening.

It must be some type of rockslide, based on the choking dust and what he was overhearing. Had it been across the hall where MacManus was working? How many people were with him? Was anyone hurt?

He strained to hear more, to decipher answers to his many questions. The chaos outside only increased, voices rising frantically. The situation must be dire. What could he do to help? Surely there was something.

He had to do something.

27

Levi watched for someone to move past the doorway slowly enough for him to catch their attention. He had to learn exactly what had happened and whether anyone was hurt.

Hurt. If there were injuries, Audrey would be there to help.

After several moments of watching the open doorway, he wasn't able to snag either of the two people who sprinted past. He could call out and hope someone heard him, but the last thing he wanted to do was pull away someone who was rendering aid.

He eyed the walking sticks. This might be the right opportunity for their first use.

He lifted the injured leg from the bed down to the floor, just to keep from using the hip too much. It had been so long since he'd even moved his injured side, other than sliding up and down in the bed. The joint ached, but that feeling had grown far too familiar.

Positioning the walking sticks, he pulled himself upright, supporting his entire body on his good leg. The poles were a good height as he placed them under his arms. Maybe a tiny bit tall, but stretching up helped him keep from putting weight on the injured hip.

At first, he tried to walk the sticks forward one at a time as he would his legs, but that forced him to put weight on the injured side. So he positioned the base of the poles in front of him, then swung his body forward. Better.

The cacophony of sounds continued outside the room as he struggled forward, one swing at a time.

At last, he reached the door and peered both ways. People were clustered in the hallway to the left. At first, it looked like they were spilling out of the Durands' apartment. But most seemed focused on the opening in the stone wall that must be the new quarters Evan MacManus was building.

The knot that had been forming in his belly pulled tighter. Had someone been injured by loose stones? That earthquake could have sent rocks rolling around. But enough to cause this much commotion?

He swung forward more slowly, staying against the wall, as far out of the way as he could. He sought out familiar faces—Audrey or her father, one of the Durands, or even one of the council members who'd come to talk with him. Anyone who might tell him what was going on. Of course, they might be just as likely to send him back to the Moreaus' apartment.

A young woman who stood back from the fray looked a good bit like Charlotte, Brielle's younger sister, the one who had brought them food during those days he'd been barely coherent from the fever.

He swung forward, tucking his crutches as close together as he could to maneuver through the crowd. The young woman stood with her hands wrapped around her middle, worry lining her face as she looked toward the crude doorway that marked the new construction. She was so focused that she didn't notice his approach.

"Miss Charlotte?" He had to raise his voice over the din around them.

She startled and jerked her attention to him. He could tell the moment she recognized him, and that recognition didn't seem to relax her any.

Her jaw worked. "What are you—"

To keep her from finishing that question and trying to send him back to bed, he nodded toward the opening in the rock. "What happened? How many are hurt?"

The distraction worked well, for her attention quickly swiveled back to the entrance. That intense worry muddled her features again, and she wrapped her hands tighter around herself. "A rockslide. Evan and another man are closed in behind it. We don't know if they're hurt or not."

Levi's senses jumped to alert. "Can they get them out? Why is everyone just standing here?"

"Brielle and Papa are helping to organize the work to clear a path. Andre said the hallway they're trying to open is tiny, only big enough for one person at a time."

He stared at the rough opening, at the people standing around outside doing nothing. Surely they would all be willing to help if a job could be found for them. But if there really was such small space inside, passing rocks out of the chamber might be the only thing these bystanders could do.

He wouldn't even be able to accomplish that small task with these crutches, though in truth, it didn't appear his aid would be missed among all these able bodies. Still, as he stood and waited beside Charlotte, the lack of action rubbed the raw ends of his nerves.

He leaned close enough to Charlotte to be heard without raising his voice. "Is Audrey in there?"

She nodded. "Her father, too."

Frustration sluiced through him. He should be there helping. He'd never been one to stand idly by when there was work to be done—much less when men's lives were at stake.

He glanced sideways at Charlotte. He could send her inside to see if there was something he could do. But what could a man hobbling on crutches possibly manage? He would be a nuisance. In the way.

So, he waited, leaning against the wall and resting the foot of his injured leg. He spent the next angst-filled minutes lifting petitions to the Father.

The group around them grew restless, conversations becoming noisier. From the rough doorway, a man stepped into the hallway, his dirt-smudged face grim as he worked his way through the crowd, turning down the corridor away from Levi.

Levi leaned toward Charlotte again. "Who is he and what is he doing?"

Her gaze still lingered on the figure disappearing down the hallway. "That's Wesley. I don't know where he's going."

The solemness the man's expression had held wound Levi's gut even tighter. The operation inside that room must not be going well. How long had it been since the rockslide? It felt like hours, but maybe only thirty minutes had passed. His leg ached, but he would bear the pain to stay here and know what was happening.

A few minutes later, a man's voice rose above the others. "Make way! Clear a path."

The people around them began to move, spreading down

the hallway toward the Moreaus' doorway and beyond. Bodies jostled against him, but Charlotte moved close to his side and acted as a barrier to keep him from being bumped. He would get out of the way if he could, but he didn't dare attempt it with this throng of people shuffling around him. His balance on these walking sticks was still precarious, and if he were knocked over . . . A shot of pain speared up his hip, as though his body was giving him a taste of the possibility.

A new noise sounded from the direction Wesley had disappeared, like a hammer striking stone. Or not a hammer . . .

Just as his mind registered the sound of hooves on rock, a horse appeared through the dim light.

A flush swept through his body. That couldn't be. They'd brought . . . Chaucer?

The gelding snorted, sidestepping shadows cast by flickering torches. Every few steps he halted, and the man leading him tugged on the rope, pulling Chaucer forward a few steps until he jumped at another shadow.

Poor Chaucer. Between the darkness and smoke from the torches, he must be terrified. Levi hadn't been there for the barn fire the gelding had barely escaped, but he'd dealt with the aftermath in the horse's behavior. For weeks, Chaucer had jumped at falling leaves or the faint scent of chimney smoke wafting from a nearby home. Even now, the horse always shifted nervously if Levi tied him too close to a campfire.

With his walking sticks, Levi maneuvered toward the gelding, weaving through the villagers still clearing the hallway. Chaucer and his handler were about ten strides away now, and the horse balked again at the shadows from the torch mounted on his left.

The handler muttered something in a low voice, then

tugged the rope. Wesley eyed Levi as though he might be part of the reason the horse refused to walk freely.

Levi eased forward more slowly and started a calming monologue for the gelding. "Hey there, Chaucer. There's a fellow. It's good to see you again, my friend."

Little by little, the horse's ears perked toward him, and his body seemed to relax.

"Walk on, fellow." As Levi drew near, the horse tensed, preparing to bolt. He must be put off by the jerky motion of Levi's swinging and the clatter of the walking sticks.

He paused and held out a hand toward the horse. "Come on, boy."

Chaucer's posture relaxed again, and Levi sent a glance to the handler. "See if you can lead him to me."

Wesley sent Levi a suspicious look, then finally gave a tug on the rope, and the horse stepped forward, closing the distance to Levi.

After letting Chaucer sniff his hand, Levi reached up to rub the spot behind the gelding's ear that always itched the most and received the usual nudge of approval. The horse's backbone still showed prominently, but his ribs no longer protruded as sharply. He'd clearly regained much of his energy, too.

As Levi continued to stroke the horse in all his favorite places, he glanced at the man. "Is he needed for the rescue?" If there was barely space for a person, he couldn't imagine how the horse would help.

"Yes, and there's no time to waste. The other horse is too lame to work." Wesley growled the words and looked like he would tug Chaucer forward again.

"Wait. Can you tell me what he's to do? I may be able to help him settle so he can accomplish it."

The handler sent him a glare. "The rocks blocking the men in are too big for one man to move, and there's not enough space to fit two people. We need the horse to pull the boulders out."

Levi worked to keep his reaction from showing. Chaucer was no cart horse. As far as Levi knew, he'd never worn a harness. Mixed with the darkness in that room and the smoke drifting from the torches, he'd never be calm enough to do the job safely.

But if he was their only hope . . .

He leveled his focus on Wesley. "Are the trapped men injured?"

The man's jaw set. "We don't know. We can't hear anything through the wall of rock."

Levi sucked in a breath. It might be hopeless, but they had to try. If he could get Chaucer to perform the job, that might be the only way they could free MacManus and the other man quickly enough.

"All right, then. This horse was in a barn fire a couple years back, and since then he's never liked dark areas or smoke. I helped him work through his fears after the fire, so I might be able to help him manage the tight spaces in there. Can I walk along with you?"

The man gave a tight nod, then tugged on the lead line. Levi's gentle stroking seemed to have settled the horse a little, for Chaucer didn't startle this time when Levi swung along beside him. He did raise his head as he neared another torch, nostrils flaring as he slowed.

Levi halted and propped the walking stick under his arm so he could reach out and rub the gelding's neck. "Easy, boy. All is well." Those same words he'd said to the horse through weeks of rehabilitating the gelding.

At last, they reached the rough doorway hacked from the wall. Several figures watched from the opening, yet one stood out from the rest.

Audrey.

Her expression was hard to read in the shadows, but her posture bespoke worry. Was it concern for his being out of bed? Or fear for the men caught behind the stones? The latter was definitely the greater cause for apprehension, but he hated that he might be adding to her angst.

When Wesley halted the horse in front of the group, they moved into action, clearing the opening. Audrey and her father both moved into the corridor, and she stepped beside Levi. Maybe she felt better able to help him if she was close, or maybe she sought his presence for comfort.

One of the men inside, a strong-looking fellow who seemed familiar, spoke up. "I have ropes tied around the largest of the rocks but they're not long enough to reach out here. Can you back the horse into the room?"

Wesley grunted. "We can try. He's skittish."

Levi stepped out of the way as Wesley turned Chaucer and tried to move him backward into the room. The horse balked, especially since the man was attempting to push the horse with brute force instead of giving the simple cues Chaucer was used to.

Levi swung forward. "Can I try?"

The fellow was clearly frustrated, and his agitation wasn't helping Chaucer keep calm. The desperate need to free the trapped men hung thick in the air, but allowing the horse to feel the panic would work against them.

Wesley allowed Levi to come alongside the gelding and take the rope. The fellow took a step back, and Levi used the moment to settle the horse with another rub behind his ears.

"All right, boy. It's time to back." After positioning the walking sticks under his arms so he could lean on them and free his hands, he tugged the lead line down to make the gelding's neck bow, then used the thumb of his other hand to press the tender spot in the horse's chest. "Ba-ack." He kept his voice in the singsong tone he'd always used for the command, breaking the simple word into two syllables.

Chaucer's training came through, and he took one step back, then a second. He'd moved as far as Levi could reach, which meant he'd have to swing forward and reposition himself before giving the horse the command again.

Audrey stepped forward before he could do so, fitting one hand around the rope just above his and placing her other thumb on the horse's chest where he had. "Ba-ack." She used the same two-syllable tone, though her sweet voice made the command much more enticing.

Chaucer waited a beat before responding, then he tucked his nose as before and moved a hesitant step backward. Levi hobbled behind her, doing his best to move smoothly enough that he didn't scare the horse.

But after two more backward steps, Chaucer's rear hoof stumbled on a loose stone, and his head reared up.

28

Levi leaned forward to calm the horse, but Audrey was already stroking his neck and whispering gentle words in his ear. Chaucer still tensed, but his head lowered under her soothing touch.

"That might be far enough. See if we can hook this rope around him." The voice sounded from inside, then the man who'd taken charge before stepped into the light.

Levi tried to move near enough to take the rope and tie it around Chaucer, but the space was so small, and with Audrey and the horse already there, he didn't have room to maneuver with the walking sticks. Thankfully, Durand and the others stood back in an open corner.

The fellow holding the rope tried to fasten it around the gelding, but the ends would only extend as far as his shoulders. At least another arm's length would be necessary to wrap around his chest. More than that in order to tie a knot.

Audrey stroked Chaucer's neck. "All right, boy. Let's take another step back." Her crooning worked the same charm on the gelding that it did every time with Levi. When she tugged the rope and pressed her thumb into the signal spot on his chest, Chaucer edged backward. Smaller steps this time, but moving the right direction.

The man holding the rope stayed beside them, keeping the thick braided leather cords raised so they could measure exactly how far back the horse had to go.

When Chaucer balked again, Levi held his breath while the fellow measured the rope around the horse's chest. "This might be enough."

While he worked with the ends to tie a strong knot with the short amount of cord he had, murmurs sounded from the group standing behind them.

One voice rose above the others. "Hurry. We still haven't heard sounds from them." The voice belonged to a female, and the desperation welling in the tone must mean it was Brielle, Evan's intended.

Levi glanced behind Chaucer to gauge how many rocks had to be moved. The shadows overwhelmed the tunnel that had been cleared, so he couldn't see how far back it went.

"There. I hope that's strong enough." The man stepped back from fastening the knot.

Now for the other hard part—seeing if Chaucer would pull. Levi shuffled to the side to allow the gelding room to step forward, then reached for the lead line.

Audrey shook her head, not releasing her hold. "I'll walk him." Stubborn woman.

"He might balk. He's never worn a harness. He might lurch forward and try to bolt." Levi shifted his position and reached for the rope again.

"I can handle it." Audrey crooned the words as she stroked the horse's nose, though they were clearly meant for Levi.

Perhaps she might have a better chance with the gelding

now, given her ability to charm him. Levi would stay just out of the way, but near enough to grab the halter in case the horse bolted.

Lord, help us.

Audrey had to use every bit of her self-control to keep calm, though the panic tried to squeeze her throat. Evan and Hugo might be lying in tremendous pain, half-buried by stone, while she quietly stroked this horse. But keeping the animal calm was the only way they could pull those boulders out.

When Levi stepped out of the way, she tugged the lead to signal Chaucer forward. Philip had taken over holding the tow rope around the horse's chest, which allowed her to focus on encouraging him forward.

Chaucer moved to obey her nudge, but the instant the rope tightened around him, he halted. He was probably following his training, as the rope pressed over the place she'd used with her thumb to back him.

"Come on, boy. Walk forward." She gave two strokes to his neck, then tugged the rope again.

He stepped to obey, but once more, when the strap around his chest tightened, he paused. She gave a harder pull on the rope, taking a small step herself. "Walk, boy. Walk forward."

Behind her, Levi's voice rumbled. "Walk on."

Chaucer hesitated, then leaned into the harness rope and took a small step. The rope pulled tight, pressing into his flesh. The horse eased back to loosen the pressure, but she added more encouragement to move forward, both with her voice and steady pressure on the lead line.

"Walk on, boy. Walk on." She used the same phrase Levi had spoken, in case the horse had been trained to it.

Again, Chaucer leaned into the rope. If it had been fastened to a cart or loose branch or something that moved with little effort, he might've been fine. But this stone wouldn't budge.

"Come on, boy. Pull hard. Walk on." She tugged harder on the lead line, using every bit of encouragement she could manage.

The gelding responded, leaning into the harness rope for several heartbeats before easing back.

"Again." Philip had moved back to the shadows where the rope was tied around the boulder.

Once more, she urged Chaucer forward using voice and touch. The gelding responded, pulling into the harness for several seconds, longer this time than before. It still didn't seem like the rock moved at all.

"Again." More urgency filled Philip's voice, infusing the same within her.

"Walk on, boy. You can do it." She tugged and coaxed the horse forward, and he leaned into the harness even longer this time.

When Chaucer eased back, he coughed as though the harness had been cutting into his air supply. She should wrap something around the rope for padding. Why hadn't she thought of that at first? She scanned the length of herself, but the only clothing thick enough that could be easily removed was her coat.

With fumbling fingers, she let Chaucer's lead line hang, then unfastened her buttons and slid her arms from the sleeves.

"What are you doing?" Levi shifted behind her. Chaucer stayed still, as she'd expected. His training really was remarkable. No wonder Levi loved the gelding.

She didn't take time to answer, just slipped her coat between the harness rope and the horse's chest, wrapping it once and stretching the padding as far around the animal's shoulders as possible. "That should help."

"Once more might do it." Impatience rang from Philip's voice, and she readied herself for the next pull. Two men's lives depended on them.

"Here we go. Come on, boy. Walk on." She put everything she had, every form of encouragement she could muster, into urging Chaucer forward. Behind her, Levi did the same, their voices weaving together as the gelding leaned into the harness. His haunches tucked underneath him as he utilized his full body in the effort. This had to work. *Lord, move that rock.*

"Keep going!" Philip's voice rang out just as Chaucer would have slackened the rope.

Audrey tugged the lead line harder, infusing her urgency into the horse.

Chaucer responded, pushing into the harness again. Straining. Then he stepped forward.

"It's moving!" Excitement filled Philip's tone as Chaucer labored even harder.

He managed another small step. But then, exhausted, the gelding eased back from the pull.

Audrey stroked the horse's neck, murmuring encouragement into his ear as a reward for the hard work. From the darkness, Philip was yelling into the rock, trying to speak to the men trapped inside.

Excited voices came from behind her. "Is there an opening? Do you hear them?" Brielle sounded more hopeful than before.

"Quiet." At Philip's snap, the entire room silenced, straining for the sound of any muffled voices.

Audrey's heartbeat thumped loud in her ears, overwhelming what she hoped to hear.

Philip waited only a handful of seconds before he began to move again. "Let's keep going. I can't see an opening yet, but we should get one with another pull or two."

She gave Chaucer's neck a final pat, then adjusted the harness and moved into position. "Let's do this, boy. Walk on."

Chaucer strained and she encouraged, pulling on the lead. Little by little, they nosed forward. First, one small step. Then another.

With the third, Philip called out something she couldn't understand. A rumble sounded. Then a shout.

Chaucer's head reared high, nearly jerking the lead line from her hand. He swung his hindquarters toward her to escape the growing noise.

Her heartbeat grew frantic as she tried to soothe the gelding. That sounded like another rockslide. Did more stones break loose from the ceiling?

A shout sounded. Philip. Was he caught amid the falling rock?

From the corner of her gaze, the tumble of stones began to rain down behind the horse. The harness rope had fallen to the ground, leaving Chaucer the freedom to dart forward.

He lunged from the apartment, jerking her hard behind him.

Levi swung after Audrey and the horse as quickly as he could manage. The thunder from the rockslide seemed to be lessening, but dust clouded thick in the air.

In the corridor, Chaucer spun, head high and eyes wide as he tried to dart away. Audrey held a firm grip on the rope, keeping him from turning completely. She spoke soothing words, but the horse's panic made him deaf to her sweet voice.

Levi eased his movements as he drew near and began speaking to the gelding, his voice resonating more than Audrey's. "Whoa, fellow. Settle down. Easy there."

He dared to draw near enough to give a firm pat to the horse's neck, a touch still soothing, yet solid enough to break through his frantic state.

Chaucer quivered under his hand but slowed his movements.

"Easy, boy. All is well." The smoke of the torches was greater out here, surely adding to the gelding's panic. Though the rock fall had ended inside the work area, frantic voices had taken up the noise.

Levi's gut churned. What further injuries had been caused now? Leaning on the walking sticks, he reached for Chaucer's lead line. "You're probably needed in there. I can handle him."

Audrey hesitated, glancing between the horse and him, her gaze dropping to the walking sticks still propped under his arms.

A loud groan—or maybe a heave—from inside the work area seemed to make the decision for her. She handed over the line, and her gaze met his for a brief moment, fear and worry swirling in her eyes. "Please be careful."

He nodded. "Let me know what I can do to help." Maybe

he couldn't do anything more than the others, but if there was something . . .

⁓⚬⚭⚬⁓

In the torchlight, Audrey stared at the mass of rock rising up before her. Removing the boulder had shifted the smaller stones jammed into that narrow hallway, sending them tumbling in both directions and bringing more down on top of them.

But now that the dust had settled, the stones formed a slope that allowed enough space between the peak and the ceiling for a small person to wiggle through.

Brielle had just disappeared over the top, and Philip and Wesley were hauling stones off the pile to widen the opening.

Audrey grabbed the chief's arm. "Are they alive?"

The only time she'd ever seen his face as grim was the day of the massacre, when his wife had been shot, along with five other villagers. "I think so. Brielle needs you in there." He placed a hand on her shoulder and gave her a nudge.

She jumped into action, grabbing the satchel of medicines she'd been carrying on the visits to her patients.

The men clearing the rubble allowed her to pass, then assisted her as she climbed up the stones. Rocks shifted beneath her, some of the smaller ones tumbling down as she stepped away from them.

The opening at the top barely allowed her to slide through, with both her back and belly rubbing against stone. But her discomfort was nothing compared to what Evan and Hugo were probably experiencing.

As she maneuvered down the other slope, she strained to see anything in the darkness. "Brielle?"

"Over here." Her voice came from the far side of the narrow chamber, and her tone sounded like she was crying.

Dear Lord, please don't let Evan be dead. Hugo, either. How would her friend take the blow if she lost the man who'd become so important to her?

Before she attempted to maneuver to Brielle, she called back through the opening. "Philip, can you hand in a torch?" She could do nothing to help the men unless she could see them.

"Let me get one." The voice sounded so distant.

While she waited, she worked up her courage and asked the question she almost couldn't bear to know the answer to. "Are they . . . alive?"

A shuddering deep breath came from Brielle. "Hugo is here, and his hand is bleeding bad. Evan is breathing, but unconscious. I don't know what's wrong." Her voice trembled with the last words.

Audrey hadn't seen her friend cry since they were girls. She longed to be there, to wrap her arms around Brielle and tell her all would be well.

But she couldn't know that for sure.

29

At last, the glow of the torch shone in the opening, and a hand passed it through. Audrey reached up and took the light, then turned to get her bearings in the small space.

Rocks littered the floor, and Hugo sat upright against the far wall. Brielle knelt near him, beside the form of her beloved.

With the torch in one hand and her satchel in the other, Audrey maneuvered over the rocks to kneel beside Evan. She handed the torch to Brielle, then glanced over both men. As Brielle had said, Evan lay perfectly still, and Hugo sat against the wall, curled into himself.

She squinted to see what he held. "Where are you hurt?"

The young man gasped. "My finger. It's gone." He always mumbled when he spoke, but now his voice also trembled, making his words even harder to comprehend. Then they registered and the pressure tightened in her chest.

A finger sliced off? She'd never treated such an accident, though one of the elders had only the stub of his thumb left from a knife accident years ago. "Let me see."

Hugo eased both hands up, and the dim light revealed

blood running down his skin. As she peered closer, the missing finger became clear. Her belly roiled, but her mind moved into action. Reaching for a bandage from her satchel with one hand, she cradled Hugo's hands with the other.

Carefully, she wrapped the damaged hand with the bandage, just tight enough to slow the bleeding. "I'll tend it properly once we get you out of here. For now, press this on the wound." She placed Hugo's good hand around the injury.

Once he had a good grasp, she moved her hand to cup his face, drawing his focus up to her. She had no doubt of the pain throbbing through his hand, but she needed to know if his mind was clear. "Are you hurt anywhere else?"

As he met her gaze, only pain registered in his eyes, not shock or fear, which could be deadly. "I don't . . . think so."

"Good." She moved her hand to squeeze his shoulder. "We'll get you out of here as soon as we can."

Turning her focus to Evan, she reached for the pulse in his throat. His heartbeat thrummed strong, though fast. She rested a hand on his chest and felt the steady rise and fall of breathing. Those were good signs. "Has he been awake at all since the rockslide?"

She didn't pull her attention from the man as she waited for Brielle or Hugo to answer, instead running her gaze and her hands over his limbs.

Hugo responded slowly. "I . . . thought I heard him talking at first. I'm not sure, though."

"He had some rocks on his legs I moved away. Not big ones, just the size of my fist." Brielle's voice strained with worry, but at least the tone sounded free of tears. She would have to make sure her friend found the chance to cry later if she needed to release the tension of the ordeal.

After a careful check of Evan's limbs, Audrey shifted her focus to his abdomen. "I don't feel any broken bones yet, though his clothing is torn. I'm sure he has scratches." *Gashes* may be the better word, based on some of the blood she'd found. But if bones weren't broken, the healing would be much faster.

Moving as quickly as she could, she unfastened the buttons on his shirt and peered at his skin. No bruising that she could see and no swelling, either. That boded well for no chance of internal damage to organs.

At last, she turned her attention to his head. She still needed to check his back, but the skull was her greatest concern, since he'd been unconscious so long.

Scratches marred his face, but nothing that would need stitching. She began working her fingers through his hair, moving slowly so she didn't miss anything.

The blood was hard to overlook. Above his right ear, thick liquid matted his hair, and a lump puffed out. Her fingers detected a gash in the area—the source of the blood, no doubt.

Evan groaned as she prodded the spot, and a layer of tension lifted from her chest. He responded to pain, which was a good sign.

She eased her probing, and his eyelids flickered open. Brielle gasped, shifting her position so he would see her better. His vision would likely be blurry at first.

He kept his eyes half-closed, just like Levi had done that first day after his fall. The brightness of the torch might contribute to his squint, but his head probably felt like it was splitting from the pain.

"How are you, my love?" Brielle's voice held a tenderness that made Audrey's chest ache. Tears stung the backs of her eyes, but she blinked them away as she waited for Evan's response.

His mouth opened first, as though he had to work for the words, or the ability to speak them. "What . . . happened?"

Brielle ran her fingers over a patch of unmarred skin on his face. "You and Hugo were building our home. Earth tremors began, and they must have started a rockslide. It took a while before we could clear enough stone to get to you. Where are you hurt?"

Brielle's fingers continued to stroke his face, working into the edges of his hair, though she stayed far away from the bloody place. She'd never possessed a gentle bedside manner—had always kept her distance from illness, if she could manage it. But now, she seemed to know exactly how to soothe her man.

Evan's brow gathered. "Head hurts."

It was time Audrey speak up so she could get a better idea of the extent of his injuries. "Does anything feel broken? Can you move your arms?"

She glanced down to his fingers as he lifted each one slowly, then shifted each arm enough to show its wholeness. "How about your legs? Can you raise them?"

A groan slipped out as one leg barely lifted upward.

She darted a glance to his face, which showed strain. He was still trying, so she refocused on his legs. He shifted both of them from side to side but seemed to struggle to lift even his feet. Maybe something was broken there after all.

She refocused on his face. His eyes had closed, but his mouth opened to speak. "I don't think they're broken. The effort just hurts . . . my head."

That made sense. A blow powerful enough to make him

lose consciousness for so long could affect movement in his body—hopefully only for a short time, but that remained to be seen.

She glanced up at the opening where the men still worked. They'd made significant progress, probably enough for a man to squeeze through.

Shifting her attention back to Brielle, she gathered her satchel. "I don't think anything is broken, but I'd like to move him out on a stretcher. His head and neck need time to rest, so he shouldn't sit up yet. I'm going to go ready things for him. I'll be back with the men when he can be moved."

Brielle's expression was a mixture of fear and hope and a dozen other emotions. She grabbed Audrey's arm, her gaze digging into her. "He's going to be okay?" Though the words might have been a statement, the question in them hung too heavily.

Audrey placed her hand over Brielle's. "It looks promising."

The relief on her friend's face brought a smile to Audrey for the first time since the earthquake. She reached out and pulled Brielle into a hug, and her friend clung to her for a long moment.

Together, they breathed in the possibility that everything might truly be all right. Maybe even better than all right.

Audrey did her best to enjoy this moment with some of the people who meant the most to her, not let her mind drift to the assembly room where the vote would soon take place.

"Philip is getting some men together to clear all the rock

from our home." Brielle sat beside Evan's bed, her eyes rarely leaving her intended's face.

After being extracted from the rockslide and brought to Audrey's apartment for her to tend, Evan had spent the rest of the day of the accident in bed. Much of the time, he'd been sleeping from the effects of the herbs Audrey gave him. Through God's mercy, the wound on his head was the only real injury from the awful ordeal. He had no memory of anything that day before awakening to Brielle and Audrey leaning over him, but perhaps it was better he didn't remember the worst of it.

Poor Hugo had, indeed, lost a finger, along with a great deal of blood. His mother cared for him now, feeding him the foods Audrey prescribed and keeping him close to home. She should go check on him again soon, but she couldn't bring herself to leave this room until news came of the vote.

The knot clenched tighter in her belly as her mind conjured images of familiar faces making their way through the voting line. The Mignot family, whose youngest son she'd nursed through influenza last month, spending long nights by his side when the fever rose highest. Did they hate her now, believing she turned against the people she'd always loved?

What of Marie Chapuis, who came to her each month for herbs to help with her women's pains? She always brought the twins, Eva and Anyette. Those two pink-cheeked cherubs could bring a smile to even the grumpiest face. Would Marie ever trust her with the babes again?

Levi's hand slipped over her own, as though he could read her thoughts. She met his gaze as she turned her hand to clasp his. The look he sent said he understood her worries.

His words from the other night rose inside her. *"The Lord has a plan in this. He'll carry us through."*

She sent a prayer upward. *Lord, whatever happens, let me not be separated from this man.* If Levi was sent away, did she have the strength to go with him? If that was God's will, *He* would give her the strength. For whatever she had to face, He would give her the strength.

A soft tap sounded on the rear door, then it pushed open and Charlotte appeared. Not at all the person Audrey expected. She stood and moved to greet Brielle's younger sister, searching her face for sign of whether she brought news.

Charlotte met her gaze. "My father wishes you to come to the assembly room. There's someone there who's asked to speak with you."

Audrey's insides coiled tight. "With me? Has the vote finished?" She hadn't expected the council to be ready to speak their verdict so soon.

Charlotte shook her head. "Not yet. Come."

As she followed Charlotte's willowy form down the corridor, she had to clamp her mouth shut to keep from asking who wished to speak with her. If Charlotte had been allowed to tell, she would have. Wouldn't she? The young woman rarely spoke up unless asked a direct question. Maybe she would become bolder as she grew into womanhood, but she'd already matured so much for a girl of sixteen, ensuring the Durand home ran smoothly with her cooking and cleaning and keeping up with Andre. Most people likely had no idea what a capable, intelligent young woman resided in this slender body.

Too soon, they reached the wide doors of the assembly room. Both were propped open, showing the crowd of people milling inside. Audrey scrambled to keep up with Charlotte as she wove through them to reach her father.

Chief Durand offered a smile and nod to his daughter, but his expression turned grave when he looked at Audrey. The coil inside her twisted into an impossibly tight knot. "Audrey, Madame Picard wishes to speak to the villagers before the vote, and she asked that you be present."

For the first time, she noticed the woman standing behind the chief. Leonard's mother wore full mourning dress, including a black cloth over her hair. The sight of her caused a wad of burning emotion to clog in Audrey's throat. She should step forward and greet the woman, take her hands and tell her how sorry she was . . . What a good man Leonard had been . . . How if she could go back and change things . . .

But she could only stand there, her mouth too dry to speak.

The chief stepped back to Madame Picard's side, then raised his hands and voice to silence the crowd. "Before we begin the vote, one of our own wishes to speak."

He motioned to the grieving woman. Madame Picard straightened, lowering her head covering to rest on her shoulders. Her chin quivered as she opened her mouth to speak, and the lines wreathing her face made her appear ten years older than the last time Audrey had seen her. Grief could do that.

"I have labored hard over whether to speak or not. I think my Leonard would wish it, so here I am." Her voice began with a tremble but grew stronger with each word.

She turned to face Audrey, and the tears Audrey had been working so hard to hold back finally slipped through her defenses as Madame Picard's gaze locked with hers. "These past days have been hard for many of us. Terrible things have happened. Things I'll never understand the reason for." Her voice broke on the last words, but she gathered herself and raised her chin as she continued. "Audrey has proven her heart for others. She's done much to help our neighbors, especially those ailing in body or spirit. I believe that same kindness is what drove her in this matter as well."

She glanced around the room. "It's not my place to judge whose choices and actions ultimately took my son's life. But this I know well—all have sinned and come short of the glory of God. But when we repent, God's grace covers our sin through Jesus's death on the cross."

Madame Picard's eyes met Audrey's again. "How can I not provide the same grace our Lord extended to me?" Then her gaze shifted to the crowd around them. "I urge each of you to consider the same. As you vote, purge any vindictive feelings from your hearts. Be the hands and feet of our heavenly Father in this matter."

As she bowed her head and stepped backward, the murmurs of the crowd rose around them.

Tears streamed freely down Audrey's face, but the only thing that mattered to her now was reaching Leonard's mother, wrapping her arms around the brave woman, and letting their tears mingle together in a river of grief and grace.

30

Audrey's emotions were spent, and she had no doubt her face bore the marks of her tears. But as she sat beside Levi, the tension in the air kept her from speaking. Occasionally, the murmur of conversation would drift from Brielle and Evan, but she didn't have the energy to even look their way.

The vote should be over now, and any moment, someone might come with the news. Or she might be summoned again.

Would Madame Picard's moving speech affect the outcome of the vote? *Lord, thank you for your grace, even if I'm not granted the same from Laurent.*

A knock sounded on the rear door, and thankfully, Brielle rose to open it. Audrey reached for Levi's hand, though she couldn't take her eyes from the entrance as Chief Durand stepped into the room. The expression on his face gave no sign of the news he brought. But he must have an update, for he would have stayed in the assembly room until the vote was complete and the council had deliberated.

Levi's thumb stroked across the top of her hand, and only then did she realize how tight she was squeezing his. She tried to relax, but only managed it a little.

"Is the vote finished?" Brielle asked the question Audrey couldn't manage.

He nodded, coming to stand where they could all easily see him. His gaze moved over Brielle and Evan first, landing on the man who would be his son-in-law. "You're feeling better today?"

"I am. Audrey won't let me out of bed for more than a minute or two, but I'm much better."

The chief's gaze moved to Audrey, then slid to Levi, finally hovering on them both. "The vote is finished, and the council conferred afterward. We've made a decision—two decisions, I guess you could say."

His gaze grew pointed. "The rockslide yesterday had far-reaching effects, even more than we realized at the time." His focus lifted to Evan and a frown touched his brow. Then he shifted his attention back to Levi and Audrey. "In your case, the results were good. The report of how you both helped free the men has been carried around the village." His gaze hovered on Audrey, and a hint of a gentle smile touched his mouth. "It was a good reminder of how you've always worked tirelessly and unselfishly for our people."

His focus moved to Levi. "And you labored like one of us, setting aside your own injury to help others. For many of our people, that was the proof they needed to make them willing to give you a chance. If you wish, you're free to remain in Laurent. Or you may leave when you're ready. I feel it only right to tell you that your behavior will be watched closely while you're here, at least for a while. Yet we feel confident enough in the character we've seen so far that we're willing to give you a chance among us."

Relief seeped through Audrey's body a little at a time as the chief spoke. With those final words of freedom for Levi, happiness nearly stole her strength.

A smile stretched her face so wide she had no ability to contain it. Levi squeezed her hand, and she pressed back, almost too exultant to speak.

His words buzzed through her mind. *Willing to give you a chance. Free to remain in Laurent.* There would be no punishment for Levi at all.

Yet a niggle in the back of her mind tugged a bit harder. Had she been so addled during the chief's comments that she'd missed the final verdict about her? Did she dare ask?

She had to know. "Was it decided what my punishment will be?" Her voice sounded so small with the question.

He raised his brows at her. "I suppose I didn't make that clear, did I?" For the first time, merriment touched his gaze, the way he used to look at her as he called her his other daughter. "The people voted to allow you grace to cover this sin, just as Madame Picard requested." He dipped his chin, his brows rising in another pointed look. "Not that the council condones your disobedience, but we understand your reasons."

Emotion clogged her throat, rising up to burn her eyes and nose. She couldn't speak, even if she had the words. Releasing Levi's hand, she pressed her fingers to her mouth to keep a sob from slipping out. Could they really be willing to forgive her completely? To allow her another chance without holding a grudge?

As her mind spun, an arm slipped around her. She turned to find Brielle at her side, pulling her into a hug. Brielle, who almost never offered affection and even struggled to receive it sometimes. This dear friend knew her too well, knew she needed a physical connection to help her mind believe what she'd just been told.

Wrapping her arms around Brielle, Audrey let the tears of joy fall.

Though his hip still ached, Levi craved to get out of this bed again. Yet he'd promised Audrey he would stay here, at least for now. When she looked at him with that mixture of concern and love—and yes, joy, after the wonderful news they'd received yesterday—he couldn't have refused her. But with the apartment empty all morning, he couldn't help but fidget.

They were both free. That awareness had barely sunk in, even after his mind raced through much of the night. Now that no pending decisions or votes held him back, he wanted desperately to tell Audrey exactly how he felt. What he was thinking for their future.

Before he could speak with her, though, he needed to have that conversation he'd promised her father. If only he could get out of this bed, he could find the man for the talk right now.

The grumbling in his belly told him it was almost time for the noon meal, and if he knew Audrey, she would return soon to prepare plates for him and her father. If her food weren't so good, he would feel bad about the way she spent so much time cooking and serving him. Well, he did regret the serving part—he wanted to serve her. To treat her like the lady she was. Yet she seemed to take such joy in doing for others. He'd never seen such a sweet, giving spirit as hers.

When the back door finally opened a while later, it wasn't Audrey, as he'd expected. Monsieur Moreau shuffled in, sending Levi a nod of greeting. The man moved toward the cookstove instead of his chair by the fire. "Audrey was delayed, but she said she has soup warming. Sent me to make sure you don't starve."

The hint of mirth in the man's voice gave Levi pause. That was the first time he'd heard a jest from the man. A promising sign. Maybe this would be a good time to speak.

After Moreau filled two bowls, he picked up both and handed one to Levi.

Before he could turn and retreat to the table, Levi spoke up. "Sir, could we talk a moment?"

Moreau paused and gave Levi a look that could only be called wary. Then he seemed to resign himself, and he settled into the chair that Audrey usually occupied beside Levi's bed. Once seated, the man gave Levi a nod. He looked like he was bracing himself for news he would hate. He surely knew what Levi was about to say, especially after their conversation before.

A twinge pinched his chest. As much as Martin Moreau clearly loved and depended on his daughter, the thought of her leaving must be devastating. Yet the man seemed to be preparing himself for that very thing. Only a strong love wouldn't hold the other person back.

Levi did his best to keep his tone level. "Sir, I love your daughter. I'm sure you know how hard it would be to keep from loving her once someone got to know her. She truly is the most remarkable and kindhearted woman I've ever met.

Now that we're both free to choose our paths, I'd like to ask her to marry me."

Even braced as he'd been, Moreau's shoulders jerked with Levi's last words.

He needed to set the man at ease. "I don't want to take her away from here—at least, not to live. I need to visit my mum and dad, and I would love for Audrey to meet them, if she wishes. But Laurent is her home. Her family and friends are here. If the people will accept me, I would be happy to make it my home, as well."

Moreau eyed him, chin dipped, his expression almost skeptical. He didn't speak for a while.

As his silence continued, Levi fought the urge to fidget. Would Audrey's father deny him? Had Levi said enough to satisfy the questions he might have? In his mind, he worked back through everything he'd said. Had he ever actually asked for the man's blessing?

He nearly slapped a palm to his forehead. No wonder Moreau hadn't answered.

Straightening, he tried to meet the man's gaze. "I didn't say that very well, but what I'm trying to ask is if you would give us your blessing. You're important to her, and that makes your good opinion important to me."

Again, he waited, and thankfully, Moreau didn't drag out the silence this time.

He nodded. "It's up to Audrey. I'm glad you're willing to stay here. Whatever she decides is my choice, too."

Levi eased out a breath and let the smile spread over his face. "Thank you, sir."

Moreau pressed his hands to his knees and pushed up to standing. "Eat up. I think she'll be along soon."

With the nerves playing havoc in Levi's belly, he may not be able to eat much.

Yet once he tasted the first two bites of her stew, his mouth craved more. He'd nearly finished the bowlful when the rear door pushed open, and Audrey stepped in.

31

Like always, Audrey's smile lit Levi's insides on fire as her gaze settled on him. "Good, you're awake."

Her head disappeared back into the hallway, then the door opened wider, and she stepped into the room, pushing a chair with two large wheels on either side and a small one positioned in front.

He nearly choked at the sight. The wheeled chair was a familiar sight, but not with this particular woman pushing it. Did she mean for him to ride in it? Just like Levi's father did.

She stopped the seat at the edge of his cot, a triumphant grin lighting her beautiful face. "I thought you might like to get out of bed for a while. I think we need to wait before you use the walking sticks again, but Louis Bureau offered the use of his chair for a few hours."

The sight of the conveyance sent his emotions warring. He would love to get out of this bed and see Laurent, maybe meet more of the people. But his father practically lived in a chair very similar to this one. In Levi's mind, he'd always matched it with his father's displeasure.

Yet it wasn't the vehicle that made his father frown. It was his situation. The fact that he couldn't use his legs to walk. But if Levi really thought about it, it was the fact that his father didn't work to find joy in the hardship. Everyone went through times of pain and trial. His father's situation had certainly lasted longer than many endured. But surely he could have found peace and pleasure in his wife and children. In the love of a heavenly Father who'd not allowed his life to be taken in that battle and given him many more years with his family.

In truth, Levi would never fully understand how hard things had been for his father. And it wasn't his place to judge the man for his attitudes. Levi's own attitude about his situation was all he could control, and he could choose to view this borrowed chair as a gift. The gift of movement, instead of being bound to this bed. A gift of love from the woman now beaming at him.

He returned her smile. "Thank you." Setting aside his empty bowl and shifting off the coverings, he scooted to the edge of the bed, where he could maneuver onto the chair. Using his arms and his good leg, he shifted onto the seat, then eased against the back support. That small bit of movement shouldn't wear him out, but he was already breathing hard.

Reaching for a reserve of strength, he straightened and attempted to push the wheels to roll the chair forward. Turning it away from the bedside proved his first obstacle, and a task much harder than he would have expected.

"Wait." Audrey scooted the bedside table farther out of his way. "Let me roll you."

Surely he could accomplish this small feat. His father maneuvered all around their house in a chair just like this. Yet getting the knack of how to make the smaller wheel turn the right direction took concentration.

Audrey finally moved in front of him, a frown wrinkling her brow. She looked like she wanted to brace her fists at her waist and lecture him, but she was too kind for such a stern act. "Wait a minute, Levi. I have somewhere I want to take you. Let me help."

And with those words, with her sweet voice and her angelic face in front of him, the frustration building in his chest eased. She'd planned this treat, this special outing, and he was stealing her joy.

Forgive me, Lord.

To Audrey, he offered an apologetic smile. "I'm at your command. Take me where you wish."

Her frown softened into a smile, and the twinkle in her eye looked almost scheming. Not anything he'd ever seen from this angel. But he liked it.

After taking her place behind his chair, she pushed him forward, turning around the end of the bed toward the front door. She maneuvered the vehicle with ease, a far cry from what he'd been able to manage.

She paused to open the door, and sunlight streamed in alongside the chilly air. When she'd regained her position behind him, her voice sounded. "Hold on as I push you down the stoop. It will be bumpy."

He gripped the chair arms as she commanded, but he was able to use his good foot to help walk the chair down the low step. As they settled the vehicle on the ground, he took a moment to scan the courtyard around them. Most of the snow was gone, and a group of children played in the distance. A few people relaxed in chairs outside their homes, probably enjoying the pleasure of the outdoors. The chill of winter still hung in the air, but the warm sun bespoke the coming spring.

"I'll be right back." Audrey's voice faded behind him as she returned into the apartment.

He took the opportunity to relax against the backrest and turn his face to the warmth of the sun.

A moment later, she moved beside him and placed her own chair beside his. Her smile turned shy as she adjusted its feet on the damp ground, not meeting his gaze. "I thought you might like to sit in the sunshine for a while. It's our first mild day this spring."

The warmth filling his chest had nothing to do with the sun, and as she settled beside him, he reached over and took her hand, weaving his fingers between hers. He stroked his thumb over hers—such a small hand that possessed so much power. Power to heal, power to care. Power to make his world so much warmer.

She finally met his gaze, and he lifted their joined hands so he could press a kiss where his thumb had just stroked. He didn't shift his eyes from hers, though.

He'd not expected an opportunity to ask her so soon, but with these moments alone with her, these moments of perfection, he had to speak. "Audrey, I think I told you in the cave that if our situations were different, my intentions toward you would be . . . different." Those days in the cave were all blended together. He could recall the conversation and what he'd meant to say, but he wasn't sure exactly how it had come out.

"Since then, God has shown me clearly that there truly are circumstances I have no power to change. Only He has that power. He's worked so much good for us these last few weeks." So much more than Levi had ever expected.

Audrey was watching him, a sheen in her eyes. She must be thinking of how far they'd come too.

"I promised myself when I watched Brielle walk you back toward Laurent that if God brought us through, I would never let you go again."

Her eyes widened a little, and he lifted their hands again to press another kiss there. "Audrey Moreau, will you do me the honor of becoming my wife? It would be my greatest honor to join our hearts before God. I'll do everything I can to provide for you, to protect you, and to cherish you. No matter what happens in our lives, you'll never lack for my love."

He squeezed her hand and resisted the urge to once more press a kiss there. He had to wait for her response. The shimmer of moisture in her eyes was the only visible sign of emotion.

Her mouth parted, and he held his breath as he waited for her to speak. But she didn't, which made his chest ache with the delay.

At last, her mouth pressed shut and the beautiful lines of her throat worked. What did that mean? Was she trying to think of a way to let him down gently?

But then she nodded, and her mouth opened with a puff of breath that sounded almost like a sob. She nodded again, more vigorously. "Yes." This time the sound that slipped out was definitely a sob, even as a beautiful smile spread over her face. "I would love to be your wife."

The knot in his chest uncoiled, and he could finally breathe. She'd said yes. The turmoil of thoughts and emotions took a moment to untangle enough to speak, but his smile came easily.

She'd said *yes*.

He lifted her hand to press another kiss there, then his

mind caught up enough for a better idea. Leaning toward her, he cupped her cheek with his free hand.

As her eyes fluttered shut, he took a single heartbeat to relish her beauty. Those exquisite features had caught him from their first meeting by the creek, yet it was her inner beauty that showed in every sweet smile, every caring word, every gentle touch. She'd captured every part of him.

He brushed his lips against hers, planning for only a sweet sealing of their promise. But the touch of her, the taste, drew him back for more.

She was intoxicating, addicting. The only way he was able to finally pull back was remembering that he would have the rest of their lives to kiss this woman.

As he worked to catch his breath, his smile stretched wide. He probably looked besotted, but he didn't mind. He'd determined to only speak the truth, so why shouldn't his face do the same?

He glanced at the children playing across the courtyard. The happy voices made the perfect background for the joy building inside him.

When he looked back at Audrey, her eyes held questions, and he pressed a kiss to her fingers. "What is it, my love?"

"Would we live in Kettlewell?" Her voice seemed tentative. Not worried, but unsure.

A wash of gratitude swept through him. Had he failed to mention that during his proposal? Even not knowing that detail, she'd still said yes.

He didn't deserve this woman, but he'd spend the rest of his life thanking God for her. "If you wish to, we can. I do need to make a trip there, and I hoped you might come with me so my family can meet you. After the wedding, of course." He squeezed her hand. "But then I thought we might make Laurent our home. If you want to, of course."

Her eyes widened again, taking on that same sheen as before. Once more, her throat worked. "Really? Are you certain?" She seemed so hesitant, as though afraid to hope.

He cradled her face in both his hands and held her gaze in his. "Audrey, I've lived many places these last years, and the one thing I know for sure is that it's not the location, it's the people around me that matter. I like your village. I would be honored to become a part of it. But even more important to me is that *you* can be in the place where you'll be happiest. I think that will be near your father and your friends, but if you ever wish to see more of the world, we can do that, too."

Even the tear that slipped down her cheek didn't tarnish the sweet smile lighting her face. "I love you, Levi Masters."

He would never tire of hearing those words. He nearly swept down for another kiss, but she spoke again before he could.

"But what of your family? Don't they need you, too?"

He regarded her for a moment. "I've saved a good bit of money from my earnings. It's back with my things in Washington, so we'll need to retrieve that on our way to England. I think that will help Mum and Dad a great deal for the next few years. Maybe we'll find things are different when we see them, but we won't know for sure until then."

He gazed into her beautiful eyes. "I do know the Scripture says that a man shall leave his father and mother and be joined with his wife. I'll always do what I can to help them, but my home will be with you, wherever the Lord calls us."

As he spoke those words, he weighed them in his heart.

He'd not consciously formed that thought before now, but the rightness of the notion sank through him.

And even more so when Audrey reached her hand around his neck and drew him closer. She paused partway, and her words filled the air with sweetness. "I love you, Levi Masters."

Then she pulled him in for a kiss that promised a lifetime more of that love to come.

EPILOGUE

Levi soaked in the activity in the assembly room as he sat with his leg propped on a chair. The place looked far different from when he'd first been brought in here. Greenery hung in swags on every wall, and the chairs had been placed in rows instead of around tables. All pointed toward one end of the room, where an arch had been erected, just wide enough for two figures to stand beneath. Three, if you counted the minister.

Brielle's father would be performing that honor, as the village's chief. How did he feel about giving his eldest daughter away in marriage? To an outsider, no less.

Levi's gaze wandered through the wedding guests milling about. Several had come by to greet him, and it felt good to receive the friendly attention. But he could also be content sitting on the sidelines watching. Waiting.

Audrey had flitted in and out of the room more times than he could count, positioning things at the food table, straightening decorations, and occasionally retrieving something. As much as he wished he could get up and help her—perhaps bear some of her load during this busy day—he suspected she loved being so busy.

She'd looked forward to this day with an eagerness that had been palpable, planning and preparing for weeks. He loved the way she took such joy in blessing others. *Thank you, Lord, that she was able to be here for Brielle's celebration.*

A figure sank into the chair beside him, and Levi glanced over.

Evan MacManus.

Levi had only seen the man a handful of times since he'd recovered from his injuries after the rockslide. The long hours of metal pounding on stone across the hall had made it clear what kept the fellow busy. That much work would have him sleeping well through the night, too. But finally, the couple's big day was here.

Evan glanced over at him, and strain showed in the lines on his face. The ceremony would begin soon, so Evan likely had nothing left to do except wait. And waiting on a day like today could drive a man mad.

As Levi searched for something light to say, Evan spoke first, his tone far from light. "You and I haven't talked much, but there's something I think needs to be said. Something that's taken me a while to come to terms with."

That old familiar knot tightened in his middle, a sensation that had disappeared after the council's vote. Did Evan really think it would be helpful to castigate him for Britain's actions during the war? *Now*, of all times, on the man's wedding day?

"I know we've had our differences in the past." Evan's eyes turned earnest. "But the war's over. I imagine we've both done things we might change if we had the chance to go back. But thanks be to God, we get to move forward. This is a new life for us both. From what I've heard about you, you seem like the kind of man I would like to know better."

His gaze flicked to the tables behind them, where women were still bustling about. "You're important to Audrey, which makes you important to Brielle." His focus locked back on Levi. "I'd like to start fresh." He extended a hand. "I'm Evan MacManus. Good to meet you."

The man's words sank in slowly, untying the knot in Levi's middle and lifting a weight from his chest. A smile tugged at his mouth as he took Evan's clasp. "Levi Masters. The pleasure is mine."

After a firm shake, they both turned to face forward.

Evan released a long breath, but it didn't seem to ease the tension inside the man. He'd probably just turned his focus back to the coming nuptials.

Levi glanced his way and lifted his brows. "You ready for this?"

Evan gave a quick nod. He ran one palm down his pants, maybe to wipe perspiration away.

Levi bit back a grin. "Nervous?"

Evan stared up at the arch, where he'd be taking his place soon enough. "Only for the ceremony. I expected the community would want to celebrate, since they love Brielle so much, but I . . . I didn't expect it to be such an ordeal."

This time Levi had to bite back a chuckle. "Just imagine that the rest of us aren't here. It's just you and your bride and the minister." He'd almost said *her father* instead of *the minister*, but that reminder might not ease Evan's nerves.

Levi had come to hold a great deal of respect for Chief

Durand. His wisdom, patience, and thoughtfulness made him an excellent governor. But becoming the man's son-in-law would be no small thing.

On the other side of Evan, Audrey approached. Her gaze caught Levi's, and she gave one of those beautiful angelic smiles that stirred his insides. This one in particular seemed special for him, almost intimate.

When she reached Evan's side, she finally pulled her gaze from Levi's. She placed a hand on Evan's shoulder, and he looked up anxiously. "She's ready."

He jumped to his feet, then tugged at the hem of his frock. His gaze found the rear doors as he rotated his shoulders then pulled his sleeves down.

Audrey patted his arm. "You look well. The perfect groom for her."

Evan's focus dropped to her face, as though checking the sincerity of her words. Then he drew in a deep breath and released it. At last, a smile spread on his face. "I'm ready."

While the groom moved to the front of the room to stand with his future father-in-law, Audrey slipped into the seat beside Levi. She leaned in, snuggling close as she slipped her hand into his.

He would never tire of the feel of her next to him. Her sweetness. Her goodness. The essence that made her so special. He pressed a kiss to the top of her head, a tiny token of what he'd one day offer her.

A glimpse toward the aisle showed her father shuffling toward them, with Brielle's younger sister and brother following behind. A hush slipped over the room as they all settled into seats. Gazes shifted back to the double doors, which parted for Brielle to enter.

She wore a full dress, much fancier than Levi had ever seen on her. It gave her a softer look, though as she approached the center aisle toward the front of the room, her bearing still carried the nobleness she wore so often.

A sheen glimmered in Audrey's eyes, though her smile stayed sure as her breath fanned against his ear. "She's wearing her mother's dress."

He met Audrey's gaze as the significance of that sank in. He squeezed her hand to show he understood. Both of these women had been forced to grow up without mothers to love and shepherd them. Perhaps that was part of the tie that connected them, but at least they had each other.

And a host of friends and neighbors and family to help fill the void.

As Audrey turned her focus toward the couple in the front, Levi couldn't help letting his gaze drift around the crowd. Two rows forward and to the left sat the tall form of Erik Le Monde, one of the men who'd come to talk with him in those first days after he recovered from the fever. Monsieur Gaume was one of the others, and he sat in the opposite section with his wife and three children. Two of their little ones might be twins, since their blond heads bobbed at around the same height.

Slightly forward from them sat Hugo, the young man who'd been trapped with Evan during the rockslide. Audrey had said he'd recovered well from the loss of blood, though he'd forever have the tiny stub of a finger to remind him of the ordeal. An older woman settled beside him, one who might be his mother.

Near the front sat a figure who'd become very familiar to Levi these last weeks. Marcellus, a fellow whose body appeared to be only a few years younger than Levi's, though his mind might be younger still. He possessed a zest for life that was impossible not to admire, and his open friendly personality drew in everyone around him.

All of these people had begun to open themselves to Levi, allowing him to join conversations and share meals with them. Helping him become part of this extended family.

He gave Audrey's hand a gentle squeeze. Soon their own special day would come. He would no longer be an outsider. He would be Audrey's husband.

His blood warmed at the thought.

He shifted his gaze toward the front, where the ceremony had already begun. Evan held both of Brielle's hands in his as her father read a passage from 1 Corinthians about love.

All traces of nervousness had left Evan's face. The intense love lingering there was impossible to miss.

Levi knew exactly what that love felt like. Even now, it took all his self-control to keep from wrapping his arms around Audrey and drawing her close. To find a tangible way to show even a small bit of how much he loved this woman tucked beside him.

Now wasn't the time, but that day would come. And after that, he would do everything in his power to make every day special for her. As long as he lived, this woman beside him would never doubt his love. That promise he could make with all his heart.

After all, he'd promised both God and Audrey he'd only speak the truth from now on.

USA Today bestselling author **Misty M. Beller** writes romantic mountain stories set on the 1800s frontier and woven with the truth of God's love. She was raised on a farm in South Carolina, so her Southern roots run deep. Growing up, her family was close, and they continue to maintain those ties today. Her husband and children now add another dimension to her life, keeping her both grounded and crazy. God has placed a desire in Misty's heart to combine her love for Christian fiction and the simpler ranch life, writing historical novels that display God's abundant love through the twists and turns in the lives of her characters. Learn more and see Misty's other books at MistyMBeller.com.

Sign Up for Misty's Newsletter

Keep up to date with Misty's news on book releases and events by signing up for her email list at mistymbeller.com.

More from Misty M. Beller

On assignment to help America win the War of 1812, Evan MacManus is taken prisoner by Brielle Durand—the key defender of her people's secret French settlement in the Canadian Rocky Mountains. But when his mission becomes at odds with his growing appreciation of Brielle and the villagers, does he dare take a risk on the path his heart tells him is right?

A Warrior's Heart • BRIDES OF LAURENT #1

HEARTS OF MONTANA Series
by Misty M. Beller

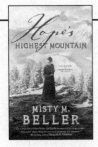

On her way to deliver vaccines to a mining town in the Montana Territory, Ingrid Chastain never anticipated a terrible accident would leave her alone and badly injured in the wilderness. When rescue comes in the form of a mysterious mountain man, she's hesitant to trust him, but the journey ahead will change their lives more than they could have known.

Hope's Highest Mountain

After her son goes missing, Joanna Watson enlists Isaac Bowen—a man she prays has enough experience in the rugged country—to help. As they press on against the elements, they find encouragement in the tentative trust that grows between them, but whether it can withstand the danger and coming confrontation is far from certain in this wild, unpredictable land.

Love's Mountain Quest

Nate Long has always watched over his twin, even if it's led him to be an outlaw. When his brother is wounded in a shootout, it's their former prisoner, Laura, who ends up nursing his wounds at Settler's Fort. She knows Nate wants a fresh start, but she struggles with how his devotion blinds him. Do the futures they seek include love, or is too much in the way?

Faith's Mountain Home

◆BETHANYHOUSE

More from Bethany House

Libby has been given a powerful gift: to live one life in 1774 colonial Williamsburg and the other in 1914 Gilded Age New York City. When she falls asleep in one life, she wakes up in the other without any time passing. On her twenty-first birthday, Libby must choose one path and forfeit the other—but how can she possibly decide when she has so much to lose?

When the Day Comes by Gabrielle Meyer
TIMELESS #1
gabriellemeyer.com

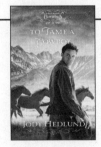

While Brody McQuaid's body survived the war, his soul did not. He finds his purpose saving wild horses from ranchers intent on killing them. Veterinarian Savannah Marshall joins Brody in attempt to save the wild creatures, but when her family and the ranchers catch up with them both, they will have to tame their fears if they've any hope to let love run free.

To Tame a Cowboy by Jody Hedlund
COLORADO COWBOYS #3
jodyhedlund.com

Michelle Stiles has stayed one step ahead of her stepfather and his devious plans by hiding out at Zane Hart's ranch. Zane has his own problems, having discovered a gold mine on his property that would risk a gold rush if he were to harvest it. But soon danger finds both of them, and they discover their troubles have only just begun.

Inventions of the Heart by Mary Connealy
THE LUMBER BARON'S DAUGHTERS #2
maryconnealy.com

BETHANY HOUSE